KAFKA'S UNCLE

and Other Strange Tales

Bruce Taylor

ReAnimus Press

Breathing Life into Great Books

ReAnimus Press
1100 Johnson Road #16-143
Golden, CO 80402
www.ReAnimus.com

ISBN-13: 978-1530692170

First ReAnimus Press print edition: June, 2016

10 9 8 7 6 5 4 3 2 1

To Ben Bova, friend and former agent whose advice, support and interest in my writing is most deeply and sincerely appreciated. Thank you.

Contents

Acknowledgements

To the memories of Marie Landis, founder of the writing group now known as The Landis Review, and her husband, Si. You taught me that the object of life isn't wealth. The object of life is the wealth of life.

To the former members of the Landis Review: Phyllis Hiefield, Brian and Jan Herbert, Joel Davis, Faith Szafranski, (the late) Cal Clawson and to the present members—Roberta Gregory, Linda Shepherd, Sarah Blum, Art Gomez and Jim Bartlett: to success! To love, laughter, connection, and a wonderful sense of a full and vibrant life well lived. What better definition of success do you need than that?

Also, many thanks to John Dalmas, great friend and enthusiastic supporter of my writing who was so gracious as to write a fine introduction to my first book, *The Final Trick of Funnyman & Other Stories*. Thanks also to Jeff VanderMeer (and family) who, through profound generosity, kindness and just plain hard work read many of my stories and selected some of them for publication in the aforementioned book (Ministry of Whimsy Press, 1997) but had plenty of good things to say about many other stories that, much to my delight, now appear in *Kafka's Uncle*. I am and will always be grateful to you. Also thanks to Patrick and Honna Swenson who reprinted *Final Trick* (available through www.fairwoodpress.com) and who have published some of the stories reprinted here in their wonderful magazine, *Talebones*. Thanks to Scott Eagle for the cover art for the first edition of *Final Trick* and Carl and Lida Sloan for the cover art for the second edition (and Thank You!! William F. Nolan for a recent and stunning review of the book who likened several stories to " —Bradbury at his finest.")

Thanks for the work of Adrian Majkrzak for the cover of *Kafka's Uncle*, who produced such a fine cover that is so true to the story. Thank you, Brian Herbert for so many years of fine friendship and for allowing me the honor of using your words to grace this book. I hope that I have been as good a friend to you as you have been to me.

Last, but certainly not least, to Roberta Gregory, my partner, my friend, who, with infinite compassion and forbearance, offered great solace and a superb eye for detail, and suggestions in the difficulties around my being challenged by computers and the proofreading of this manuscript. And to Karen Townsend who has been an outstanding editor and wonderful to work with, and Mike Toot who, through his fine understanding of computers, steered me through, at times, incomprehensible electronic waters and prevented crashes on the ever-lurking computer reefs. And with deep appreciation and a thank you to Andrew Burt and ReAnimus Press for publishing the second edition of Kafka's Uncle. Such are these people, upon entering one's life, you know that no matter *how* many times you say, "Thank you," it never seems enough. But that being said, "Thank you. Thank you all, thank you so much."

— Bruce Taylor
Seattle, Washington

Introduction

The first thing to understand about Bruce Taylor is that he's an esoteric original. He doesn't copy other writers and doesn't care a whit about commercialism, though if you look deeply enough you might think you see sprinklings of Ray Bradbury and Franz Kafka, set in a Taylorian universe of magic realism. Bruce cares most of all about his art, which places him far above the petty and mundane concerns of other purveyors of the written word. He's not plastic or phoney. He's real.

Trained as a psychiatric counselor, he is a stream-of-consciousness writer, a person who lets it flow in high-energy bursts. This is especially remarkable when you realize that he has, for many years, suffered from diabetes, a strength-sapping illness that has required much of his attention. Through sheer willpower he has controlled this debility and has created a remarkable life for himself, and a remarkable life's work. He is a prolific writer of short stories, and has garnered considerable acclaim for them. I am one of his admirers, and I am not alone. More and more, this man's talent is being recognized.

One day critics will say that so-and-so writes like Bruce Taylor, because by that time Bruce will be so incredibly well known and (horror of horrors!) commercially successful that people will begin to copy him. At least they will be *trying,* but I don't know to what extent such an effort can be successful. Bruce isn't a formula-type person who is easily subject to analysis, and is undoubtedly resistant to any sort of replication effort, whether computer aided or otherwise. He writes what is on his mind, in whatever manner suits his fancy.

He's also my backpacking buddy, on many a trip into the untrammeled wilderness of the Pacific Northwest. On a regular basis — whenever he feels overwhelmed by the burdens and B.S. of civilization — Bruce needs to go out and commune with nature, where he recharges his batteries. I remember one evening in particular when we watched the incredible gathering of dusk over the Enchantment Lakes. The sky changed as the purple swept over us, and moments later — far to the west beyond trees and mountains — we noticed an eerie, sickly yellow glow, reminding us that we had not escaped after all. It was the lights of Seattle against the sky, from seventy-five miles away.

Bruce and I are in an eclectic writing group that comprises quite a range of personalities and talents, including: Linda Shepherd (a feminist writer who is also a Ph.D. biochemist); Cal Clawson (a writer of math books and western novels); Marie Landis[1] (a science fiction/fantasy writer who is an accomplished painter); and Phyllis Lambert (a scientist who writes about human aging and about monkeys in car washes). Somewhere in all of this Bruce and I seem to fit in, or at least we haven't been asked to leave yet. At our Friday evening sessions the conversations are catholic (with a small "c"), ranging from Plato, Einstein and vampires to debates over whether the fisherman in one of our stories should haul up a human toe or an eyeball. To categorize the members of our group (and Bruce to a large extent), it might be said that we're interested in everything, and we're a support group for the fragile creative psyches of writers. Bruce is an integral part of this, and for years I have appreciated his intellectual input and emotional support.

In his writing and in his life, Bruce is on a journey of the soul and of the imagination, stretching the limits of consciousness and perception. To a large degree this has to do with his attempt to understand his parents and in particular his father, and in this regard I am a kindred spirit with him.

Joseph Campbell once said that the quest for one's father is a hero's journey, and I know from personal experience that it can be an arduous, painful pursuit, but one that can lead to incredible enlightenment. Much of Bruce Taylor's prose is written from the perspective of a bright child, one who is in some pain but overcomes it by seeing the world of adults as truly bizarre, whimsical and weird. It's important to realize that Bruce's stories are not strange; the world is, and he's separated himself from it in order to show us new realities, with remarkable clarity and insight.

— Brian Herbert
Bainbridge Island, Washington

---

[1] Since this introduction was written, both Marie Landis and her husband, Si, sadly have passed away.

Kafka's Uncle

What the red haired girl in this novel might say if she were to read this manuscript:

"This really should be dedicated in loving memory of certain Republican presidents of the last quarter of the twentieth century and their fellow fascist followers who, by thinking they invoked God in justifying their *cause, actually believed they were totally different than the worst Communist followers who invoked Marx to justify* their *cause. Sorry. Totalitarianism is totalitarianism, no matter if it's right or left."*

What the author might say about this manuscript if he were so inclined:

"To the generation of the seventies and eighties and — alas — the nineties. There are no words for the ache and the despair. It is so sad. May this give laughter to the tears"

She sees nothing and hears nothing; but all the same she loosens her apron-strings and waves her apron to waft me away. She succeeds, unluckily. My bucket has all the virtues of a good steed except powers of resistance, which it has not; it is too light; a woman's apron can make it fly through the air.

"You bad woman!" I shout back, while she, turning into the shop, half-contemptuous, half-reassured, flourishes her fist in the air. "You bad woman! I begged you for a shovelful of the worst coal and you would not give me it." And with that I ascend into the regions of the ice mountains and am lost forever.

The Bucket Rider
Franz Kafka

Chapter 1

Kafka Dreams

Anslenot walks down the street with the flames gushing from the fire hydrant and the sky turning purple. Planes screech overhead and confused pilots fire upon their comrades. Anslenot realizes that he can never remember a time in his life with the world at peace. Always a war raging somewhere. He sits on a bench and watches the chaos; a big tarantula, wearing four pairs of cowboy boots, comes wandering up to him. "Howdy pardner," it hisses.

"Hello, yourself," replies Anslenot.

"Bitch of a day, ain't it," says the spider. Anslenot isn't exactly sure how the spider does it, but it spits what looks like tobacco juice. Anslenot doesn't know if spiders can spit or not. Maybe this tarantula has a special Tobacco Spit Gland. He is not sure.

"Yeah," says Anslenot. "Sure is. No different than any other day."

"Yup," says the Tarantula. "Understand you like Kafka."

Anslenot stares ahead. He watches the Bucket Rider sail across the sky, leaving a contrail of ice.

"What business is that of yours?" says Anslenot. "How do you know?"

"Lucky guess, pardner."

"Quite a guess," says Anslenot.

"You related to him?"

"Not really," says Anslenot, "though I might as well be."

"Why?" asks the spider.

"Insane," says Anslenot, "utterly insane."

"You? Me? Him? Everything?"

"Yes," says Anslenot.

"Which?"

"Yes," replies Anslenot. He looks straight ahead. The contrail from the Bucket Rider has frozen; it falls around them like chunks of white coal. Anslenot looks at the spider. "Were you a man once?"

"Nope," the spider says. "Never was."

"Were you an insect, metamorphosized into a spider?"

"Nope," says the spider. "No, siree, I is what I is. Arachnid with a Western Spin. Weaver of tall tales, at least for now. No guarantees how long this will last, pardner."

"What about you?" asks the spider. "What were you?"

"Hopeful."

"Huh," says the spider.

Anslenot gestures to the chaos. "Once everything seemed hopeful."

"General harshness of this society gettin' you down?"

Anslenot sighs, looks at a burning building in the distance caving in on it-self while the firemen watch, for whatever reason, not putting it out. The spider turns to look in the direction Anslenot is staring. "Instant urban re-newal interest you, pardner?"

Anslenot shrugs.

At that point, a beautiful white stallion with orange saddle comes gallop-ing up the street. "Well," says the tarantula, "gotta get on my trusty steed."

Anslenot watches as the tarantula tries to climb upon the horse but just keeps falling off. Finally, the spider simply attacks the great, white horse; the spider bites; the horse falls. While the horse is still alive, the spider wraps it in silk and begins to drag it away; it turns to Anslenot. "Gonna eat tonight," it says. And long after the tarantula and the horse disappear into a nearby gutted building, long after the weak whinney-ings of the horse give way to noisy sucking sounds, Anslenot looks around and then gazes at the sky, only to see the stars — exploding.

Chapter 2

Kafka Dreams 2

Anslenot sits on a bench and dreams that he wakes up. In front of him, the sun shines down from blue sky, a fresh wind blows and it's a pleasant day. Startled, Anslenot looks around. He smiles, *My God*, he thinks, *it is truly a beautiful day. What has happened? Where have I been? It's all normal again.* Abruptly he turns and sitting on the bench, squatting rather, is a large taran-tula, white, with sequins and rubies all over its body.

Just then, a Mercedes Benz pulls up. In the front seat, a young man, hair combed back. He stops in front of Anslenot, rolls down the window, and says, "Howdy, stranger, how are you?"

"Do I know you?" asks Anslenot.

"Oh," says the figure, glancing away, "I'm famous. You've probably read some of my stuff." He grins. "Kafka. Kafka's the name."

Anslenot looks at the famous author. "You've done rather well."

"Yes, I have, haven't I? Time has been kind to my strangeness," he says. "So I decided to cash in on it all. I mean, why not? Don't I deserve the best? Oh, sure, I was a little screwed up way back then, but it happens. Say, I'm looking for James and Boren Avenue. Know where that is? I'm supposed to meet my wife there on the corner."

"Uh—" says Anslenot.

"Gotta meet 'er," says Kafka. "Real jewel. Sexy babe, too. Wow. Got a couple of kids, well, hell, with money taken care of, I'm rich. I can afford it." He pointed at Anslenot. "Fame. That's what you need, fame and fortune. Now, that's great security. Just write a bunch of weird shit and everyone will buy it because they're fascinated by their own pathology and weirdness, you know? Oh, I tell you it was a real market gamble, you know, but it paid off. Now, you, you gotta get a suit, and get all fixed up, and get yourself a pretty little lady and you'll be set for life. I mean, nothing wrong with a little money now and then. You know? I mean, look at me. I'd never thought I'd own a Mercedes or really be truly happy, I mean, *really* happy—boy, you gotta see this mansion I got over in Kirkland. Right on the lake—8000 square feet and maids, would you believe it? And I got masseuses who give me these great massages. And hey, I get to go golfing with Bill Gates in the morning and I'm gonna get together with Ross Perot later for a little strategizing. You know, gotta get in some local politics here—"

Then Kafka stops and looks at Anslenot for a minute. "You know, kid, there's something about you that reminds me a bit of me, even as I was sailing across the sky there not long ago. When I crashed into the ice mountains, I kinda came out of it, you know? Got my act together, you know?" Kafka gets out of the car and comes up to Anslenot and puts his arm around him. "Kid, I like you, you know. I think you're gonna go places—now, it's true I don't know you but, you know, I kinda do, if you know what I mean. So, I'm gonna make you my uncle and you can carry on my tradition—see where it took me? Here I am, made it big—you can be my honorary uncle. What say—?"

Stunned, Anslenot stands transfixed and finally says, "Uh—"

Kafka claps Anslenot about the shoulders. "*Knew* you'd see it my way, kid, just *knew* it. Well, hey, pardner, I gotta go—have yourself an interesting life. Boy, I sure have, and look how I turned out. You take care now."

Anslenot simply stares, almost uncomprehending, while Kafka gets back into his car and slams the door. He leans out the window.

"Oh, hey, good talking with you kid—where'd you say James and Boren was?"

Dazed, Anslenot raises his hand and points down the street.

Kafka grins and nods his head. "Got it. Thanks. No problem, no problem. It's a great life. Boy. Who woulda thought? What a metamorphosis, eh? Who woulda thought. Just take it from me, my friend, invest in Microsoft stock and get yourself a lady. Man, no more bucket riding for me. You know what

I did to those fuckers who wouldn't give me coal? Bought the place and became their new landlord—oh, they didn't own the place and they didn't recognize me—but remember that real cold stretch back last winter—three weeks of sub-freezing—oh, them bastards. Raised their rent 600%. They couldn't afford it. Out in the ice. Served 'em right. Well, hey, pardner, I gotta go—you take care now."

And with that, he roars off. Anslenot stares, sits back against the bench, closes his eyes and when he opens them again, in front of him is a 1958 Blue T-bird, and in the front seat, the white, sequined spider; it looks over to Anslenot, not even trying to sound like Elvis Presley, hisses the lyrics to *But Love Me*.

Abruptly, the white of the spider fades and becomes black, and the rubies and diamonds fall off in rattling cascades.

Anslenot looks around; in the distance, an explosion and the trees are defoliated; the air becomes a yellow murk. "What—" says Anslenot, "what—what—where?"

"Your friend?" whispers the spider. "He's gone. He's gone forever. You're on your own now. Ah, it's too bad it wasn't what you thought it was. But then, what is?"

"But what do I—where—"

"I don't know," says the spider. And with that, the T-bird goes roaring off, only to lose control and flip end over end, down the street and off into the distance.

Chapter 3

Busride

Anslenot decides that it may be time to be moving on; he decides to take the bus. By the time the bus comes, it is dark. Anslenot climbs on board, and, while paying his fare, looks to the busdriver. "Romano?" he says. "Is that you?"

"Indeed it is, dear brother."

"Good God," says Anslenot, "how long have you been out in these parts?"

Romano pulls away from the curb. "A while," he says. He is still lean and small, thinks Anslenot; how different we are.

"You're looking well," says Romano. "You always were a muscular brute."

Anslenot laughs, then looks around. "Empty bus?"

Romano smiles. "Not for long."

"How long has it been?" asks Anslenot.

"Ten years," says Romano, slowing for another stop.

"Ten years," says Anslenot. "I haven't spoken to anyone in the family for ten years," he sighs. "It was just as well. It was too crazy. Good to leave it all behind, not have to deal with it anymore."

Romano says nothing but opens the door to the bus and a young lady steps on. She pays her fare and looks at Anslenot.

"You jerk," she says. "What was the idea of leaving *us* to take care of the parents? Why should *you* have gotten away?"

"Christina," Anslenot says, "my sister Christina—I didn't know you were up here—"

She sits across the aisle, opening her purse and rearranging the contents thereof while she speaks to him. "—it was a mess, God it was a mess and I don't blame you for leaving but God it was *such* a mess..."

"I don't understand," says Anslenot, "I don't see either of you for ten years and now, all of a sudden, I'm meeting you."

It's as if no one hears Anslenot's comment.

"...yeah," Romano says, "it was pretty rough all right."

"Listen," says Anslenot, "while I'm glad to see both of you, I don't need to hear this bullshit. You could have left too. Are you angry at me for leaving or are you angry at yourselves for not having left like I did?"

But before anyone can answer, the bus slows, stops and—

"Uncle Aba, Aunt Jana—" says Anslenot.

"Howdy, pardner," says Uncle Aba, vigorously shaking Anslenot's hand. "Ain't seen you in years. Where ya been keeping yourself?"

"Dear," says Aunt Jana, extending her hand like something delicate, made of fine china. "Dear," she says again, "how *are* you?"

Anslenot shakes his head. "I don't know. I haven't seen you folks in years, and all of a sudden, you're all over."

"Dear," says Aunt Jana, withdrawing her hand as though a queen having somehow beknighted a suitor, "such things are in the realm of Providence and are not to be questioned."

"Yeah," says Uncle Aba, grabbing a vertical pole as the bus swerves out from the curb. "Funny how it all happens you know? Funny how it works. Yeah, it's been a long while, but I sure can't blame ya for leaving, boy, I really can't. Boy, yer parents were drunken sots if I ever saw. Yeah, I thought you had guts when you left. You really did."

"I'm glad *you* think so," says Anslenot. "Some of my family don't think it was such a great idea."

His aunt and uncle sit down behind Christina. "Gotta follow your heart, boy," says Uncle Aba.

"Dear," says Aunt Jana, to her husband.

"It's true," says Uncle Aba, "just as I was born naked, it's true."

"Well, it sure made it hard on *us*" says Christina, looking into a pocket mirror and putting on lipstick.

"Trapped," says Uncle Aba, "loyal and trapped. That was the problem with you and Romano. Loyal and trapped by your loyalty. Ah," he says with disgust. "You gotta get out there. You just gotta go out there and do it, you know?"

Anslenot licks his lips. Finally he looks to Romano. "This is too strange. This is *really* strange. I haven't seen anyone for years and all of a sudden, I'm seeing everyone on this bus ride. I think I want off at the next stop."

Christina snaps her purse shut. "There you go. Running away."

"Atta boy," says Uncle Aba, "but..."

"Better look outside," says Romano.

Anslenot does. Outside it is snowing. "What?" says Anslenot, "*What?* Where *are* we? It was 85 degrees and July when I got on the bus... where the hell are we? What happened?"

"Good questions," says Romano. "I'm just the bus driver and a long forgotten brother. I just drive the bus."

"But... but..." begins Anslenot. He then sighs and says, "I'll take my chances. It's got to be less crazy out there than it is in here."

"Look again," says Romano.

Anslenot does. Through the snow, he sees a reddish sky and an immense volcano in the distance and... no vegetation. Stupefied, he stares.

"That's carbon dioxide snow," says Romano, "and this is Mars."

"What?" says Anslenot. "It *can't* be."

"Nothing but," says Romano.

"But... but... but," begins Anslenot, "you can't drive on Mars."

"Oh, yes I can," says Romano, "and so can this bus—"

"But... but..."

"Told you it was going to be an interesting ride," says Romano, pulling over to let on even more passengers. And somehow the door has been replaced with an air-lock and the figures who come on are suited. The two figures remove their helmets.

"Oh, my God," says Anslenot, "oh, my God. Mother and Father."

"Well, look who's here," says Anslenot's mother, "it's the little renegade, himself." Anslenot's father saddles up behind his wife. "Enjoy your ten years of freedom, boy? Enjoy that? You really thought you could get away, forget, blot out your family?"

Anslenot looks up from his seat, stricken. "I'd hoped," he whispers, "that might be the case."

Anslenot's mother laughs. "Oh, how the younger generation thinks. As if they are independent of their past, their roots. It's all *so* amusing."

"Is there no escape?" whispers Anslenot, beseechingly.

As if an answer, the bus pulls over again, and through the airlock, four *more* figures. Removing their helmets, Anslenot sees who they are. "Oh, my God," he wails, "*my grandparents.*" He shivers. "Are they sober?" he whispers. "Are they going to hit each other?" Then looking up at his mother and father, "You? Are they going to hit you? Are you going to end up hitting us? Does this start all over again? Is there no escape? Is there no escape?"

In answer, everyone on the bus bursts out laughing; shamed and embarrassed, Anslenot looks out the window and watches the red sands of Mars roll by.

Chapter 4

Elvis Martian

The bus passes through a long, unlit tunnel and it is suddenly quiet. Abruptly, the light returns. Anslenot is in a room and a Martian stands in the doorway. The Martian is dressed in Levis, leather jacket, and stands with a guitar dangling from his shoulders. He has an Elvis wig on, mod sunglasses and looks hauntingly similar to Elvis Presley, except for the pale, blue skin.

Anslenot glances out the window to the Martian countryside with canals running toward the low hills in the distance under a deep blue-black sky. "Well," he says, "now that you're here—"

"Don't Be Cruel," says the Martian Elvis; it strums an off-key chord of his guitar.

"I hadn't planned to be cruel," Anslenot says, "I just wonder what you are doing here." He looks back to the scene of Mars outside. "I wonder what *I'm* doing here." Anslenot looks around the room. On the wall are pictures of a woman he knew when he was young—or younger. Slender, green eyes, long brown hair. And others on the wall, another lady, ah, what *was* her name—Mindy, he remembers. She was short, had a little vertical cleft in her chin and a delightful laugh and liked to dress in flowered dresses. Anslenot feels a longing.

Elvis the Martian strums another off-key chord. "Heartbreak Hotel," it says.

Anslenot knows the lyrics to *that* song all *too* well.

Elvis says nothing. It glances around the room. Abruptly, it sneezes; *yeeeek-kac!*

Anslenot startles. He's never heard a Martian sneeze before, much less an Elvis Martian.

"Gesundheit," says Anslenot.

Elvis strikes another off-key chord.

"I don't understand," says Anslenot. "What am I doing here? What do you want?"

Elvis gyrates its hips like the real Elvis did when he first was becoming famous. An image shoots through Anslenot's mind of Elvis on the Ed Sullivan show and the network censors blacking out Elvis' swivel hips from the bottom part of the picture. "Doncha have a girlfriend for that?" Anslenot asks.

"Lonely Town," replies Elvis softly.

"You and me both," Anslenot says. "Look at all these pictures, all the people that I've known, all the women, and where are they now?" He thinks for a minute. "Is it any wonder? Several I sure didn't treat very well."

Whang, "Hound Dog."

"I don't deny it," Anslenot says. "I didn't treat a lot of people very well." He looks out the window, "Least of all—myself. Wonder if that has anything to do with me being on Mars. Although," he pauses, staring out the window to the lush beds of vegetation, and to the nearby cities, buildings of spires, onion domes and strangely angular and baroque buildings, reminding Anslenot of a mixture of prophetic views of cities in the future by science fiction artists and Stalinist Neo-Gothic Architecture, "I can't help but wonder—I mean, it's pleasant out there. Innocent and pleasant."

The Martian adjusts its Elvis wig and mod sunglasses. Anslenot looks around the room again, and looks at a picture of his mother. "And her," Anslenot wonders out loud, "what about her? What did she want of me?"

"Teddy Bear," says the Martian Elvis. *Twang.*

Anslenot nods. "Probably lots of truth to that, 'ol, buddy," he says, "lots of truth to that."

The Martian begins to gyrate its hips again and says, "Love Me Tender."

"You got it wrong," Anslenot says, "I'm not into that sort of thing. Get your life patched up. Talk to Priscilla."

"Jailhouse Rock," Elvis responds.

"That bad, huh? So what are you going to do? I mean, you standing there in Elvis garb, plunking on a guitar and you may sort of look like Elvis but I know you're not, so exactly what do you want? What is this about?"

"Are You Lonely Tonight?"

Anslenot shakes his head. "You got it bad. You got it *really* bad. I told you, I'm not into what you're thinking. Sorry. Wish I knew what *else* I could do for you."

The Martian strums another off-key chord. "Blue Suede Shoes."

Anslenot glances out the window. Something is changing. He doesn't know what it is, but something bad, real bad, is beginning to happen out there. "Somehow," and Anslenot looks at the Martian, "somehow, I think that that's the least of your problems, our problems, Mr. Elvis, Mr. Martian, whatever you are. Behind all the fame and fortune or quest for it, I can't believe you're really happy—or that such things would make anyone *really* happy—"

Crash, the guitar drops to the floor and the Elvis Martian yells, "Caught In A Trap—" and it madly flees from the room, screaming, "I can't get out—" Anslenot hears the slam of the outer door to the building. Turning, Anslenot looks out the window to see Elvis Martian wildly running about. Abruptly, the sky turns pink, the cities vanish, as do the canals. A massive Jupiter rises, filling the sky with red, orange and yellow clouds and just as the Great Red Spot lifts over the horizon, Elvis stops, staggers—and explodes.

Chapter 5

Phobos Comes A Stumblin'

All shook up by what he sees, Anslenot decides he needs to relax and climbs into a bathtub. Out the window, he sees the pink Martian Sky. He is glad for the thick glass. It's chilly out there. The bathroom is tiled in red and blue. There are depictions in the tile of a once-proud race, of cities, of pastel and gentle colors. The bathroom is vast and as he looks around, he discovers a Martian, a different one, sitting in the corner reading a *PLAYBOY*. When the Martian gets to the centerfold, its eyes suddenly glow blue and it emits a high-pitched whine. Anslenot glances over. "Horny or just blowing off steam or did you just come?"

"Eeeeeeeeeee," says the Martian. It folds the centerfold back, sighs, presses a button on the wall. The surrounding area of the wall becomes a display panel. Immediately, the bathroom is filled with the sounds of a jungle. There are roars, raspy bird calls and the sound of something massive crashing through brush.

"Your idea of music?" says Anslenot, scrunching down into the bathtub further.

"Bleek," says the Martian. It picks up another magazine, *The Pink Tattler* and Anslenot reads the headlines. "No!" "Yes!" and "Maybe."

The sound of an elephant trumpeting fills the room.

Anslenot sighs. "Is it *absolutely* necessary that Martians accompany their guests when they take baths? Are you curious or just afraid guests will make the water somehow unfit for recycling or what?"

"Ga-heeb," says the Martian.

"It can't be because you're afraid of wasting water—this tub is huge! Was your civilization known for bathing orgies or what?"

The Martian smiles and thumbs through the *Pink Tattler*. The call of something fearsome reverberates through the bathroom. Anslenot sinks lower in the water, suddenly feeling *very* vulnerable and abruptly noticing that he can't locate his clothes or a towel. "Where's my clothes?" he calls to the Martian. "What'd you do—" He stops.

The head of a spider begins to rise like some sort of strange sun over the rim of the tub. In a weird, insectial hiss, it says, "You ask too many questions. Just enjoy the pleasant incongruities of life. Have fun—"

Anslenot screams to the Martian, "Save me!" Strangely modest, he covers his privates with his hands.

The spider has its front legs on the rim of the tub. "We all spend too much time worrying about minor, inconsequential matters," it says. It begins to clamber over the tub rim. Anslenot, frozen in fear, cannot move.

The Martian grabs another *PLAYBOY*, opens up the centerfold and goes, "Eeeeeeeeeeee!" again. It points a finger at the display again and the Beatles song, *Help!* blasts out.

The spider hisses the lyrics to *Help!* and pauses on the rim.

"*Help!*" screams Anslenot.

The spider, poised as if it's contemplating going into the water continues to hiss the lyrics to *Help!*

"Help!" screams Anslenot to the Martian, "Help!"

Splosh—the spider falls into the bathtub—and begins to dissolve, turning into black ink; mortified, Anslenot watches the blackness then fill with stars and galaxies. And as the first, terrible cold touches Anslenot's toes, the Martian throws the *PLAYBOY* above his head, screams "Eeeeeeeeeeee!" and its eyes blaze blue.

Chapter 6

Lovefire

—and Anslenot just falls into another dream only to find himself driving a 1978 battered Pontiac Firebird down a road in a swampy part of Venus. The Martian is with him again. Anslenot says nothing. The blue Martian picks up a bottle of wine off the floorboard and takes a gulp.

"You really like that shit, don't you," says Anslenot.

"Quee-brd," says the Martian. It takes another drink.

"That's the third bottle and we've only been on the road five hours. Are you alcoholic?"

The Martian vigorously shakes its head. "Kwud."

"I think you're in denial," says Anslenot. "Alcoholics usually are." He reaches over. "Gimme a drink."

"Kraee-ruptla-squuz," says the Martian pointing at Anslenot as he gives the bottle to him.

"Nope," says Anslenot, "I'm just a social drinker and just like the taste of it. I've only had three bottles over the last week... hardly an alcoholic. I don't have to drink."

"Gh, gh, gh, gh, gh, gh," laughs the Martian. From a paper sack beneath the seat, it pulls out long ropes of black licorice and begins to eat it. The wet, steamy Venusian vegetation rolls by in a grey-green blur. In the distance, buildings. Anslenot points. "C. S. Lewistown."

The Martian shrugs, "Kwup."

"Okay, maybe it's not as great as the cities in *Martian Chronicles*, but it is still an impressive city." They ride the curve of the road and there, by the roadside, a green Venusian, in shimmering scale-dress, thumbing a ride. She lifts her skirt up a ways like Anslenot remembers actresses doing in some movies; he does not feel particularly aroused by the reptilian thigh nor the lizard-like head with orange eyes and horizontal black pupils.

"Qut, qud dut," says the Martian.

"I am slowing down and I am picking her up," says Anslenot.

The Venusian runs up to the car and peers through the window on the driver's side.

"Ssr rsseem hseeshj shieeemi."

"Yeah," says Anslenot, who, having never heard Venusianspeak before, still does not find it odd that the Venusian or the Martian can understand him or he them. "I'm going all the way to Slime City, the Fungi-side part of town."

"Hsss sh sh seem sh sheem."

"No insult intended, but I'm not feeling really sexy today. Won't cost you nothing."

"Hiss sre reseesh."

"No, not even a blow job."

"Shuu iere rees?"

Anslenot looks over to the Martian then back at the Venusian. "That's a Martian. What he/she/it does about sex—I don't know but it looks like you have lots of choices."

"Hrssshee?"

"Sure," says Anslenot. "Hop in."

The Venusian does—she gets in the back seat—and the Martian does as well.

Anslenot starts out on the road and hears part of the conversation in the backseat.

"Sss sreesh seemshh."

"Ik il tregzzyz ki treg."

"Shee ip?"

"Qud."

Anslenot glances up to the rearview mirror to see them passing the bottle and laughing.

"Gh, gh, gh, gh, gh—"

"Sh, sh, sh, sh, heesh, sh, sh, sh—"

When Anslenot looks up again, they are locked in a steamy, passionate embrace. And when he looks up *again,* he sees glittering fabric and pale robes flying about in the air and then feels the car moving side to side.

"Twuz! Ik kwill gudr!"

"*Shee!* Iee shree ee! Ee!"

"Uk! Uhk! Uukk-uuk!"

"Ee! Ee! EE!"

"*Gu! GUK!*"

"*EEEEEEE!*"

Suddenly, a searing white light fills the back seat; unable to see, Anslenot pulls off the road and looks. Among blue robes, there is a pile of pink sand; among the shimmering scalecloth, something green and slimy oozes and there is the intense smell of cinnamon. Anslenot stares. Then he turns around; the clouds part, the brilliant sunlight pours through; in seconds the vegetation around him bursts into flames, the asphalt softens, the car begins to melt and in the distance, through the choking air, Anslenot sees the mountainous highlands of Ishtar Terra, like a massive, blunted erection, high, mighty and naked in the searing light. And Anslenot screams, "Venus! Now I see you as you are! This is not a dream!" And the steering wheel melts in his hands.

Chapter 7

A Little Deimos, A Little Phobos

Anslenot simply falls into yet *another* dream: he is driving across Mars in a 1965 red Pontiac. The sands are frozen, hard-packed and the road is an ancient roadway built by Martians God knows when. It is early morning and his friend and traveling companion is, again, a Martian. A typical Martian wearing a pale, translucent robe, quietly tinkling earrings that must have been made out of some sort of light alloy, Anslenot assumes. The Martian's skin is light blue, the eyes yellow this time and cat-like. From the Martian's pale four fingered hand, dangles a Marlboro cigarette. The Martian blows smoke out the window.

"You don't know how lucky you got it," says Anslenot, roaring past a billboard for Adidas tennis shoes with super air cushioning that let you jump ten meters — up. "You just don't know how lucky you are not to have come from a fucked-up family."

"Bleek," says the Martian, taking a drag of the cigarette.

"Yeah, well," says Anslenot, "it was bad. All that criticism. Man, they never gave me a moment's peace. Never good enough."

"Spizzak-ek-ke-blurt," says the Martian, sneering. The black pupils narrow.

"Bad news," says Anslenot, "really bad news. I'm glad I never got married. Too afraid I'd repeat the mistakes. But still I wonder..." he sighs.

The Martian says nothing, takes a drag, crosses its long legs and looks away from Anslenot to the Martian countryside flowing along outside as they barrel across the red-sanded road. They pass another billboard fastened to an ancient tower in a once-elegant city. The billboard is for Coors Beer and shows a bunch of Martians partying it up on the side of a canal. They are all discreetly poised away from frontal exposure; the Martians knew no shame; advertising must teach them. The caption on the billboard reads, "Ancient Races, Brand new fun. Coors."

Anslenot turns onto New Route 66 — Xxytyrouy 300 km. McDonald's Hamburgers, Yyyxxzy City, five km.

"I'm glad you understand," says Anslenot, "though I'm surprised Martians do. Your people seem so peaceful and loving to each other. You're lucky."

"Glrk," says the Martian.

"Must be nice to never get lonely," says Anslenot, "to never be afraid. It must be nice to trust that wherever you go, your past won't necessarily rise up and screw you over again, make you act out things that you hoped you'd be done with by now."

The Martian looks over, smiles, and takes another puff on the cigarette. Then it reaches down and picks up a Budwiser. *Ks-spsshhhh.* The spray from the can splatters the inside of the windshield.

"Gh, gh, gh, gh, gh," the Martian laughs. Then it drinks the beer down, opens another one and drinks *it* down.

"I remember all the drinking," says Anslenot, "all the boozing, and the fighting." He reaches out with empty hand. The Martian opens up another beer and gives it to Anslenot. "Glad I don't have that problem. Oh, sometimes I have a bit much, but I can always stop when I want to. Once I went for three days without a drink. Proud of that."

They drive on in silence for awhile, passing several old cities; Syrtis Major, Kliygc; once-proud cities, now in decay, once-high towers, shattered, broken. Finally Anslenot says, "You guys once had a great civilization. Wonder what happened?"

The Martian just dozes, head centimeters from the dash board.

Anslenot muses, driving beneath that pink sky, muses, saying, "You guys had it so easy. Luxury, high living. Wonder what the hell happened. You don't know how good you got it. Or had it. Even if you are two or three sexes, you still got it easier—"

He has just passed another billboard advertising Martians in Jockey shorts and Maidenform bras when the Martian suddenly sits bolt upright and yells, "Skedge!" Then, "Skedge! Skedge! Skedge!" and it yanks the steering wheel from Anslenot's hands; the car swerves off the road, slows and stops. The Martian leaps out from the car, runs to a fluffy, buff-colored Mars bunny sitting beside the road and grabbing it, grins as it walks up to Anslenot's side of the car, and daintily pulls off the creature's arms and legs and tosses the screaming, bloody, wriggling mass into Anslenot's lap. "Gh, gh, gh, gh gh," the Martian laughs and bounds away, into the ruins of an ancient city.

Anslenot screams, wakes up and frantically, looks around the room. *It's o.k.*, he thinks, *it's o.k.* "*Jesus*" he whispers, "*Jee-zuz!*" He swallows. "It's o.k. It's the city of 'S', it's Earth, it's—"

He draws in a shaky breath. "It's o.k." He lays back down, swallows again, then looks out the window—looks out only to see two small moons tumbling, falling across the pink sky.

Tink, tink, tink, the sound of something tapping on the glass. Anslenot turns; a Martian looks back at him, then pointing to Anslenot, grins and laughs.

Chapter 8

Syrtis Major Blues

Dazed, Anslenot slowly notices he's walking the pink sands of Mars. Soon he comes to a road and after a few minutes walking on the pink stone road, he comes to a car. It is red, and on the back of it, below the hatchback window with a cartoon image of skiers skiing down the volcano Olympus Mons in spacesuits with the K2 emblem on the back, there is the car model name: SYRTIS by MicrosoftNabiscoToyotaFord. Anslenot peeks in the driver's seat. No one there. He glances upward to see a giant dirigible in the sky, shaped like a spider and there is a visual display on the abdomen: "Armstrong Spiders Grip the Road." Pause. "7:30 AM." Pause. "Temperature, -40 F." Anslenot momentarily wonders why he is not frozen as hard as the rocks. He shrugs. "It doesn't make any sense," he says to himself. "Nothing makes any sense. Why am I here? How did I get here? What happens next?" He notices keys in the ignition. The door is unlocked; he starts the car and zooms off down the road. In ten minutes or so, he comes to a huge red, white and blue diner built as a huge tarantula. A sign dangles above the opening at the "head" of the spider: "Delicacies Inn." Anslenot walks in, pushing open the wet doors; looking up, he sees a constant drool leaking down from digestive glands cleverly designed as pipes. His fingers burn from touching the glass. Inside, Anslenot is met with Elvis Presley's music; *Heartbreak Hotel* ends and then is followed by *Don't Be Cruel*. Martians skate around on rollerblades delivering orders for other Martians sitting at tables that are, again, designed like spiders. There is a dance floor and two Martians are doing break dancing.

"Gleep."

Anslenot looks up. "Oh, you."

"Glurz," says the Martian, and it looks at Anslenot.

"So, why'd you dismember that Mars bunny and throw it in my lap?"

"Gh, gh, gh, gh, gh," laughs the Martian.

"Sure had me fooled. I thought you Martians had it all figured out. But boy, you sure don't. You're every bit as obnoxious as anything I've ever seen. Whew."

"Gh, gh, gh," laughs the Martian again.

"And then there was that thing on Venus," says Anslenot. "You making it with that Venusian chick. Wow. Was that an orgasm or does love lead to annihilation?"

The Martain smiles dreamily. "Gweewizzzzz."

"I'll never have the answer, will I?" says Anslenot.

It is at that point that a little silver spider lowers itself between Anslenot and the Martian. The little spider looks at the Martian for a minute and then somehow manages to turn in mid-air to look at Anslenot. "I don't think you're going to like it here," it says.

"Why am I not going to like it here?"

"Believe me, I just don't think you will. You don't know what you're getting into."

"What am I getting into?" asks Anslenot.

"Believe me," says the little silver spider, "you don't want to know."

"Why don't I want to know?"

"Don't ask," replies the spider.

"But I *am* asking," says Anslenot.

"You're going to wish you hadn't."

"Why would I wish I hadn't?"

"You don't want to know."

"But I *do* want to know."

"If you knew, you would be very unhappy."

"How do I know that unless I know?"

"You don't want to know."

"But I *do* want to know."

"You *really* don't," says the little silver spider. "You really, *really* don't want to know."

Abruptly, the lights above begin to jiggle and then pull up. The Martians cheer. Elvis belts out *Jailhouse Rock*.

"I think," says the little spider, "you had better leave. This is the Martian's pathology — not yours. You already have yours."

"I do?" asks Anslenot. "What is it?"

"You don't want to know."

"Yes I do," says Anslenot. "Tell me what my pathology is."

"No," says the little silver spider. "You don't want to know. No one wants to know what their pathology is."

"What about the Martians. What is their pathology?"

"You don't want to know that," says the silver spider. "Besides, no time."

Abruptly, the ceiling panels began to pull back, revealing tubes, and structures that remind Anslenot of intestines; a gentle mist begins to drift down. Abruptly, Anslenot understands. The Martians dance in a frenzy and shriek in joy. Anslenot grabs a chair and, jamming a descending inside shutter, breaks the window and crawls out. Outside he dashes to the car, gets in and drives. In the rearview mirror, he sees the spider, now black, settle down in the sands, to feed, absorb and... bloat.

It Will Just Get Worse...

Chapter 9

Little Truthful Fibs

Anslenot sits on a rock staring over the reddish sands of Mars. He shivers. "Boy, it's cold."

Ray Bradbury, sitting at a typewriter perched on a rock, smiles. "No, it's not. It's a wonderful summer day. And if you look real hard, you can see sand ships way out there."

Anslenot looks to the direction Bradbury is pointing. "Sand fleas, maybe, sand ships, no." He shivers. "Not even sand fleas. Their little asses musta been frozen off a long, *long* time ago."

But Bradbury shakes his head. "Would you listen to that. No imagination. That's sad."

Anslenot sighs. And looks away. When he looks back, Bradbury is gone. Instead, Percival Lowell is sitting there with a small telescope. He sighs in wonderment. "Ah, what those Martians did. Built those amazing canals to transport water from the poles to save their dying planet."

"'Scuse me," says Anslenot, "but I think the planet has been dead a long, *long*, time-before the Martians ever came along which means they never came along at all."

Percival Lowell sighs again. "There's Syrtis Major. And there is the Grand Canal."

Anslenot stares. "Boy, you got better eyes than I do. I don't see *nothin'*."

But Percival Lowell just keeps staring through his telescope and when Anslenot looks away, he hears a *clink*. He looks. Percival Lowell is gone, but his telescope remains. Anslenot picks it up with great trepidation and looking through it, sees great sand ships slipping across the silicate floors of vast silent seas. He watches the Martians toiling, digging the canals, to save their doomed civilization. He looks in another direction and sees the Martians lifting off for their invasion of Earth as told by H. G. Wells and looking again, sees John Carter adventuring on Barsoom. Then, looking up, Anslenot sees a glint of silver in the sky; training his telescope on that, he realizes it is a craft like the Viking lander. It lands. Anslenot sees a door slide open and a figure climb out, down the ladder, then stare at the pink sky, the frosted, reddish sands. The figure turns, then falls to his knees and Anslenot realizes it is himself, on the sands of Mars, weeping, weeping, weeping.

Chapter 10

He Dreams of Watches

Anslenot looks up from his weeping and realizes he is not on Mars. He does not know *where* he is and his head, his vision fills with scenes of watches and of crawly things with faces prehistoric and a land of melting landscapes and he wonders where Mindy, an old girlfriend, is. As as he wonders, a tarantula wanders by in the leaden twilight and Anslenot screeches in fear, "In the name of all that is holy, why am I here again? What is the occasion?"

The spider stops and it says, "Who knows why any of us are here? We're all slogging through this, waiting, waiting, maybe for magic, maybe for the End, maybe for something Grand and Glorious." The spider hisses for what reason Anslenot cannot comprehend. Disgust? Irony? Derision? Despair?

"I've been here before," says Anslenot plaintively, "yet I'm back again."

The spider begins to move on. "So you want a medal, or a cookie or what?"

"I want an answer," says Anslenot.

"Don't we all," says the spider, slogging away, "don't we all. And yet there is only one real answer. You know it as well as I do." The tarantula moves away.

"Wait, stop, I want the answer!"

The spider continues, not heeding Anslenot's plea.

Anslenot turns, and in the twilight, the landscape congeals enough for a store to emerge, ooze up from the goo of a land that more often than not flows like molasses. He walks into the store which turns out to be a book store. In the middle of the floor, a newspaper brightly burns but it isn't doing any harm and everyone ignores it. Anslenot goes up to a check-out person, a tall, blond, bearded man reading a blue book with no title. He wonders if there is significance there and decides that maybe it doesn't make a lot of difference. The man smiles grimly. There is no glass in his glasses. He wears a red tie with a picture of Gorbachev on it. The birthmark on his forehead has been changed to look like a dollar sign. The salesman waits.

"I need information," says Anslenot.

"You may have to cross my palm with lots of silver, buddy," says the salesman. "Tell me what you want and I'll tell you how much it's gonna cost..."

"Reality," says Anslenot. "What has happened to reality? What is the answer to everything?"

The salesman nods. "That's a cheap question," he says. "Won't cost you a thing because it's so easy."

"Well?" says Anslenot.

"Well what?"

"Reality. The answer."

The salesman points. "Look over in the cookbook section."

"Wouldn't it be over in the philosophy section?" asks Anslenot.

"Do you work here?" says the salesman.

"No," says Anslenot.

"Then don't fucking tell me what to do."

"I wasn't—" says Anslenot.

"Furthermore, in response to your other implied accusation, I did not kill my father nor marry my mother. You got that? Not only *that*, I did not best my father and my mother did not then reject him because of her love for me. I did not do that."

Anslenot backs away and heads for the cookbook section.

"Nor do I hate my father and lust after my mother—" the salesman yells.

Anslenot turns a corner and picks up a cookbook. There is a picture of a recipe for a banana loaf; it sits on a plain that looks melted and is draped by melted watches. When Anslenot looks up, the bookstore vanishes; he is again outside, on the plain and looking off into the distance, he sees another beast lumbering toward him and it is ridden by a figure. And as they draw close, Anslenot sees the face of the beast is human, and contorted with great sorrow. The figure looks down. Anslenot looks up and finally says, "Are you Dali, the painter?"

The figure smiles and tosses Anslenot a limp watch.

Anslenot points to the contorted face of the beast. "What's going on? Why...?"

"'Human condition', my friend. The great human condition; joy and sorrow, hopes and despair, dreams and death."

Anslenot looks to the dark beast, to the melting landscapes, to the dark brooding sky and feels a chill wind blow. "What?" he whispers, "what is the nature of all of this—"

Dali tosses Anslenot another melted watch. Then he kicks the beast in the flanks. "Come now," he says, "you know the answer as well as I do."

"No," says Anslenot, "I don't know the answer."

"Bah," says Dali, "everyone knows the answer. It's just that we keep forgetting it and even when we remember it, we can't act on it." He mutters the answer and Anslenot cannot hear it.

"Wait!" yells Anslenot. "Wait! I didn't hear the answer."

"*Hissssss.*"

Anslenot turns. The spider lords over Anslenot. "Hisssss," and the spider sighs or rages—Anslenot cannot tell which. "Hisss. You know the answer. Everyone knows the answer. How can you not know?"

Anslenot stands, looking up at the spider and shakes his head.

"You don't know the answer," hisses the spider. "You don't know the answer. Without *that* answer, *this* is the all the answer you have; *this* is the *only* answer there is." And the spider descends.

Chapter 11

The Crossing

The spider descends and Anslenot covers his head, waiting for the inevitable. Suddenly, it is black. Slowly, the darkness fades and when Anslenot can see again, he sees that the sky is the color of frosted lead with parallel bars of darker grey. Anslenot sits on a ferry boat watching the City of S. fade into the greyness, watching the brutally carved and ossified erections of buildings become smothered in the deepening twilight. He sits, then stands and shivers silently and thinks to himself, *And this is one of the better days.*

The ship shudders and rumbles. Black, oily smoke drifts down in a putrid mist. Water rushing alongside the ship is the sound of hissing snakes. *Oh, God*, thinks Anslenot. He turns and stumbles into the dark interior of the ship, passing the walls once yellow and gay, painted with scenes of mothers embracing their daughters, fathers and sons smiling at each other—the walls are badly stained and discolored by streaks of yellow and brown from leaking plumbing. Other scenes of a flag, and a statue of freedom, have large areas where paint has blistered and peeled away to reveal the red and dried scab-like crustation of color and tortured and rusted metal beneath as if the very structure is decaying and rotting from within.

This, too, was once new, thinks Anslenot. *Oh, how the artists believed. Oh, how time showed them to be liars.* He wraps his thick black coat around him not for warmth, but for protection. He glances at the smudged windows of the ferry. The long, low hill of the opposite shore looks like a horizontal leg, but stripped of the coarse hair of vegetation. Left are the black sinews and musculature of rock and tendons exposed. Some enterprise on top of the leg-like ridge of land is excavating and blasting; vast volumes of drifting brown dust billow up. Anslenot says nothing to himself. He remembers someone saying that on another part of the ridge, there once was a golden statue of a woman, standing proud, draped in long flowing gowns and a hand reaching to the sky, fingers extended. And it was said that sometimes at sunrise, the sun could be seen, from a special vantage point, to balance on the statue's finger tips. A long time ago, thinks Anslenot, before the greyness, before the razing of the statue for its gold and metals, before stink and stench and vileness rotted away what was left. Anslenot sighs. "When was the last time I felt well? Ate a decent meal? Cut my hair? Brushed my teeth? How long ago?"

The ship heaves, shudders, rolls and the water is dark and disturbed as though something vast, dark and unknown moves through the depths of the littered sea. A cold rain smelling of sulphur begins to fall. Where it touches paint, the paint hisses, pales, blisters and peels off, again revealing the scarlet, the rust of the metal beneath.

Anslenot gropes in the twilight of the passenger deck. Abruptly the lights come on—then go out again—and finally come on as a flickering glow, a spastic, pathetic trickle of feeble light—but it illuminates little. A television shows the President speaking; behind him, a vast window, smoke boils in the distance. The President looks haggard—his tie askew. He is pleading, his arms open wide, but the sound is off and someone is retching violently nearby, *It makes no difference*, thinks Anslenot. *It makes no difference at all. I can tell no difference.*

Anslenot sits. A woman nearby with hair the color of burning strawberries and smelling of rancid chocolate and eggs looks at him. A long, fresh scar runs down the side of her face. Her front teeth are broken. Her look turns to numbness and it looks like she is trying to mouth some words. "Love?" guesses Anslenot. "Father?" She continues to stare and Anslenot gives up trying to make any sense of her.

"There's hope, brother!" says a fat priest nearby with mirror sunglasses and three fingers on his left hand. His black cloak has holes in it as though something has gnawed at the fabric. "There's hope," and he draws in a long, shaky breath.

Anslenot says nothing. The priest leans toward him and opens a Bible which, from the way the priest holds the book, Anslenot can see that, for the most part, is filled with blank pages. The priest or someone has tried to fill the pages with crayon drawings that a child might do—a green lawn, on which sits a crudely drawn orange house with a tilted rectangle of a door and windows on each side. A stick figure—a child, Anslenot thinks—is swinging on a brown tree with red blotches on the branches. In the upper left, a big smiling sun pours rays across the page. "Believe brother," says the priest and Anslenot notices sweat inching, halting down the priest's face and neck. The priest turns a page and there is, pasted on the page, a picture of a 1957 Chevrolet. On another page is a crisp and green dollar bill protected by Saranwrap. On yet another page is pasted an unopened condom. "Believe," says the man and his voice somehow reminds Anslenot of a spider's hiss. His sunglasses reflect Anslenot's image.

Anslenot pulls back, shakes his head, and looks away. Nearby, another man, with hair combed as though by a typhoon, sits looking out at the coming darkness of the approaching shore. "Fuck," he says, "God damn mother fucking son of a bitch." He then abruptly yells it, over and over again. He smashes his fist into his head.

A little girl in a pink ballerina tutu and silver slippers dances around him and then running up to him—suddenly looks horrified, then runs away—only to return, dance and run up to him, look horrified, run away and dance again. Nearby, a boy hides behind deck chairs and watching the man, slowly and religiously practices the words the man speaks. When the man smashes his head with his fist, the little boy does the same.

Anslenot looks down. A mongrel has just peed on his foot. The dog looks up and a red and pus-filled socket marks the place where an eye had been. The dog smiles to reveal white, perfectly white, small needle-like teeth. Suddenly, two large black spiders drop into Anslenot's lap and fight, scramble and bite each other.

"Oh, shit," whispers Anslenot. He pulls the sleeve of his coat down over his right hand and brushes the spiders away. He stands, watching, then wishing to go back to the City of S. *But I can't go back to it*, he thinks. *It's even worse there—people coming into contact with the lies and screaming,* He swallows and pulls his black coat closer. *At least people here know.*

The ship rolls again and shakes sharply as if something beneath has bumped it hard, perhaps even grabbed it. Silverware slides off tables, and glasses and bowls crash and shatter on the steel floor. The lights go out completely. Anslenot gets up to see how close the ship is to the shore—but it is impossible to know for the shore is lost in darkness—forever.

Chapter 12

The Truth

Crunch. The ferry plows into a pier. In the darkness Anslenot scrambles off the ferry and discovers, as the sky lightens, that he's in a city; as he walks, he walks past the dying men in doorways, past the laughing women flouncing stained shirts at passersby. The sky is filled with grit, dust and smoke; overhead another jet screams by and launches missiles at the Opposition headquarters. As Anslenot passes a doorway, he is seized, his arms pinned behind his back and someone unseen says, "Here's a message for your friends. Tell them that we know. It's all over with. Tell them! The Militant Lambs are through."

He is shoved out from the dark doorway. Dazed, frightened and confused, he stumbles. Nearby, loudspeakers blare militant music and then a strident voice. "Citizens. The Opposition is crumbling before our mighty onslaught. With God on our side and the women toiling in the great factories turning out glorious weapons of Peace and our men fighting on the front, our victory is assured. Keep heart and know victory is at hand. God rest you merry, citizenry, there is nothing to dismay..."

A nearby blast sends Anslenot to his knees; the brilliant white light bleaches gutted and burned skyscrapers. Anslenot gets up, stumbles on and suddenly he is grabbed from behind, an arm around his neck, and pulled into a doorway.

"The Militant Lambs have a message for your Opposition. Tell them to call off the attack or else they are through. Finished. Got it? Good. Tell them."

He is pushed out of the doorway and he again stumbles on.

"Migod," he whispers, "I haven't got the *faintest* idea *who* these people *are*."

More jets screech overhead; the blood-red jets of the Opposition striking back at the white jets of the Militant Lambs. From loudspeakers come sounds of a struggle.

"...Fascist Lambs... take your God..."

"...Kennedy Lovers — baby killers — atheists — get your hands — "

More struggle and finally a triumphant voice, "Citizens, we are free of Hardliners of the Right, free of the Fascists — Liberation is at hand. A new Dictatorship of the Proletariat is now here. For the time being, the press must serve the state and all art must convey socialist realism — "

Gun shots, screaming and another voice on the loudspeakers. "In the name of the Militant Lambs, this radio station has been freed from the leftist fascists. The Militant Lambs are now the supreme rulers of this section. In observance of this victory, everyone is ordered to drop to their knees and pray to God; those that do not will be regarded as totalitarian supporters and executed. Also, the press will serve the Will of God, not the state, and all art will be for the glorification of God, so you see, citizens, how much freer you really are."

There is strident, militant music and Anslenot runs to a parked car, climbs into the back seat and hides. The radio is on, the radio is always on, while overhead the jets scream and which ones they are he cannot tell and he covers his head, waiting for he knows not what.

Chapter 13
The Lure

When Anslenot thinks all is clear, he gets out of the car—a flash of light, an explosion; Anslenot runs to a doorway. He turns and hears rock and gravel rattle in the doorway, feels himself pelted by debris. "Oh, my God, he whispers, does it ever stop? How long has this been going on now? How much more? How much more!" He huddles closer to the door and—it gives. Quietly, furtively, Anslenot pushes again; the door opens—suddenly he is yanked inside. Darkness. Whoever pulled him inside throws him against the wall and someone else grabs his arms and pins them behind him.

"Listen," the voice says, "it's just going to get worse. Much worse. There is little time. So little time left. But we do what we can. You must do what you must do."

"What—" says Anslenot.

"Don't talk," whispers the other, yanking back on Anslenot's arms. "Just listen. There is a great evil out there; a great war is going on, by whom we do not know, for what reason we cannot guess and there is only one way the war can be fought and stopped. The enemy is cunning; they play with our minds but we have a way of finding them out. You're going to help us."

In the blackness, Anslenot can see nothing but he feels the closeness of the speaker, can smell his breath; a sickly sweetness as if the speaker has been chewing mint. "You will know what to do. And if you do it right, you can change the course of events. You do have power, more than you realize. We will save you—you and others like you can change things. Farewell."

Abruptly, he is let go; his assailants, like rats, scuttle into the darkness. Anslenot falls against the wall; he shivers, brings his arms in front of him and rubs them. The building shakes. Another explosion. Abruptly, he is blinded by color and light and when his eyes adjust, it is as though he is right up against a television screen or perhaps in it, he cannot tell, but what he can see is that he is between two people: on the right, his mother, on the left his father. They are seated at a white, glass-covered iron table. Beneath the glass, interlocking loops of metal and open spaces; like stencils, thinks Anslenot. His father looks as Anslenot remembers, with his walrus mustache, his tan, but slightly sunken cheeks and those sad but stern blue eyes. He is dressed in white, a white cap and a blue bow tie.

Anslenot looks to his mother. She sits, looking at him, her hand around a tall glass of something pale, lemonade, perhaps. She too, is dressed in white, her grey hair is cut close to her head and she wears a white hat, wide-brimmed, with a small blue feather. Her eyes are greener than Anslenot remembers, and her cheeks pinker. She motions to Anslenot. "Sit down. Join us."

Anslenot shakes his head. "This... is... a movie...? I can't sit..."

"Sure you can," she says. "Even if this is a movie, well, humor us. Sit down."

Anslenot unconsciously begins to sit and... sure enough, there is a chair beneath him. Anslenot looks at his parents, then beyond them, to the white split rail fence, the high apple trees, and a field behind where a pale grey horse nibbles grass.

"We haven't seen you for a while," says the father.

Anslenot shakes his head. "Before I saw you in the bus, I thought you'd been dead for—for awhile."

"Oh, yes," says the father and he laughs; a drink abruptly appears in his hand. "These things happen. The silly war. Oh, this country—if the taxes don't get you, the lasers, the smart bombs will. Dreadful. Dreadful."

In the background, the horse is changing into a coyote.

"But how are you, dear?" says Anslenot's mother.

"How—did you—get here," Anslenot asks. "Before the bus, the last time I saw you, you were being—choked... beaten—by the People's Democratic Militia after the civil war—"

"Patriotic War," says his mother.

"International Fight for Freedom and the Enslavement of the Majority War," says his father.

Anslenot's mother and father stare at each other, then laugh easily. "Same thing," the father says. "But how are you?" they both ask.

A waiter then appears, bringing lunch. He serves Anslenot's mother. "Ah," she says, "fried scorpion and maggot soup. Oh, it looks so yummy."

The waiter then serves Anslenot's father. "You ordered the filet of harelip dog and cockroach salad."

"I did," he says.

Mesmerized, Anslenot watches this then looks off into the distance to see a huge spider leap upon the coyote and, bringing it down, bites it, then wraps it in silk and drags it away. "How—have—I been?" says Anslenot. "It has been dreadful out there, the wars, they never stop. The lies, the lies, always the lies—I know there's an answer, but no one will tell me."

His mother gently sips her soup; her social graces are perfect and she says, "Wars are difficult things, they really are. Make people late for work and give babies colic. And sometimes the—" she gestures with a hand, "—the things they use in the bombs must play havoc with the genes—dreadful—three-headed children, two-fingered babies, black roses, early deaths — dreadful, dreadful. But my son, what brings you here aside from shelter from the war?"

"But," says Anslenot, "why are we fighting? Why does the war go on and on and on?"

"Care for some soup, dear?" says his mother, "or would you like to order? They still have Rattus Norwegian with mustard sauce or slightly decayed trout with active Hanford Radium potatoes — gives you a *wonderful* glow."

"The war," says Anslenot, "the war."

His father finishes his drink and stares at his meal. "You need some new clothes. When was the last time you had a bath?"

"I don't —" says Anslenot, "it has been so long..."

His mother smiles. "And to what do we owe your visit this fine day?"

"It was an accident. A bomb fell, I took shelter in a doorway, the door opened..."

"My," says Anslenot's father, "what a strange coincidence that that should happen... but now that it did, what have you heard about the war? We've been hearing about the Rainbow weapon — since you seem to be so much out there you must know — it sounds wonderfully curious —"

Anslenot shakes his head and closes his eyes. "Oh, God," he whispers, "God dammit —" He blinks his eyes and shakes his head again, then says, "Yes," and he pushes the chair back and says, slowly steadily, "yes, yes, it truly is interesting that I would be here now, isn't it? Tell me about the war —'"

"Honestly," says the father, "do we really need to talk of it? The war goes on, no one can stop it —"

"Why am I talking to two dead people?" says Anslenot.

"Dead?" his father says, "how can that be?"

"That I missed you so much," says Anslenot, "that I *missed* you *so* much... but somehow, somewhere I knew..." He closes his eyes and when he opens them, the split rail fence has vanished, the grass is gone and his mother and father look to each other; abruptly, their faces crack and behind them, the mandibles —

"*The enemy!*" someone shouts.

"*Duck!*" someone else yells.

Anslenot does; a blaze of light; the smell of burned flesh and Anslenot is on the ground. He feels hands on him, lifting him and someone is whispering to him, "You unmasked the enemy — you will be remembered and honored... remembered and honored..." and Anslenot sobs in rage... and sorrow.

Chapter 14

Strange Interlude In Four Parts: 1

On the corner, a nicely dressed man stands. He wears a grey, pin-striped suit, white shirt, red tie. In one hand, a briefcase. In another, a copy of the *New York Times*. Near his side, a huge tarantula crouches. A spider as big as a dog. Anslenot, curious, approaches the man.

"Wow," he says, "nice spider you got."

The man looks down. "Not my spider. Must be yours."

Anslenot shakes his head. "Nope. It was standing by you when I approached."

The man looks unimpressed.

The spider just stands there, squats there, whatever it is that spiders do when they're on all eight legs. The eyes are dark and it might as well be a statue except for minute movements of the pedipalps.

"Well," says Anslenot, "if it's not your spider and if it's not *my* spider, whose spider is it?"

The man studies the business section of the *Times*. "Got me."

"How'd you get so lucky as to not have spiders?" Anslenot asks.

"Perfect parents," the man says, scanning the stock market listings.

"Hm," says Anslenot examining the spider from a safe distance.

A big grey dog, drooling and slobbering, comes wandering over. It sits near the spider and drools copiously. The spider does not move. The dog gets up, wanders over to a nearby fire hydrant, pees an unbelieveably long time, and then pads off. Overhead, a jet explodes.

Anslenot looks around. "Is there any meaning to any of this?"

The man shrugs, "'Toys R Us' has gone up in value," he says. He studies the paper some more. "Sony is down."

"That's it?" asks Anslenot.

"As far as I'm concerned," says the man. He folds his paper up. He looks down at the spider. "Sure am glad that's not my beast."

He turns, and, almost as if absent-mindedly, shoves a grandmotherly woman in front of a bus. The spider moves and follows the man.

Chapter 15

Number 2

On the corner, a nicely dressed man stood. He wore a grey, pin-striped suit, white shirt, red tie. In one hand, a briefcase. In the other, copy of the

New York Times. Near his side, a huge tarantula. A spider as big as a hog. Anslenot, curious, approached the man.

"Wow," he said, "nice spider you got. Quite some spider there."

The man looked down. "Not my spider. Must be yours."

Anslenot shook his head. "Nope. It was standing by you when I approached."

The man looks unhampered.

The spider just stood there, squatted there, whatever it was that spiders did when they were on all eight legs. The eyes were dark and it might as well have been a statue except for minute movements of the pedipalps.

"Well," said Anslenot, "if it's not your spider and if it's not my spider, whose spider is it?"

The man studied the business section of the *Times*. "Got me."

"How'd you get so lucky as to not have spiders?" Anslenot asked.

"Perfect parents," the man said, scanning the stock market listings.

"Hm," said Anslenot, examining the spider from a safe distance.

A big, grey dog, drooling and slobbering, came wandering over.

It sat near the spider and drooled copiously. The spider did not move. The dog got up, wandered over to a nearby fire hydrant, peed an unbelievably long time and then sauntered off. Overhead, a jet exploded.

Anslenot looked around. "Is there any meaning to any of this?"

The man shrugged. "'Toys R Us' has gone up in value," he said.

He studied the paper some more. "Sony is down."

"That's it?" asked Anslenot.

"As far as I'm concerned," said the man. He folded his paper up. He looked down at the spider. "Sure am glad that's not my little toy boat."

At that point, the bus came, stopped. The man turned and walked away as the doors opened and the spider clambered on.

Chapter 16

Number 3

On the corner, a nicely dressed man will stand. He will wear a grey, pin-striped suit, white shirt, red tie. In one hand, a briefcase. In the other, a copy of the *New York Times*. Near his side, a huge tarantula, a spider as big as a hog. Anslenot, curious, will approach the man.

"Wow," he will say, "nice spider you got there. Impressive."

The man will look down. "Not *my* spider. Must be yours."

Anslenot will shake his head. "Nope. It was standing by you when I approached."

The man will look unimpeded.

The spider will just stand there, squat there, whatever it is that spiders do when they're on all eight legs. The eyes will be dark and it might as well be a statue except for minute movements of the pedipalps.

"Well," Anslenot will say, "if it's not your spider and if it's not *my* spider, whose spider is it?"

The man will study the business section of the *Times*. "Got me."

"How'd you get so lucky as to not have spiders?" Anslenot will inquire.

"Perfect parents," the man will say, scanning the stock market listings.

"Hm," Anslenot will muse, examining the spider from a safe distance.

A big, grey dog, drooling and slobbering, will come wandering over. It will sit near the spider and drool copiously. The spider will not move. The dog will get up, wander over to a nearby fire hydrant, pee an unbelievably long time, and then wander off. Overhead, a jet will explode.

Anslenot will look around. "Is there any meaning to any of this?"

The man will shrug. "'Toys R Us' has gone down in value," he will say. He will study the paper some more. "Sony is up."

"That's it?" Anslenot will ask.

"As far as I'm concerned," the man will say. He will rip his paper up then look down at the spider. "Sure am glad that's not *my* beast."

A black and shiny Mercedes Benz will pull up; the man will get in. Anslenot will shake his head, turn to walk away and stop. He will look back. The spider will be following *him*.

Chapter 17
Numero 4, For, Fore, Four

On the corner, a man, dressed, stands. He wears grey, pin-striped shoes, red shirt, white tie, white suit. In one hand, briefs, in another, a tabloid titled *Sluts Today*. Near his side, a zebra colored tarantula. A tarantula as big as a fog. Anslenot, curious, approaches the man.

"Zwiff," he will say, "spider you got."

The man looks clown. "Not my spider. Must be yours."

Anslenot will shook his shlock. "Nup. It was tap dancing by you when I approached."

The man looks. Unimpressed.

The spider just stands there, squats there, whatevers there, or what it is that spiders do when they're on all eight legs give or take a few. The eyes are dark as congealed blood mixed with chocolate and it might as well have been as much a statue of David except for minute movements of suckerets.

"Well," presumes Anslenot, "if it's not your spider and it's not my spider, then—?" He will raise his eyebrows up until he looked like enterprising Spock.

The man rubs his eyes with his tie, then turns the paper upside down. "Dunno. Just dunno."

"How'd you get so flamboyant as to not get webbed with spiders? How'd you out-slick them? Chewing gum in their spineretts or what? Say?"

"I had a parentectomy," the man says, taking stock of the market in the busy-ness section of the paper he was also conjecturing with.

"Gwiff," will muse Anslenot, perjuring the spider from a safe distance.

A big, grey fog, droolingslobbering, comes wandering over. It will sit near the spider and drool copiously. The spider does not move. The fog gets up, wanders over to a nearby fired hydrant and damped an unbelievably long time and then will drift off. Overhead the moon explodes.

Anslenot looks around. "Is there any *angst* to any of this?"

The man hiccups his shoulders. "'Gamed Are Us' is down in value," he says. He studies the paper some more. "Sony has moved to a different star cluster."

"That's it?" will ask Anslenot.

"As far as I'm festooned," muses the man. He folds the busy-ness section of the paper up and down and inserts the stiff section into the crotch of the rest of the paper as he looks askance/askewed at the spider and ejaculates. "Sure am glad that's not my little legged pony."

Kwa-foom! The spider explodes in blood and light and eggs; a massive monarch butterfly arises from the remains of the spider; it grows even larger, seizes a city bus and screams lines from T. S. Eliot's *The Love Song of J. Alfred Prufrock*, "I grow old! I grow old! I shall wear the bottom of my trousers rolled! Shall I part my hair behind? Do I dare to eat a peach?"

Chapter 18

The Treatment

Still foolish, Anslenot thinks that he might be able to get help. He gets on the elevator in a famous hospital in the city of S. The hospital, which has a commanding view of the bay, is known for its innovation and down-hominess. Anslenot notices he is the only one on the elevator.

The music, which is a lighthearted musak rendition of Stravinsky's *Rite of Spring* which is basically carried by harmonica and xylophone and background chorus of howling cats in heat, abruptly stops. "You are Anslenot," comes a voice over the loudspeaker.

The elevator doors, which have closed, seem to Anslenot that somehow they will never open again. Anslenot says nothing.

The voice. "You are Anslenot."

Anslenot looks around the elevator. He pushes "door open," but the doors remain closed. The elevator starts moving up. Floor two.

"Just because you are not answering me, doesn't mean I don't think you're there, Anslenot." Anslenot wonders what type of innovation this is. Finally, he bites. "Why do you want to know who I am and what difference is it to you?"

"We know all about you," comes the voice, "we are an innovative hospital. We know everything. Everything is tied into me, TRAUMA, the computer. TRAUMA, by the way, stands for The Radically Automated Underutilized Major Annoyance."

"Can you take me to the eighth floor?"

"Of course I can," says the voice, "but I won't. We have all sorts of floors to stop at first."

Anslenot swallows.

"Floor two," says the voice, "Cardiology, Vascular and Nightmares."

The door opens and Anslenot sees himself smacked across a room by his grandmother because he simply, at age two, wanted another Nabisco Shredded Wheat biscuit.

"Gods, *why'd* you show me that—" and Anslenot cringes at the back of the elevator, suddenly sweating, his arms wrapped about him.

The door closes. "Floor three," says the voice. "Orthopedics and Young Adult Violence."

The door opens and Anslenot sees himself pinned against the door by his father as he twists Anslenot's shirt collar and says, "By God, you little son of a bitch, you're gonna *remember* this." Why Anslenot didn't pee in his pants then is unknown to him. The doors close.

"Why," sobs Anslenot, "*why* are you showing me this?"

"New program," comes the voice, "computerized therapy. Making the most out of your stay and any time you spend here. A little therapy never hurt anyone. How many times have you done a Bradshaw Spontaneous Age Regression just because some event in the present reminded your subconscious of an event long-forgotten consciously but still on-going subconsciously? Wouldn't you like to be free of such torment?"

"Oh, God," Anslenot sobs, "I want to be free of *you*."

"Have to wait for your proper floor. Floor Four. Rehabilitation and Terrors."

The doors open and Anslenot looks out into a tropical jungle with strange, misshapen beasts lurking about in the foliage. It gets darker and suddenly the scene is filled with glowing, staring eyes, looking right at Anslenot.

Anslenot flattens out in horror against the back of the car.

The doors close. "Fifth floor," the voice says, "Major Life Traumas and Zero Medical Insurance Coverage Department."

The doors open, and Anslenot looks out at an appalling scene of people with broken minds and souls and bones and Medical Insurance examiners going around to each one and saying, "Nope, not covered. Sorry. Nope, need to be five minutes younger, coverage denied. Nope, can't be male or female in order to get covered, coverage denied. Nope, nope, your common cold is far too pedestrian and the medicine not expensive enough. Coverage denied. Sorry."

Finally, the elevator gets to the Eighth floor but the doors will not open. "I want off," says Anslenot. "This is my floor."

"No, it's not," says TRAUMA, "this can't be your floor."

"It is," says Anslenot, "this is the floor and I must get off."

"No," says the voice.

"How do *you* know?" says Anslenot.

"Because I say so."

"Fuck you," says Anslenot and he rushes the door. It opens and Anslenot bolts out, out to the far, far away arms of the galaxy Andromeda, waiting to embrace him.

Chapter 19

Job

The great galaxy Andromeda embraces Anslenot and for a brief moment, he feels peaceful and then finds himself back at the hospital as an employee, and thinking, "Your eyes are brown and it's just too bad you're mad," and Anslenot sees himself going out a door, leaving the nurse standing there, looking impatient, weird, and thinking everyone else is nuts except her. The door closes with a good solid *chunk* but then the madness begins. Who knows why it begins or how; it begins and that is all that matters. Once outside the door, he sees the door opposite him open, and the hallway on the other end stretches off to infinity, off to a starry sky.

"Oh, shit," Anslenot says, and he turns to get back on the unit, but, of course, the door is locked and his key—his key is gone. He does not understand his sudden panic; he turns about and decides that now that he is out there, then perhaps he can be useful, put the fear aside, be useful. "Yes," he thinks, "be useful." Then he thinks, "How do I get out of here? Do I want to get out of here?"

From nowhere, a baseball comes flying out of the other hallway, splats against the nearby wall and then rolls across the white tiled floor to the door which opens to the stairway.

Klip, klop, klop, klip, klop, and the ball bounces down the steps. He hears the ball fall down the stairs and for some incomprehensible reason, he decides that's the most important thing he can do—retrieve the baseball. He runs down the stairs and at the bottom of the stairwell, thirteen steps later, he grabs the baseball and says to himself, "Thirteen steps—wasn't that how many there were in the moneylender's flat in Dostoyevsky's *Crime and Punishment!* Thirteen steps. Is somehow, someone going to die? Why would I think of this now?" He turns to climb the steps, but every time he steps on one, it yields and becomes flat with the inclined surface. He steps on another step; it, too, flattens down. He leans over to examine the situation; his pen drops from his pocket and turns into a rattlesnake; it shakes its tail and slithers on up the steps—which do not yield to it. He drops the baseball and it brightly bounces back up the steps and at the top, the nurse appears, the strange nurse with the brown eyes and she looks down at him. She stands there in her ill-fitting brown and baggy dress, and she tosses the baseball up and down, up and down, and says, "I sent you to the lab to get Kx red-topped Flasticine Punctual bottles with the XG Sedimentation for the experiment on Patient X. He has died because of your delay. You never could do anything right. You're worthless." She stands there, her brown hair frizzed out as if the bride of Frankenstein. Her nurse pal, the one with the blonde hair and bright blue eyes who loves to see the patient in everyone except for herself and her friend, says, "I knew he was schizophrenic. I knew it. Boy, everybody is nuts in this world." She looks at her friend. "Glad I'm not. Glad you're not." She looks down at him in the stairwell with the impossible steps and says, "What do you suppose is wrong with him?" She leans over and, as if calling to a dog, says, "Here, boy, come here, boy." She whistles to him and pats her ample thighs; at 340 pounds, her thighs are ample indeed. "Come on up and come back to work. Mr. Williams has barfed and pooped in his bed and you have to clean it up. Betsy and I have just ordered three pounds of chocolate and we're going to sit nearby and watch you clean up the room while we eat chocolate."

He is well aware of the hostility and, unable to act on what he feels in a way that is self-protective and assertive, grovels instead and says, "I'm sorry, I'm sorry, I'll be up as soon as I can get up these stairs."

"What's wrong with the stairs?" says the dark haired one, hands on her hips, looking disgusted.

He puts a foot on a step. Nothing happens.

Both nurses sigh, roll their eyes, and the blond haired one says, "He's worse than I thought."

God damn, he thinks, *the universe is conspiring*. But when he puts his full weight on the step, the Universe concedes a small favor; the step vanishes. The blond haired one sees it, but in her ample, hostile way, she sneers. "Now he's making it up. He's rigged the stairs up somehow."

Both nurses sigh; the one with the brown hair squeezes the baseball until it screams and turns to blood in her hands. "Oh," she says, "that's what I want to do to that psycho in room seventeen. I just want to grab his nuts and just *squeeeeze*—that'll knock the schizophrenia right out of him."

Both of them laugh and walk away and beneath him the stairs remain absurd and obnoxious and he finally gives up and notices a horizontal window, two feet high, three feet wide. He kicks, the glass shatters and he crams through only to realize that he is falling, falling, thirteen stories, ten stories, five stories and he knows that this is it, he knows this is gonna be it. But he hits pockets of super dense air, layers of styrofoam fog and finally trees, brush; his fall broken, he rolls down the hill and comes out alive. He stands, able to move and walk. The hospital looms beside him like a mid-evil fortress, but he runs now, he runs and, coming to a street, runs up it, seeing in the distance a highway, bathed in light, a part of town that is luminous, in white light, like glowing from fluorescent lights and he runs, runs to the light, the highway, the shining buildings, running, running to the great white way.

Chapter 20

Surprise!

... only to discover that the Great White Way lands him on the twelfth floor of the hospital in the city of S, known for its innovative style and its great view of the bay. Anslenot gets on the elevator and punches the button for the first floor. The door closes and it's like the elevator cable snaps. Freefalling, Anslenot is slammed against the ceiling of the elevator and wants to scream but at that point is beyond screaming. Suddenly, the elevator snaps to a halt on the fifth floor and Anslenot crashes to the floor. The doors open and an immense, grey dog, slobbering and drooling, wanders on. The doors slam shut and the elevator plunges downward and Anslenot and the dog are both slammed against the ceiling; the dog's face is somehow smunched against Anslenot's face and Anslenot realizes, even while this is going on, that the dog continues to slobber and drool and Anslenot closes his eyes to the saliva tide of bad fortune and they continue to free fall and Anslenot guesses finally that hours have passed. Maybe days. The elevator stops; the dog and Anslenot crash against the floor.

The doors open and Anslenot crawls out on a surface that is mighty cold. He looks up; the air is thick and pink; the haze thins to reveal Saturn, massive in the sky. *Chump.* The elevator doors close, and the elevator, with the dog, continues on down, down to God knows where.

"Oh, my God," whispers Anslenot, "where am I? Oh, where, oh where *am* I?"

There is no answer. For some reason, the word "Titan" comes to mind. "I just wanted to go to the cafeteria for a gutburger," he whimpers, "and I end up on a moon of Saturn. How the fuck—?"

An idle wind blows a newspaper and it wraps around Anslenot's ankles. It's the *Seattle Post-Intelligencer,* but no date appears on the paper. He unwraps it from his legs and sees a headline, "Hospital Experiments with Interdimensional Travel. First practical applications due fifteen years ago." Abruptly, the paper tears out of his hands, wads up and catches fire and brightly burns.

"Oh, dear God," whispers Anslenot, and, as if on command, he hears a *woosh* and right behind him, another elevator appears, the doors opening. Eagerly, Anslenot gets in, happy to hear the Muzak rendition of Beethoven's *Ninth Symphony*; a guitar carries the chorus along with the dogs barking out the various notes. Suddenly, the elevator is moving—*sideways.* Anslenot is slammed against the side of the elevator and somehow, days? later, it stops, the doors open and Anslenot crawls out to a grassy meadow. Nearby a volcano erupts furiously and birds fly backwards overhead.

Chump. The elevator doors close... and it vanishes.

Chapter 21

Timeless Answers

Anslenot sits in the grass in the country. A few miles away, a volcano violently erupts. Above, birds fly backwards. He looks to his watch, but, like a Dali painting, the watch is melting and oozing off his wrist.

He sighs. He remembers back to many things, to steamships exploding at sea, to stars winking out, to hot air balloons floating off to God knows where. Abruptly, he is aware of a presence. Looking about, a great grey dog sits and drools. His master, a young lad of fourteen or so, walks up to the dog and sits down. The young man wears orange shoes and a bright yellow bow tie. Aside from iridescent green bathing trunks, he wears nothing else. A large diamond ring on his little finger flashes wildly, though not exposed to sunlight.

"Strange days," the young man says.

"Indeed," says Anslenot, "like all the days these days."

"Do you believe in anything?" the young man asks.

The dog drools more copiously. An especially violent tremor shakes the land and growling rock vomits from the volcano.

Anslenot watches the eruption. "Is that meaningful?" He shrugs, then looks back at the young man. "In response to your question," he says, then closely examining the threads in his threadbare sports coat, "I used to."

"Not anymore?" the young man says.

"Not really," says Anslenot.

"Do you believe in an afterlife?"

Anslenot laughs. "After life, what?"

The dog howls, but it is difficult for Anslenot to see if there is meaning in that or if it's just coincidence. He finally assumes it's without meaning. Abruptly, the sky flashes to green then back to blue.

"Do you want to pet my dog?" asks the young man.

"No," says Anslenot.

"What are you doing here?" the young man asks.

"Who knows?" says Anslenot. "I wasn't born with an instruction manual. Being produced, like a T.V., is easier. At least you get a set of directions and instructions."

"Huh," says the young man.

The dog now is practically a waterfall of drool. A great bald eagle soars and dips and acts meaningful as if there is great meaning or purpose in the act but if it is so, Anslenot gives up on trying to guess what it might be.

"Well," says the young man, bathing trunks sparking brightly in the sun, "I have to go, I guess."

"Where?" says Anslenot, "where is there to go?"

"Somewhere," he frowns. "Maybe find a new frontier if there is one."

"And if you find one?"

The young man shrugs. "Find another one, I guess."

"And if you find *that* one?"

"Find another one, I guess."

"Oh."

The young man with the grey, drooling dog, gets up and walks away. The dog drools some more, gets up too and follows him. The country becomes quiet, the air still and for a second, it is pleasant. Abruptly, minute fractures and cracks appear in the sky and it begins to bubble, peel away, flake off like old paint, revealing an ancient Coca Cola sign behind the blue.

Anslenot imagines he is protected by an umbrella and lets the pieces of the sky fall where they may.

Chapter 22

Clowning With Honesty

Anslenot stands in a meadow with the erupting volcano in the distance. Around him are pines, jagged, angular rocks like you'd find in the mountains and ankle-high, bright green grass. The pines are spaced perhaps a few meters apart, no more than a few meters high and Anslenot looks up to see the blue sky, the sun shining. He breathes in deeply, and then notices a clown approaching. The clown is dressed in a silly, floppy white clown suit, with big fluffy red buttons and big floppy blue shoes. He wears a pointed hat with blue, fluffy brim. He has blue greasepaint around the eyes, red around the mouth and white on the rest of his face. His neck is blue with little stars glued on. As he approaches, he giggles uncontrollably while smacking his fist over and over again into the palm of his hand. A dark light blazes from his eyes. He comes up to Anslenot. Anslenot backs up a little. "Who are you?" he asks.

The clown giggles. "Tartar Control Krest."

Smack. Smack. Smack. Over and over again, the fist into the palm of the other hand.

"What do you want?" says Anslenot.

The clown reaches toward Anslenot's heart. Anslenot backs up and the clown grins. "Tao lets you do great things."

Anslenot says nothing but edges even farther away.

"Have you driven a Furd, lately?" asks the clown, looking at Anslenot but not really looking at him.

Anslenot shakes his head.

Giggling, the clown's eyes take on a more intense darkness and he points to a tree. It explodes into flame. Then the clown turns, leans over and picks up a thread on the ground. And he begins pulling. Anslenot watches the scene before him unravel, just like cloth. And after a few minutes, everything is a pile of shiny threads in front of the clown and the entire scene is grey. Abruptly, the clown suddenly sits on the pile of thread and a wild thrashing occurs in the costume. Claws rip through the fabric of the clown suit and a giant scorpion emerges. It looks up to Anslenot. "Fooled you. Bet you thought it was something else—an alien or a spider. Didn't think about scorpions, did you?"

Anslenot just shakes his head. He watches the scorpion change colors; red fades to white, white fades to blue, blue fades to red and the cycle repeats.

"Figures," says the scorpion. "Spiders, cockroaches, ants, flies, ticks get all the attention. We scorpions somehow just don't exist. Well, we do I tell you, we do. And we're just as nasty as the next bug or insect. Worse, actually." It waits for Anslenot to respond. "Well," it finally says, "*say* something."

"I don't know *what* to say," says Anslenot.

"This will not stand," says the scorpion, "but I don't know what else to do. And don't try to stop me from doing what I must do. I'm dangerous, you know. Very dangerous. Work to do. Gotta make things standing— unstanding. Unravel, unravel, unravel. So much to unravel. Gotta make the world safe for me. Got that?"

Anslenot nods. He watches the scorpion drag the clown suit, enmeshed and entwined with the unraveled scene of sky, sun and world, he watches the scorpion drag it away into the vast, unending grey.

Chapter 23

Odd Tale for Strange Times

The grey becomes even greyer—then, abruptly it lightens and Anslenot finds himself walking down the sidewalk and three crows fly in a perfect "v" formation overhead. And as Anslenot comes to the intersection, he looks east, just as the sun rises. Crossing the street, he sees a woman like his mother staring at him.

"Hello," he says.

"No," she responds. Her grey eyes show no emotion other than that of no emotion. Her hair is blond, her eye makeup smudged, her hat, blue and low, tipped to the right. She smiles, hands in the pockets of her long, blue coat.

"What?" he says.

She shrugs.

"Well," he finally says.

"Microdyne stock is selling poorly," she says, smiling. "Other stock is questionable."

Just at that point, five UFO's slash overhead, traveling south to north, flashing in the morning sun.

Anslenot digs into his pocket, produces a mortgage receipt, and hands it to the woman. But she shakes her head and walks on. Just as she nears a telephone pole, a blue Mercedes Benz slows down, as if to stop, but then speeds away. The woman, halfway across the street, steps into what An- slenot could not guess—she simply vanishes into the air.

He places the receipt back in his pocket, continues on. Approaching a store, he notices employees engaging in a squirt gun fight. And a block later, he suddenly finds two cats fighting in a vacant lot. As soon as he draws near, they stop fighting, crouch and stare at Anslenot. Then abruptly they manage to produce lit cigars, sit on their haunches and smoke. A little boy runs out from an alleyway, an immense butterfly perches on his hand. The butterfly flaps golden wings and abruptly, carries the little boy up, up and the little boy yelling, "For the sake of art I do this! My creative expression is sincere!"

After a few more minutes, Anslenot comes to a bench and sits. Picking up a newspaper that was left there, he reads the headlines: "Yes and No!" "A Stitch In Time Saves Nine," "Gosh," "Give Me Liberty, or Give Me Death or Get Me a Coke," "Pa-Too." Smelling smoke, Anslenot looks down the street to see the fire station on fire, but the fire hydrants are dry and the firemen just watch it blaze. Abruptly, the cosmic-circuit board short circuits and for an instant, the sky turns the color of Karnation Chocolate Instant Pudding and then again returns to blue, more or less. Anslenot finally gets up again and after a few more moments, stops, then falls as a mighty earthquake hits. Right in front of Anslenot, the earth slips away, slips out as though a picture torn in half and Anslenot looks out toward space, stars and galaxies. He scoots over to the cliff edge and peers over. No land. The McDonald's is long gone as well as the bank and parking lot and it looks like the rest of the city. Anslenot looks at all of this, then sits on the edge of the cliff, feet dangling over the edge. Looking out, he notices he is staring at a galaxy; Andromeda, perhaps. He isn't sure. After a few seconds more, he discovers he is thinking about an old girlfriend. Mindy? Marsha? One of those two. Damn. What *was* her name?

Chapter 24

Somewhere Around the Square Root of X

Anslenot remembers walking down a crooked, broken street. It is snowing and sleeting. His coat is soaked. His hair, plastered to his forehead. In the ditch, a yellow cat retches violently and for a minute Anslenot sees...

... yellow flowers waving in the wind, the grass was summer green. He walked with a woman hand in hand; her name was Marsha and her hair was dark and down to her shoulders. They swung their arms and the air was warm...

... Anslenot shivers violently. It is getting darker. A beautiful, new Cadillac, gold and white, skids out of control, hits a child on a sled and crashes into a telephone pole. The windows shatter and Anslenot hears laughter. "Whooo, honey! You sure drive my stick shift hard —"

"Eee-liee — you old horny bastard — teach you to diddle me — shoulda kept your hands on the wheel —"

Anslenot walks on. The sled is splintered over the road. He sees the body of the child and thinks about calling the police, but the neighbors shoot all strangers who approach their doors. In the distance, a white tornado slams into a school for deaf-mutes. Anslenot shrugs, pulls his coat closer......

... they were friends, walking those fields of summer — they laughed and bought each other ice cream cones on that July afternoon. *Could life be really all that grand, that fun*, thought Anslenot at the time...

... it becomes even darker. Attack jets fly overhead and strafe the rush hour traffic on the nearby freeway. All the grass and shrubs are brown and flattened by the recent worst snows in history. Mounds of grey snow remain, rapidly being whitened by new snow that is to become, according to forecasters, "The blizzard of the century."

A child, standing in the driveway to a burning home has a red and swollen face from extreme radiation...

...on that sunny day, they came to a field full of the yellow of buttercups and tall with spring bright green grass. They followed the trail through the meadow, marveling at the bees in the flowers and watching swallows slice the air in curves and turns from some inherent neural logic that even surpassed the state computer spy system...

... *it all ends here*, thinks Anslenot, *it all ends here — on this day, this moment — here —*

In the distance, the tall, city hospital is on fire. Anslenot nonetheless keeps walking, coming now to a neighborhood business district — needles litter the sidewalk. A drunk pees into the gas tank of a car and he says to himself, "When a man gotta go, he gotta go! *Lord!*" A junkie on the sidewalk is convulsing, vomiting and screaming. Anslenot does what everyone else does: nothing. Walking on, he notices that the liquor store has been looted; a television in the store is on, advertising religion. Anslenot stops. "... and in these days of strife," the Holy Man is saying, his hands holding a Bible, "we must ask ourselves about the benefits of brotherhood and clearly it is unacceptable, for the shared thinking of everyone has led us astray—we must submit to the Leader for he is the voice of God—"

"Amen," sings the choir. The camera pulls back; the choir consists of the Soldiers of the Way. They hold AK-47s at a forty-five degree angle from their groins. Anslenot travels on—

... and they had a picnic basket with them and they found a place in the grass, behind an apple tree and they spread the blanket out and placed the picnic basket between them...

... a monument, once tall and proud lay shattered. Anslenot looks at some of the inscriptions on the stone, "... to the idea that all are born equal... the pursuit of joy—" the rest of the inscription is broken and lost; Anslenot says nothing, thinks little. The snow and sleet is worse and Anslenot detours into the street to avoid the explosions in the courthouse. The ice creamery is busy and the Major and his Slaves sit ordering and eating Rocky Road ice cream...

"...we get along so well," Marsha said, after they made love, "why do you suppose that is?"

"... I don't know," Anslenot said, holding her close, "my parents were terrible models—"

"Mine were too," Marsha says, "but somehow we seem so—" and she smiles, "—so *right* for each other—"

And Anslenot sighed, "Yeah, I never thought I would find anyone—"

... and Anslenot continues on, past the sewage spewing up from manholes, he walks out of the city into the neighborhoods, now deserted, littered with burned out automobiles and destroyed houses, past the old woman sweeping the street with an imaginary broom. She smiles at Anslenot and says, "Isn't it lovely weather? The sunshine is so welcome this time of year." She looks down to her imaginary sweeping. "I think the new government is so wise to investigate opinions it doesn't like—don't you?" Her red housecoat is torn. She is bruised about the face. She blinks. "We're so much safer now, Alice," she says to Anslenot, "so much safer now. I am sorry they sent your child to jail, but after all, he didn't sing the national anthem correctly—"

Anslenot moves on and...

... Marsha sighed. "I never thought I'd find someone either—oh, my parents were such a mess—my father always getting down and smacking my mother around—oh, I really hated my father—I hated him a lot—"

"... Yeah," said Anslenot, "with me, it was my mother always belittling and trashing my father — I really got to hate my mother — a lot — "

Then they both looked at each other for a long, *long* time. *Creeak.* They both looked at the picnic basket. A huge spider with a bright red apple in its mandibles began to crawl out of the basket...

... the sleet lets up. The sky clears. Anslenot looks up to see Venus floating in the sky. "Venus," he muses, "Venus, the Goddess of love." Abruptly it explodes. The clouds come back; the sleet begins again and changes to snow. Anslenot passes the Great Old Party headquarters where children, dressed in white robes and hoods club and burn puppies, kittens and baby fur seals. In several more blocks, he passes a square-dance in progress on the shores of a lake that doubles as a toxic dump which is simultaneously exploding and burning. Some people, dressed in western clothes, sit on the shore roasting wieners and marshmallows —

... they got dressed then, and the spider with the apple between two legs now, looked at them. "What's the matter," it hissed, "why are you getting dressed? This union is fateful indeed. You have loyalties to keep. Traditions to pass on before *you* sleep — "

They got dressed and then walked out of the woods. Instantly the grasses browned, the leaves turned tan, red and brown and fell —

"Wait," hissed the spider coming after them. "Wait — "

They got back to the road. Marsha and Anslenot did not look at each other. They simply went different ways... and the clouds rolled in...

... and Anslenot continues and stops when he comes to the woods again on that snowy day and in the darkness he finds the trail —

"You there!" and a search light from the Friendly Peoples Militia Unit nails him in a white spike of light. "What are you doing!"

Anslenot does not respond and keeps walking.

"A fifty dollar fine for acting like a child when you are adult," comes the voice.

Anslenot keeps walking.

"Seventy-five dollar fine for not staying on the sidewalk that the government has graciously provided for your benefit — "

Anslenot continues to plow through the snow...

... through the sunshine, through the grass, Marsha was there, waiting — *it could have worked — we made love that day and the sun was warm —*

"Fire!"

Anslenot falls. He then sees the spider appear with a photograph. "For you," says the spider. "A picture of Marsha. Oh, my, how your life flies. How about some lies with which to die? 'There will be no problems.' Is that good? 'Love conquers all.' Is that better?"

Anslenot closes his eyes; the spider sighs and says, "Well, I tried. So many baskets in which to hide. It's such a task I do; to help recreate bad love and spew that poison into the world." And it goes scrambling off through the snow while overhead the sky fills with a curious glow from yet another human error.

Chapter 25

Spider Claus

Anslenot opens his eyes; he's in a room and stares at a dried-out Christmas tree, sparsely decorated. He turns on the television. As soon as he does, a spider clambers out of the screen wearing a Santa's hat and a white beard. "Hiss, hiss, hiss," it says.

Anslenot frowns. "It's Christmas. Don't you mean, 'ho, ho, ho'?"

"No," says the spider. "I mean 'hiss, hiss, hiss'. 'Ho, ho, ho' implies joviality. This Santa is sinister. Hiss, hiss, hiss."

Anslenot sneezes and notices that the snow outside is abruptly melting. He looks back at the spider. "Cookies? Milk? Flies? What?"

The spider squats, or crouches; it is difficult to say what it does; its eight eyes somehow all seem to focus on Anslenot. "Do you see eight separate me's?" Anslenot asks. "Or eight separate bits of me that add up to a total me?"

"Don't know," says the spider, "never thought much about it."

"Well," says Anslenot, "now that you're here, you have a gift for me?"

"Got it wrong," says the spider, "*you* got something for *me*."

"What? Aren't you the giver this season?"

"Like I said," the spider says, "you got it wrong. Close your eyes."

Anslenot looks at the spider, then at the rug on the floor with its woven designs of chimpanzees experiencing orgasm. He looks around the room, to the picture frame on the wall with the image of Andromeda slowly turning. He looks outside to see a fire engine on fire, screaming down the street and finally he looks back to the spider, Santa Spider, sitting there, this time with an empty sack by its side. "Well?" says the spider, "what are you waiting for?"

"For why would I close my eyes?" says Anslenot. He yawns briefly.

"Just do it."

The phone rings. Anslenot picks it up. A voice yells, loud enough for the spider to hear, "Just say no!"

"Sorry," says Anslenot, "you are my grandmother who beat me. I am not experiencing in the present the terror I had in the past and I am not consumed with a compulsive need to please, so—" He hangs up the phone and closes his eyes.

"Dream," says the spider.

Anslenot does. He dreams of standing with another girlfriend, Wondra, in the meadow, and the sun is in the west, shining bright and warm and she is crying and saying, "I wish you knew how to love—I do love you—but—I can't go on—I wish—" She held him then; he held her and his heart was breaking and he said to her, "I'll learn how to love—I will, so help me—"

Darkness.

Anslenot opens his eyes, and sees the spider heading out the door, its bag filled with something struggling, fighting. "Hiss, hiss, hiss," says the spider. "Merry Christmas. Hiss, hiss, hiss."

It is snowing again. Anslenot gets up, closes the door. He sits in a chair and watches the snow, watches the space between snow flakes, watches the clouds beyond the snowy space and stares into the unforgiving black of space—beyond the clouds.

Chapter 26

Acts of Love

Dazed, empty, Anslenot walks out of the room, down a city street and finds himself standing by a flaming newspaper and wondering what the headlines were. He imagines the news, suddenly turning yellow in rapid oxidation and then turning to blue air. He thinks back to comic strips in the past—to *Dondi*, to *Twin Earths* and *Mandrake the Magician*. He wonders this as the newspaper burns on the sidewalk and then is blown into gridlocked traffic. He remembers when he was small and the newspaper was large, a whole yellow and red and blue and green world he could get lost in on Sunday morning.

Out in the traffic that has been stalled for many days now, there is a scream of a newborn baby.

It had to happen, Anslenot thinks, *birth, life, death, right in the middle of the intersection of Madison and Boren Avenues.*

Overhead, the sky is bright. There is the smell of petroleum and rotten hamburger. Nearby, a mother cat methodically drops her kittens, one by one, into an open manhole. Distantly, there is a splash and a frantic mewling followed by silence.

Even the animals know, thinks Anslenot, *that these are not good times. Bad times in which to raise a family. Bad times in which to be born.* He sees what the mother cat was doing as not an act of cruelty, but the supreme act of love.

He continues to walk on, past a shop with broken-out windows. A beggar of a woman drifts past him. "For the first time in your life, feel really clean," she says. "Hee, hee, hee. Things go better with Coke." She walks a little farther, muttering, muttering, then, "Advanced medicine for pain relief." *Mutter, mutter, scuffle, scuffle, scuffle*, "The quality goes in before the name goes on."

Shots ring out in the traffic jam. By reflex, Anslenot drops to his knees. The old woman falls, hand over her heart. "Sure," she whispers, "you've had a rough day, but don't take it out on your mother."

Sobbing from somewhere.

Anslenot stands, wanders back. "Meeewwwweeeee — *splash*."

Anslenot smiles. An act of love. The only act of love he's seen in a long while.

He again hears the newborn baby cry. An act of hatred, of passing on misery; why should the next generation be exempt, after all?

He looks for the burning newspaper, but today's news is all blue smoke now, its message dispersed and meaningless.

Chapter 27

News

Anslenot finds another newspaper; opening it, he studies the ad for hamburger. Someone in a white dress is smiling as she holds out a plate of hamburgers. "You should eat one," the figure says. "You look thin."

Anslenot wonders why the woman is so much like his mother. Same voice, same grey eyes. "And you should also eat your vegetables," she says, in another part of the ad, holding out a large bowl of peas. "Peas make you big and strong. Plenty of Vitamin P."

Anslenot turns the page. He sees his father in an ad for Sears, selling aluminum boats. "You need to row a boat once in a while," his father says. He smiles. "Oar —" he pauses for maximum effect, "do something else to build up your muscles. You should have taken weight training in high school. You should have been just like me and taken in college sports. That's what you should have done. Here. Buy a boat. They're reasonably priced, only at Sears."

"Fuck you," says Anslenot and he wads the newspaper up and throws it on the ground. It abruptly bursts into flames and he hears the paper-thin scream of his parents, "You'll regret this! You're bad! You're a bad child and we're the only people who can love you. No one can love you like we can, you worthless, pitiful thing."

Overhead, the sky turns red and then changes again into a blue and white checkerboard pattern. Anslenot walks down the street and nearby, a building caves in on itself. An eagle soars, turns into a Saturn Five rocket and heads toward Mars. And finally, Anslenot sits on a flimsy park bench and feels some of the boards give beneath him but he does not move. A baboon on roller skates and wearing a blue tee shirt with a picture of some little known vice-president spelling the word "potato" wrong, rolls on by and drops another newspaper in Anslenot's lap. Anslenot opens it up but the pages are blank except for a lead story on the front page, titled, "Anslenot Endures Great Pain in Strange Reality." And there is a picture of him with a great grey dog slobbering and drooling on his feet. Anslenot does not bother reading the rest of the story and slowly folds the paper up and as he does so, a door opens up in the air before him. A thin voice says, "Congratulations, by folding the paper just the right way and just the right time, you opened up an alternate reality, a new dimension. Won't you come in." Anslenot looks ahead at the doorway that has opened, wondering at how the buses come to it, somehow go behind it only to continue on the other side. Anslenot stuffs the paper inside his shirt, stands, and pokes his head in the doorway. "I dunno," he says, "this is pretty strange."

"Here or there?" says the voice. Anslenot notices how dark it is inside in the doorway.

"Maybe it makes no difference," he says, "but this does look a little stranger than where I am right now."

"Come in all the way," comes the voice. "Step in and see wonders and possibilities."

Anslenot shrugs and does so. He abruptly is surrounded in brilliant light and when the light fades, he finds he is standing knee-deep in a toxic waste dump. The air is thick with fumes and Anslenot gasps for breath. Not far way, a steel drum explodes in a lavender light and sparkling things arch up and shimmer as they drift back down. And he hears the voice again, "Now, doesn't this offer more comfort than the place you were? This is reality and reality is so much more comforting and comfortable than the fantasies you probably entertain. This is reality. This is where you need to be. Give something people can relate to." Something explodes on the horizon in a brilliant blue-green. Abruptly, Anslenot finds something thrust into his hands; he is suddenly aware that his feet are beginning to itch and burn furiously. He pulls up a foot and finds that the shoe has been totally dissolved by the goo in which he stands. He hurriedly climbs upon a half-sunk steel drum which he finds so hot that he can't stand on it. He jumps and then wearily, slogs to the shore, passing through areas of cooler water, and he hopes, less contaminated, but he wonders as he watches the three-headed, six-armed frogs flounder about. Finally, he gets to an embankment and sitting, pulls the paper back out from his shirt and opens it. "New Epidemic Outpaces AIDS Epidemic." "Detroit Gutted In Latest Riot." "President Denies Kickback Scheme With South American Drug Lords In Spite of Evidence." "Tap Water in Newark Found to be Toxic." "Earthquake Destroys Nuclear Respository; Thousands Die of Exposure. Major Catastrophe." "Gas Prices Hit Seven Dollars a Gallon; Oil Companies Deny Price Fixing, Cite Seasonal Price Fluctuation."

Anslenot folds the paper. *"This* is better than where I've been?" he asks.

"Why certainly," comes the voice. "We always—"

Something deep in the dump goes *ka-woomph*. Anslenot falls to his side from the concussion. In seconds, the surface of the dump begins to boil. Anslenot stands quickly. "Which way do I fold the fucking paper?" screams Anslenot.

A green glow radiates from the chemical dump and intensifies and deep within the dump, more explosions. *Ka-thud, ka-thud. Ka-Woomph.*

"—to your left," comes the voice, "crease it, then fold the top down—"

The chemical dump is erupting into a flaming geyser and looks like a miniature hydrogen bomb going off. Frantically, Anslenot folds the paper—abruptly, the door opens; Anslenot leaps through the opening, rolls to the side and through the door, green-blue flames and smoke billow out as well as bits of steel drum—suddenly the door closes. Anslenot looks up to see the spider there, the grey drooling dog, notices the birds flying backwards overhead. *"God,"* he sighs, "it's *great* to be back."

...*Much* Worse

Chapter 28

Good Guy Anslenot

Anslenot stands on the street corner waiting to cross a street. A robin alights on his shoulder. "Tweet?" it says.

"Newhaven?" Anslenot points east. "3000 miles that-a-way."

"Chirp," says the robin. "That's a long way. Is there an interstate that runs that way? At least I can stop at McDonald's parking lots and pick up fries along with my worms along the way."

"Shouldn't have any trouble," says Anslenot.

"Thanks," says the bird, and away it flies.

The light turns green, but Anslenot, an adventurer, waits for the light to turn some other color so he can dash between the cars going about in their confused and often gridlocked ways. A police car, empty, in the middle of the intersection, is repeatedly rammed by other cars. The policeman sits on a nearby curb, plugged into his Walkman, rocking to the music.

From somewhere, a squirrel runs up Anslenot's pantleg, bright orange sportcoat, and thence up to his shoulder. "Portland?" it asks.

Anslenot points south.

"How far?"

"Maybe 150 miles," says Anslenot.

"Whew," says the squirrel sitting up on its haunches, and looking to the south. "That's a couple of pawfuls of walnuts away." Pause. "Well, gotta go. Big convention. 'Effective Rodent Infestation.' Weekend program. Sounds good. Thanks."

And the squirrel scampers away, hightailing it south, through the gridlocked traffic, past the father kicking his child.

An old, drunk man stumbles up to Anslenot. "You a good man?" he asks.

"I don't know," says Anslenot, "am I?"

The drunk looks at Anslenot. "You look like a good man."

"How can you tell?"

"I just know," says the drunk. "I just know these things. I know you must be a good man."

"How much do you want?" says Anslenot.

"$100. That will keep me in coffee for the rest of the week."

"Nope," says Anslenot.

"Well," says the drunk, drawling, "can you tell me where I might find people who would do that?"

Anslenot points. "Try the bank. For a fee, it's truly amazing how good-hearted they can be."

"Oh," says the drunk. "Never thought of that. Thanks." He stumbles to ward a bank that, when he approaches, automatically locks its doors, calls the police, and sounds the fire alarm.

Anslenot then crosses the street, occasionally climbing over the hoods of stalled cars, and finally getting over to the appliance store on the other side. It is then that a filmy, wispy apparition appears. A business card materializes in Anslenot's hand. "*Spiritbeing*—Seeking beings in which to embody love, trust and truth." Anslenot points to the television in the store window. The being drifts to the window, through it, then to the blank TV screen. Instantly it comes on and a blur of commercials appear: new cars, beer, washday products, clothes; abruptly the television explodes. Anslenot smiles wickedly and walks on, past the newspaper burning, burning, brightly in the light of day.

Chapter 29

Pet

Anslenot continues on; overhead another jet explodes. Nearby, a hand grenade, tossed by a member of the Extremism in the Defense of Pro-life group, explodes, killing a child. Anslenot ducks into a store and finds it is a pet store. The owner/proprietor, with a few too many legs and eyes, sits in cobwebs behind a desk near the door. He is dressed in a tuxedo. In the corner, near a large window, squats the large tarantula, now with a bright blood-red bow behind its head. There is a price tag with a question mark dangling from a leg. Anslenot goes up to the proprietor. "How much is that spider in the window, the one with the waggling pedipalps?"

"You don't know what you're getting into," says the proprietor.

"What am I getting into?" asks Anslenot.

"You don't want to know."

"Why don't I want to know?"

"Because you wouldn't like what you might be getting into."

"Why wouldn't I like what I might be getting into?" asks Anslenot.

"You just wouldn't," says the proprietor.

Anslenot turns to look at the tarantula sitting in the window. It simply stares back at Anslenot. Anslenot digs into the pockets of his jeans and pulls out a rubber band, a worthless Corporate State dollar and a bottle cap and places it on the dusty counter.

"You don't know what you're doing," says the proprietor.

"Why don't I know what I am doing?" says Anslenot.

"Because, if you did, believe me, you wouldn't be doing it."

The proprietor takes the rubber band, stretches it and flicks a large fly out of the air overhead. He then leans forward and the fly plops into the proprietor's mouth. There is a slight sucking sound followed by a faint *pop*. "I bet you wouldn't like to really know what I just did," says the proprietor.

Anslenot looks away. "This time, I think you're right. I *don't* think I really *do* want to know what you just did."

With an arm ending in pincers, the proprietor reaches out for a plastic squeeze bottle filled with something red. A label on it reads "Type-O Cola."

"I bet," says Anslenot, "that isn't ketchup."

The owner nods slightly. "You probably wouldn't like to know what it is."

"Why don't you think I'd like to know?" says Anslenot.

"You might be uncomfortable."

"Why would I be uncomfortable?"

"I just think you would be," says the proprietor. He takes the bottle and places the straw in his strange mouth and sucks noisily. Just then, another bomb explodes nearby, and another child is hit; blood and flesh splatter against the window. The proprietor immediately becomes excited and leans forward, trembling; the cobwebs pull taut.

"What a mess," says Anslenot. "I wonder how you're going to clean that up?"

The proprietor, still trembling with excitement, says, "Oh, you *don't* want to know how I'm going to clean *that* up."

Anslenot swallows and says to himself, "*Would* I *really* want to know how he's going to clean his window?"

"No," says the owner. "No, I don't think you *really* want to know. I really *don't* think you do."

Anslenot goes over to the tarantula and says, "Do you have a name?"

The tarantula moves toward Anslenot. "Tide. Tide is my name. I get your clothes bright and clean and looking New! New! New!" Somehow the tarantula gets a hold of Anslenot and manages to deftly flip him on top so that Anslenot rides the tarantula like some existential horror pony. "Is Tide really your name?" asked Anslenot.

"No," says the spider lumbering through the pet shop, "my name is Cadillac. Cadillac is my name. Buy me and get the good life, the mansions, the vacations, any woman you want any time you want her. And all the Grey Poupon you could *ever* need."

They approach the front of the store and Anslenot points to the tarantula. "What have I bought? What have I spent all my money on?"

The proprietor, still trembling at the sight of the gore and blood on the window, says, "Oh, no, no, you don't want to know what you have bought."

"Why don't I want to know what I have bought?"

"Because you will finally see just what you *have* bought."

"What would happen if I saw what I have bought?"

"You will see what it is for what it is."

"Don't I want to see it for what it is?" asks Anslenot.

"No," hisses the owner, tearing out of his cobwebs, "no, you do *not* want to see what it is for what it is."

The tarantula, with Anslenot riding it, goes through the doorway with the proprietor scrambling behind them, making strange sucking sounds.

"What is this all about?" shouts Anslenot, "What is this all about? What's the solution? What's the answer?"

"Preparation H shrinks hemorrhoidal tissue!" hisses the spider. "Buy some today!" And they lurch out onto the street.

"You don't want to know," screeches the proprietor, "you don't want to know!"

"Things go better with Coke," says the tarantula, "oh, yeah."

Chapter 30

Various Truths

Anslenot rides the spider like a strange, existential horror pony. They pass the grey, slobbering dog and Anslenot says, "What is the meaning of all of this?"

The tarantula replies, "Beats me. Besides, we've been through this before."

Anslenot looks around to the charred posters and can still make out the political slogans: "War is Peace," "Freedom is Slavery," "Ignorance is Strength."

"How'd *1984* get into this?" asks Anslenot.

The spider keeps moving. "Don't know," it finally says. "Maybe someone figures that these days are no different than those of *1984*."

They keep going, past the burned-out buildings and blasted candy stores.

"What do you know about this?" asks Anslenot.

"Nothing."

"Where are you taking me?"

"I don't know," says the spider. "You want off?"

Anslenot doesn't know what to say. "Is your name really 'Tide'?" asks Anslenot. "Or 'Cadillac'?"

"Not really," says the spider. "Try 'Rolaids'—for acid indigestion."

Just then, they meet a little girl. She walks along with Anslenot and the spider. "Bet that's not really your spider," she says.

"God, I hope not," says Anslenot cringing, "but I paid a corporate dollar, a bottle cap and a rubber band for it. Guess it's mine now."

"You paid a small fortune," says the little girl. "Glad it's not my spider. Bet you're not really happy riding it."

"You're probably right," says Anslenot.

"Bet you don't have to ride it if you don't really want to."

With that, Anslenot jumps off. "Guess I needed permission."

"That's what I suspected," says the little girl, "and I shouldn't have enabled you like that—but I saw that you were powerless."

"You're right," replies Anslenot, now walking beside the spider which is half-whistling, half-hissing a mid-1960's melody for Alka Seltzer. "You did enable me and I was powerless and now I'm co-dependent on you. What *ever* will I do?"

"You can't ask me that," says the little girl with her hair blowing in her face from a capricious wind.

"I know I shouldn't have, but I did."

"I know you did and you shouldn't have."

"Does that make me a bad person?"

"I don't know," says the little girl, "does it?"

"Should I feel ashamed? Should I be full of shame?"

"I don't know," says the little girl. "You can't really ask me that."

"I know," says Anslenot, "but I did anyway."

"I know you did."

"Should I feel bad? Should I feel ashamed?"

"I don't know," says the little girl, "but somehow this conversation seems familiar."

"Maybe it's because we just had it," says Anslenot.

"Very likely," says the little girl.

The three of them walk on in silence. Suddenly, the spider breaks into tears and eight separate tear tracks centimeter down the various parts of its 'face'.

"What's wrong?" asks Anslenot, "I just can't stand to see grown spiders cry."

"I'm hungry," says the tarantula. "I haven't eaten in pages."

"What are you going to eat?" asks Anslenot, backing away.

"Not you," says the spider. "I'm too civilized." It nears a semi-gutted laundromat, leaps through the broken window and attacks a serviceable and intact Twinkie and Ding Dong vending machine. The spider topples it, wraps it in silk and, dragging it away, hisses the latest Twinkie tune from the state regulated Total Freedom of Choice Channel.

"Well," says Anslenot.

"Well," says the little girl. "Certainly not my choice. Bet it's not your choice either."

"Bet you're right," says Anslenot.

They continue on in silence. Nearby, a newspaper spins about in a whirlwind. Anslenot tries to catch the headlines, but they abruptly disappear. Anslenot can only assume that the news is being recalled for repairs.

Chapter 31

Pictures

Anslenot walks with the girl; he watches the grey, drooling dog cross the street in the distance as it heads to a different part of reality. Overhead, the sun flares briefly then settles down into middle age. Anslenot wonders if Old Sol is having a midlife crisis. *What is it about*, he wonders. *What could it be about?* The traffic is, as usual, hopelessly snarled and somewhere a building burns but no fire trucks can get to it. Bells from the nearby church ring loudly, celebrating the death of spirituality and the ascension of mediocrity and materialism. He glances to the headline of a tabloid in a melted newsstand: "Materialism Is the Replacement for Spiritual Death." Anslenot ponders this as they continue to wander along until they come to a bench. He sits. Nearby is a trashcan. Anslenot glances down and pulls out a photo album. As he opens it, the little girl says, "That is not my photo album."

"Should I be sorry?" asks Anslenot.

"Yes," the little girl replies, not looking up at him, "you should be sad that it is not my photo album. My photo album was wonderful but the Communist Fascists took it from me and said that I wasn't to be happy—that the only way I could be happy was to be as miserable, miserable and totalitarian as they were but they couldn't admit that to themselves, they said, so they had to take my photo album. When I became unhappy, they were happy."

"Oh," says Anslenot. "I guess I sort of see."

"No," says the little girl in the red dress, "I don't think you do."

She climbs up and sits by Anslenot, plopping the album between them. She points to a picture of a man with white hair. "That is not my father," she replies. "My father was short and covered by warts like a toad. He was not a nice man, not even a decent man. Like a cockroach, he existed." She looks up at Anslenot, "I am wise beyond my years."

Anslenot nods. He points to the picture. "That isn't my father either. He sort of looks like my uncle who had no socially redeeming qualities whatsoever. He was like a spider. Just kind of sat in his web of misery and somehow thought he was a butterfly instead."

The little girl turns the page. "I didn't hear what you said," she says.

"I didn't say anything," replies Anslenot.

"I didn't think so," says the girl. "I just wanted to trouble you."

"You did."

"Good," she says. She points to another picture. "That isn't my brother. My brother has prematurely grey hair and sings terrible tunes on broken guitars. He never got far in the recording industry."

"I know," says Anslenot, "I've never heard him sing."

"That's because he never recorded anything," says the little girl wearing white gloves and a pink carnation on her dress. "Had he recorded anything, he wouldn't have been very good. A large spider attacked him one night and stole his voice for his own use. It was terrible. Terrible. But my brother did sound better afterwards."

"I see," says Anslenot, not seeing at all but, being as co-dependent as he is, and fearing loss of any affection or care, says he understands, when, in fact, he does not.

"You don't understand, do you," says the little girl with the bright red hair, "you're just saying that because you're co-dependent and fear being yourself for fear that I'll withdraw any affection from you."

"I have to deny that," says Anslenot, "because I am still in a state of denial, which means I can't face the truth about me that you see, so I have to say I didn't hear you."

"I know," says the little girl with the freckles. She points to another picture of a car. It is a late model car, suddenly obsolete and disintegrating the second it crosses the property line from the car dealership to the road.

"This isn't my parent's car," says the little girl with braces on her teeth. "That's like no car I ever saw. My parents had a Rambler American that was painted lime green. My parents were sort of ramblers themselves—American Ramblers—never staying in one place—always drifting. I speak well for my age. I am not an adult."

Anslenot wants to say something but fears if he does, he would be branded as being co-dependent again, so he says nothing.

"You can't get away from it," the little girl, who appears to be about age nine, says, "even if you don't respond to my statement, you're still codependent. It's the fear."

"Oh," says Anslenot, "I didn't know."

"I know," says the little girl in the Adidas tennis shoes, "that's why I decided to say something to help you be more aware."

"I'm not surprised," says Anslenot. He points to a picture of a cat. "I bet that's not your cat."

The little girl with the braided hair nods. "You're right. That isn't my cat. I never had a cat. I bet that's not your cat either."

"You're right," says Anslenot, "it's not."

They turn to another page of the album. There is a picture of a priest.

"That certainly isn't my Father," says the little girl with a silver bracelet on her wrist, "and I don't think it's your Father either."

Anslenot nods sagely. "No, it isn't my Father. I wonder whose Father it is?"

The little girl just turns the page, pointing to an elderly woman in white hair, holding a wilted bouquet of roses and a with a yellow canary perched on her shoulder. The little girl, with no other features with which to describe her further except that she frequently has a pouty look and keeps her head basically down except for glances of confirmation from Anslenot, points to the picture. "That looks like my grandmother. My grandmother died young of some horrible, incurable disease from some unnamed source."

"I'm sorry," says Anslenot. "I didn't do it. I didn't know her. It isn't my grandmother although I think I must have had one. I know what happened to her and I wish that I didn't. She could have been a grand woman but that's only conjecture."

The little girl nods and points to a picture of a spider. "That isn't my spider," she says. "I don't know if I have a spider. I may be too young to know this or my dark side."

Anslenot looks at the picture of the spider. "It's not my spider. It isn't wearing a name badge with my name on it so it can't be mine." The little girl closes the book. "No," she says, "no, I definitely don't know anyone in here. It's a shame, I wish I did."

"Well," says Anslenot, "I don't know anyone in there either and I wish *I* did."

Without another word, the girl places the album on Anslenot's lap, hops off the bench and continues on her way. Anslenot continues to look at the photo album until he senses movement nearby. The spider sits there. "*Mine,*" it hisses.

Anslenot nods and gives the photo album to the spider which grabs it and holding it with its pedipalps, continues on its way.

Chapter 32

Bushwacking

Anslenot watches the spider wander off and decides that maybe going someplace else—anyplace else—might be helpful. He gets up, walks around the block and finds himself in a gutted building and to his surprise, discovers a television on in the back of the room. He pulls up a serviceable chair. There is an advertisement for Coca-Cola. It shows a policeman in riot dress; he is sweating; in the background, a city burns and the voice-over says, "Hard work demands hard refreshment. This is it." The policeman smiles, drains the Coke, tosses the can up and blasts it to oblivion with an assault rifle and the scene fades in smoke and screams and gunfire. Another commercial comes on. President MaoTseBoosh, of the Corporate State, stands with one hand on a new car. Anslenot has seen this commercial before, but nonetheless, still stands, hand over heart, as he listens to the music of the *War Hymn of the Republic* and the president talking, "... your patriotic duty is to buy. That's what this country is all about—freedom and liberty to purchase, to own, to accumulate property. This is what God has in mind for you. And as your President, during my lifetime term in office, I will do my best to enact laws that will punish those, by death, if necessary, who think ownership is wrong..." Outside the store, Anslenot hears gunfire as smoke drifts through the building. The commercial over, Anslenot sits and notices that someone has written in white spray paint on a charred wall, "Godless Communism = Godless Capitalism." When he looks to the television again, he sees an old girlfriend on the screen; she looks intently at him.

Anslenot drops to his knees. "Mindy," he whispers, "Mindy, how I've missed you..."

She looks at him and shakes her head, "it wouldn't have worked," she says. "You don't believe in money. And you don't believe in President MaoTseBoosh's—our comrade in arms—way of thinking. Heil MaoTse-BooshThought! Consumers of the world unite! You have nothing to lose but your money!"

"But there is more to life—there must be more to life—money for the sake of money—*time* is life, not money—"

"Can't live off love," she says. "That's a Yankee Imperialist notion. You're demented. I'm comfortable. You're not."

"But—but—"

"I had to turn you in to the Freedom Squad. You have no right to make our fellow comrades uncomfortable by not wanting to own anything. People lose jobs because of you. I couldn't go on anymore—I'd be implicated in the crime as well—I can't do that... if you would have just worked a seventy hour a week job and gone in debt—but no, you were selfish—"

"But this is wrong—" whispers Anslenot, moving closer to the screen. "This is terribly wrong—so many are enraged from constantly being shown false realities—the pretty lies only designed to get people to part with their money—this is wrong—"

Mindy shakes her head. "No," she says, "you're poisoning my mind. MaoTseBooshThought is the only thinking that gives freedom. It's not too late to join the Democratic Dictatorship of the Corporate Proletariat. Can't you see how immoral, how disgusting you are, what a counter-revolutionary you are to not be a part of what is right?"

Movement in the shadows. A spider, shimmering in colors of red, white, blue, emerges. "She's right, you know. Buy or die. That's what it's all about."

Outside, explosions, the sounds of guns.

Anslenot shakes his head. He points toward the chaos. "What is *that* all about?"

"Unhappy shoppers who missed a K-Mart Blue Light Special!" whispers the spider. "If they would have just bought more in time, charged it at 25% interest, they would've been happy. So would you."

"I don't have money," says Anslenot.

"Because you don't work," says the spider. "You're a parasite on the sacred breast of the Motherland."

"Because you're lazy," says Mindy. "You're a running sore on the sacred heart of the Fatherland."

"This can't be all there is," says Anslenot. "The purpose of life *must* be more than material."

The spider hisses. "That's dangerous. That's Anti-MaoTseBooshThought. What would happen if everyone were content? What would happen to this country if people thought that money didn't buy happiness? What would happen to our society? You're a dangerous, *dangerous* man. People like you must die."

The spider comes scrambling toward Anslenot; Anslenot hears Mindy call out to him, "I still care for you, you counter-revolutionary scum! It's not too late to buy a new car—have you driven a Ford, lately, *George?*—I mean—*Alex*—I mean—" And the television explodes.

Chapter 33
Bus

Still dazed by the explosion, Anslenot wanders until he comes to a bus stop on a strangely deserted street, surrounded by the high, ugly buildings in the city of S. He decides to try to visit an old friend who lives in the town of T, hoping he might have some answers. Soon a bus comes and stops. It is empty. There is no destination anywhere on the bus. The door opens and a wizened driver, shrunken like a prune, lined by the years until he looks like a troll, peers out. "Well," he says.

"I need to get to the city of T," says Anslenot.

The bus driver, dressed in the brown and gold of City Metro, laughs and says, "Well, that all depends on what time of day you want to go. As you know, the City of T doesn't exist on every third Thursday of the month between ten a.m. and three p.m. unless there is a Christian-pagan holiday the week before, at which point, the city of T somewhat exists—"

"Somewhat exists?" says Anslenot.

"Somewhat," says the bus driver. "Don't ask for details because I don't have any. I just drive the bus. Why the city fathers of T did it that way is still incomprehensible to me."

Anslenot looks around. "What's today?"

"Wednesday."

"So T exists."

"No," said the bus driver. "Not today. It's the major's birthday and he has decided that, arbitrarily, a few cities need not exist today and T is one of them. This is to happen in five minutes."

"I have to get to T," says Anslenot.

"Today?"

"Yes."

The bus driver shifts in his seat and simply shrugs. "Why don't you go to the city of T Squared? It looks just like T only four times as large."

"You mean in area?" asks Anslenot.

"No, the buildings are four times as large."

"Well, I guess that will do."

"There is a drawback," says the bus driver.

"What?"

"The people are, of course, four times as large. You could get stepped on; maybe get knocked over by a hundred pound pooch or knocked unconscious by a two pound pigeon."

Anslenot sighs. "I *really* have to get to T."

"Why today?" says the bus driver, "Why today?" He stares ahead and thumps a fist on the steering wheel. "What has happened to serendipity? Coincidence? Chance? Everyone has to be at a certain place at a certain time. Ridiculous, I tell you, totally ridiculous. It's not necessary. It's just not necessary, I tell you and look here, look here," and he glares at Anslenot. "Look at me. Look how old I am. I've run my life on chance and coincidence and look how I've fared. Have I fared so badly? Don't answer that question because it's obvious that I have fared well; I drive this bus wherever I want to or to what plans the capricious fates have decided for this day and I tell, you. Have I fared so badly? Have I? Look at me, young man and answer me. No, don't answer me because it's obvious. Obvious, terribly, *terribly* obvious how right I am. Now aren't I right? Of course I am."

Somewhat taken aback at this outburst, Anslenot stares. Then, with exasperation Anslenot sighs. "Look, you go where you want. If you drive an express bus to Hell, good, the devil be with you then. I have to get to the town of T. I must visit someone there. Why are you making this so difficult?"

The bus driver looks a long time at Anslenot then, lifting the phone off its cradle on the dashboard, gives it to Anslenot. "Here," he says, "call up your friend and tell him that you can meet him on the way to the town of Z. I'm eventually going there and I can pick up your friend on the way."

"What?" says Anslenot, "What? No way is that going to work. My friend is way out of the way—" Then he stops. "Z you say? I've never heard of it."

The bus driver smiles. "See? Wherever your friend is, I can pick him up on the way to Z. But hurry."

"Wait a minute," says Anslenot, "this doesn't make any sense. I have to figure it out..."

"No," says the bus driver, "don't do that. It doesn't make sense, it's not supposed to make sense. You *can't* figure this out—"

But Anslenot is momentarily lost in thought. After some minutes he asks, "Where the heck is Z?"

But the bus driver sighs, slams the handset on the dash and thumps his fists on the steering wheel. "See what you did?" he cries, "See what you did? In trying to figure it out, you promptly unexisted the city."

"I couldn't have," says Anslenot.

"You did."

"I couldn't have."

"You did. You truly, really did. I hope you're happy. I was looking forward to going to Z. I haven't been there in three hundred years and they would have really enjoyed seeing me driving this contraption, especially my Aunt Sally Jean who was related to a Troll who used to live beneath a bridge in Medieval Europe but that's of little consequence now."

"And I still want to get to T," says Anslenot. "Isn't there another bus coming?"

"Nope," says the bus driver. "This bus, and me, your friendly driver — we're it today."

Anslenot's mouth drops open. "What?" he finally says, "what? This city has three hundred buses! What do you mean yours is the only bus and you the only driver?"

"You heard me," says the bus driver. "We're it today."

"But how do I get to my friend and to T?"

"You can't. Don't forget, the town of T doesn't exist today and won't exist for a few hours tomorrow which is Thursday. So your friend doesn't really exist either... unless..."

"Unless...?"

"Well," says the driver, "you know, I really haven't decided quite where this bus may end up. I mean, things change quickly, you know? 'The best laid plans of mice and me,' or was that 'men'? Oh, well, so forth, so on, yak, yak, yak, you know. Now, it is possible, that the town of T, while it doesn't exist here, *could be* existing somewhere else while it isn't where it's supposed to be. Now. There's a chance, just a chance that if you were to get on this bus, I mean, who knows? Who knows what we might run into in our travels? But you have to have faith. Faith, agreed? Much faith. A great deal of it. Get it?"

Anslenot stands in the entrance of the bus and looks at the driver. "I don't understand," he says. "I just don't understand. All I want to do is get to the town of T so I can see my friend whom I want to see today — if T wasn't to exist by some Major's command, why didn't my friend tell me?"

The driver smiles. "Maybe he didn't know. Things change fast."

"And if I get on this bus, I still have no certainty of getting to my friend."

"True," says the driver. "But look. Now, what were you going to do instead of this? O.K. Your plan of getting to T didn't work. But maybe there are other cities like T. If T squared didn't work, then how about T minus T? Maybe the city might be less than regular T, and maybe your visit with your friend won't be as long or as much as you thought it would be, but it would still be a visit. Or maybe even... there is a T plus T. Now there would be a city. Extravagant! Even more of a city than the T you want to go to. Maybe brighter colors. Maybe your friend will be ultra rich and he, out of his increased generosity, will invite you to stay, give you money, and perhaps be more a friend than you could ever ask for. Maybe his house will be bigger, the flowers more lovely. Who knows? Who knows? Or perhaps there is T double T where you get twice as much as everything or maybe it exists right next to T but a day behind which means you can go to one city of T, enjoy that day, and go to the parallel city of T which is a day behind, and do it all over again. No, look at the possibilities, young man, look at what you might be missing if you don't take this bus. Am I being so unreasonable? I ask you. Am I being so unreasonable? Don't answer that because it is terribly obvious. Now doesn't all of this sound better than what you were planning if you just walked away in bitter disappointment because merely one form of your silly, precious city of T and your friend didn't happen to exist at the precise time when you wanted them to exist? Now I ask you, doesn't this make more sense? Don't answer this question because of course it makes sense. Doesn't it? Of course it does." And with that, the driver sits back in his chair, folds his arms across his chest, nods his head vigorously and his lips form a determined line.

Anslenot stares. And stares. And for whatever reason, hypnotized or simply unable to think, walks up the stairway, puts in his recently found but worthless corporate dollar, sits in the seat, and doesn't blink an eye, even when the bus starts up and heads off—to the stars.

(Author's note: With appreciation to *The Switchman* by Juan Jose Arreola and for Dick Reuther.)

Chapter 34

Dreams?

—but immediately Anslenot falls asleep, only to awaken with a start. The bus driver is not there. Anslenot gets off the bus—the first thing he sees is Saturn impossibly huge in the blue sky. "Oh, my God," he whispers, "now what? Where am I now?"

"Sleep well?"

Anslenot turns. The big tarantula is squatting there.

"Where are we—am I—?"

"Not Kansas, Toto, *that's* for sure," says the spider.

"Is this a dream?"

"Couldn't be," says the spider. "Look around you."

Anslenot does. Everything is covered in a snow. In the distance, a mountain range with spires as one might find in a fantasy. Lights of a nearby city twinkle in subdued daylight.

"Why couldn't this be a dream?" asks Anslenot. "Everything else has seemed like a dream. Why not this?"

"Don't know," says the spider. "Any more questions?"

"Uh—" says Anslenot, "I guess not. But for someone or something that doesn't know a lot, you sure know a lot."

"Can't say," says the spider. "Gets too complicated."

"Aren't things complicated enough?" asks Anslenot.

The spider moves as if somehow to make a shrug. "Things can always get more complicated or so it seems to me."

Anslenot gets up. "Might as well head to the city."

The spider says nothing but follows dutifully behind. After a few yards, Anslenot picks up a newspaper. The banner headlines spell out, "AGGGGHHH!" Abruptly, the paper bursts into flames and a sudden wind carries the flaming pages high into the air. Anslenot shakes his head and moves on. After several minutes, he comes to an icy pillar. Anslenot stops, then steps closer. Then he stares at the statue for a few minutes. He sighs, his breath forming a rainbow-colored cloud which condenses and multicolored flakes fall as snow. "It's my father in there," Anslenot says. He shakes his head. "Always was a cold man." The tarantula says nothing. They continue on. And after some distance, they come to another pillar. Again, Anslenot steps closer and scrutinizes the statue. The statue is holding a newspaper with headlines that read, "Anslenot Remains Little Boy," "Anslenot Sick, Needs Constant Care," "Anslenot Incompetent." Anslenot sighs. "My mother's been reading that newspaper ever since I can remember."

He turns away; they continue on and Anslenot picks up another newspaper. The headlines read, "Reality Is Fantasy Is Reality!" And suddenly, *that* newspaper bursts into flames and is swept away high into the air.

Anslenot turns to the spider. "What is the meaning of all of this?"

"You keep asking me that," says the spider.

"Can I ask you again at some future date?" says Anslenot.

"Sure," says the spider, "but I probably wouldn't tell you."

"Why?" asks Anslenot.

"You already know the answer."

"No, I don't."

"You do."

"No, I don't," says Anslenot. "Tell me."

The tarantula hisses. "No one can tell you what you already know. No one can tell you what you don't want to hear."

"I don't understand," says Anslenot.

"Use your eyes," says the spider.

"You've got more than I do—"

"You have enough."

They suddenly come to an embankment; below, a turbid, black river flows. And the sounds of sobbing and shrieking and cursing come from the river. A big, informational sign, like you might find in an National Park, stands nearby. Anslenot goes up to it and reads, "The River Human Condition. Fed by the Black Lake of Broken Dreams, Nightmares, Sorrow and Despair, this river permeates the landscape and acts as a barrier to the City of Illusion Beyond. See other sign to right of this one. This sign erected by the Local Chamber of Disillusionment in any given year. Your tax dollars at work." Anslenot frowns and goes over to the other sign that has a big glittering silver arrow pointing to the sparkling City of Illusion across the river. Anslenot reads, 'The City of Illusion, often thought obtainable by people in their twenties, who, jacked up on hormones, think their power is unlimited. For those who actually can cross the River Human Condition, and enter the City of Illusion, they find that the city suddenly goes dark. See other sign to right of this one. This sign brought to you by City Light, lighting your way to darkness'." Anslenot chews his lower lip and moves to the third sign. "The City of Disillusion. To best understand this City, 1. Stare at it intently. 2. Make a wish upon a star (Understand clearly that it *does* make a difference who you are) and close your eyes. 3. Open your eyes." Anslenot does. The city is dark. He sighs, "I feel so disillusioned," he says to the spider. "Where do we go from here?"

As if on cue, Anslenot notices movement nearby.

"I think you're about to discover what happens next," muses the spider.

In a few minutes, Anslenot makes out a sleigh being pulled by a team of spiders and on the sleigh, something wrapped in shrouds of cloth. The sleighmaster, dressed in a Santa Claus suit, cracks a whip and Anslenot realizes the voice sounds familiar. When the sleigh draws near, it slows, then stops. The Santa Claus figure pulls the hood back—

"Mindy," Anslenot stares at his old girlfriend. "You've come back."

"I felt sorry for you, you dirty little counter-revolutionary. I'm giving you another chance." She turns and pulls on ropes which pull off the tarps to reveal—

"... a giant Coke machine—" whispers Anslenot.

"For seventy-five cents, you can recapture the illusion, the youth, the image of life, love, and happiness—you can remember back to your youthful vigor when you thought all was
possible—"

"Seventy five cents—" whispers Anslenot, "but, but—I don't *have* seventy five cents—"

"Then life and love has just passed you by—again—you parasite on the breast of the Motherland."

"You rotten pustule on the soul of the Brotherland," whispers the spider.

"Whose side are you on?" says Anslenot.

"Mine," says the spider.

Anslenot looks back at Mindy. "... and I don't believe anything you say anyway—" says Anslenot.

"He-ya, mush, you arachnids—" she turns to Anslenot. "I tried. I tried to get you to see the ways of Chairman MaoTseBooshThought and the Shining Path of the Right Way, but I was foolish. I really will have to turn you into the Freedom Squad." And she continues on her way. Anslenot watches her leave, then he turns to the City of Illusion only to find it still dark. Listening to the River of the Human Condition, Anslenot then looks up at Saturn— which has now turned into a car. And in the distance, he can hear Mindy singing, "... Oh, beautiful, for spacious skies, for amber waves of grain—"

Chapter 35

A Message

Rather out of sorts, Anslenot finds a bench and sits, watching the sky turn ghastly colors from another, as yet, undisclosed disaster from somewhere. As he sits, he is aware that the tarantula is coming toward him and there is something fastened on its back. The tarantula comes up to him then crouches. The thing on the back of the tarantula is a television. The sky turns dark and the picture can be seen with little trouble.

"Should I thank you?" asks Anslenot.

"Later," says the spider.

"What are you doing?" asks Anslenot. "Is this a message of some sort?"

"Might be," hisses the spider.

"What should I do?" asks Anslenot.

"Watch."

Anslenot watches and the picture is clear and in color. The picture is of a desolate landscape, snowy, and the sky is black and at the bottom of the picture a caption reads, "Pluto," and then other words appear at the bottom of the screen, followed by a little bouncing ball above each word; there is a voice-over:

"Come, sing along with us, just follow the bouncing ball." Anslenot stares and the song begins:

"Pluto is a very-y cold place;
Pluto is oh, so lost in space."

Anslenot tries to place the melody and it sounds remotely like the sound-track to *The Sound of Music,* but the words don't fit the melody and the melody is terribly off key.

"In any case
It's a rotten place,

A place that you'd like to avoid
For a thousand years."

The music fades, the words and the bouncing ball disappear and suddenly, Anslenot sees his father on the screen. He doesn't see his face looking at him, rather he sees a profile and his father is dressed in rags and is pulling a sleigh in which sits his father's mother. She is dressed in fur and looks elegant. There is a samovar in front of her and she drinks tea and eats scones and throws out bread crumbs to Anslenot's father and she calls out, "Be grateful that I care so much about you. Why, if it weren't for me, you wouldn't be here. Hurry up, you're dawdling."

"Thank you, Mother," says Anslenot's father. "I always knew that eventually, I'd get your love."

Anslenot's grandmother sits, sips tea; she puts the tea cup down, throws out more crumbs which Anslenot's father cannot eat because he's busy pulling the sleigh and she cracks a whip over him and says, "Gidd-yap, you worthless son. You never did care for me."

Anslenot's father turns, a look of horror on his face; he says, "That's not true. I do love you. Honest I do. I'll show you," and he pulls the sleigh even harder and his mother sits and drinks tea and munches a scone.

Anslenot stares and then his father pulls the sleigh around and stares out at Anslenot; he puts his hands, his face against the other side of the picture tube and scowls at Anslenot.

"You're getting too big for your britches sonny boy when I see you again I want you to cut my hair and shave the hair off my back you're so thoughtless you never think of anyone but yourself and you should be grateful why if it weren't for me you wouldn't be here and don't feel guilty or obligated!" And Anslenot's father then turns away; the sleigh swings near the screen and Anslenot's grandmother leers at Anslenot, winks and says, "Oh, didn't I train him well? Oh, my, look how he passes it on. It is *so* much fun to have a slave. How I *do* adore it." And the sleigh moves on, out of the picture. Behind it, a rope and far, far off in the distance, a red flyer sled attached to the other end and on it, Anslenot's mother, asthmatic, left out in the cold. When the sled draws near Anslenot, she gets off it, trots over and presses up against the picture tube on the other side and says, "Please don't grow up and leave me like my baby brother did when he died please be sick so I can take care of you why don't you come back and live with me you can come and crawl in bed with me like you used to."

Anslenot puts his hands over his ears. "Oh, God," he says, "this is unbelievable." He reaches over and turns the channel selector and there appears a scene of strange planet, with a magnificent spiral galaxy rotating majestically in the sky.

"Oh, geeze," says the spider, "why'd you do that? Just as it was getting good."

"God," says Anslenot, "how do I escape this madness? Is there no answer?" Beseechingly, he looks to the sky. Abruptly, the stars begin moving and forming letters—

"O-N-L-Y," whispers Anslenot.

"Look!" says the tarantula, "a parade—"

"Huh?" says Anslenot, glancing over to the sound of trumpets and the sight of the clown in red, white and blue greasepaint leading mighty elephants pulling great sleds—Anslenot glances to the sky—

L-O-V-

Ka-pow, ka-pow and cannons go off; the smoke billows up, clouding the sky. Upset, Anslenot glances over again, and then, despite himself, looks longingly at the sleds piled high with dishwashers, cars, and nude women rubbing orgasmically against televisions—Anslenot pulls his eyes away and tries to read the sky again. "M-A-K-S-"—suddenly, Anslenot hears singing and he glances over again and sees Dinah Shore sitting on the front of a 1957 blue and white Chevrolet and she's singing, "See the Yuu Ess Aaa/In your Chev-ro-let/America is asking you to buy—" For a moment, Anslenot does stare, but then he again tries to read the sky—"T-O-L-R-B-L-" Then smoke gets in the way. The parade passes close to Anslenot and then Mindy appears riding a bucking white stallion; behind her, another sled, and on it a laser light show with male nude dancers, thrusting and writhing to a Muzak version of *Handel's Messiah* and again, Anslenot turns away and looks to the sky but the smoke and the light make the message difficult to read. Nonetheless, Anslenot makes out more letters, "T-H K-N-L-D-E O-F -R" *crash, crash, crash*—and Anslenot closes his eyes, unable to even guess what the parade is doing now, but he glances up again—"M-R-T-A-L-T-Y." Then, as if exhausted, the stars go out. Just as suddenly, it is quiet. Smoke drifts and Anslenot turns and sees the parade, the participants, all looking at him, grinning, then all burst out laughing pointing to Anslenot, pointing to the sky.

Anslenot turns to the spider, munching red, white and blue carnations. Beseechingly, he asks, pointing to the sky, "What was the message?"

The spider pauses as though thoughtful. "Hm," it muses, "could have used some steak sauce. Bland." Then, without another word, the tarantula moves up the street. Abruptly, it explodes and the sky is filled with a rain of small tarantulas; Anslenot holds out his hand and one lands in his palm, "is this some weird symbol of hope?" Anslenot says.

The tarantula answers in a high-pitched voice. "I don't know. Is it?"

"Is there anything to be hopeful for?" asks Anslenot.

"I don't know," says the tarantula, "Is there?"

"What is the meaning of all of this," says Anslenot, waving his arms at the chaos. "What is the meaning?"

"Should have paid close attention," says the spider.

"But how could I—" he whispers, "I was distracted."

"Indeed," says the spider, "aren't we all. And perhaps the message has been lost for all time. And most likely it's been lost for a specific reason. Most likely it has. Now that there is all that emptiness—oh, well, too bad. Too bad. Now it's just all unknowable. And nothing to deal with the unknowable. All lost. All gone."

Anslenot sighs. "Might as well be, might as well be." He leans, places the tarantula on the ground. "Maybe in the end, what it's all about now is dealing with a thousand small curses, rather than one giant nightmare."

"Or," says the small tarantula scampering off, "maybe it's all one vast nightmare presenting itself as a thousand small curses."

"Or maybe," says Anslenot, watching the tarantula scamper off, "maybe in the end it is just not knowable any more." He begins to walk up the street, under that uncertain sky, with the traffic hopelessly snarled and gridlocked, the birds flying backwards, and two cats, sitting on a table on a balcony of a burned-out building, smoking cigars.

Epilogue

Anslenot walks. He walks past the gutted buildings and the jets of the Freedom's Friendly Loving Forces (formerly "The Militant Lambs") fighting with the Glorious People's Pacifist Front (formerly "The Opposition"). The little red haired girl walks past him, shaking her head, obviously assuming that Anslenot is unsalvageable. Little tarantulas become big tarantulas instantly. The traffic continues to be stalled and Anslenot walks and soon he comes to the ice mountains—and the bucket of the Bucket Rider. Anslenot sighs, and then as if with sudden resolve and with great purpose and intent, climbs into the coal bucket and ascends into the regions beyond the ice mountains, into the regions... beyond the ice.

End

The Humphrey Bogart Blues

Chapter 1
Space-Time Barbiturate

It is a picture of Marilyn Monroe in a plain, beige sweater; she is leaning over a balcony of a high building, looking down to the traffic below; there is a half-smoked cigarette in her right hand. Perhaps she's had a bit too much alcohol this morning. Maybe it's the uppers she had earlier to counteract the effects of the downers and the sleeping pills she had the night before. Maybe she's just really in a stupor from the drugs, but it does appear that she is looking at something. If so, could it be that she—

1. Is she looking at the past events that have led her up to this point, this place, now. So she isn't really looking at anything *per se,* but the past memories are so real that they are reality itself and while she sees the "present" reality, she doesn't see it at all. Maybe she's looking at the little girl inside. Maybe she's looking for the little girl inside. Maybe she doesn't even know if there *is/was* a little girl inside. Whatever. Perhaps she does know a question: if there was/is a little girl inside, is *this* the life that she *really* had in mind?

2. It is difficult to know exactly when this picture was taken. The cars have humps and bumps and look like elongated blobs rather than the sleek, streamlined blobs of the time this writing occurs. But it is probably the mid to late fifties; say 1957 perhaps. The newest architecture surrounding Marilyn is late forties to early fifties—massive, bulky, like strange, deformed stone erections by engineers and architects who wouldn't dream to consider the possibility that their skyscrapers really *are* phallic and so they've tried their best, in their controlled, repressed, bestial unconscious way to not make it too obvious. Marilyn is on a high level on this phallitechtural monstrosity. Perhaps on some level she knows that this is the gauge of success in this culture, for her, perhaps, for all women—by how high you can crawl up on

these things. Certainly true for her. Yet, her look is dour, somewhat depressed. One can only wonder why. Certainly, she's made it. She's successful.

Isn't she?

3. Looking out over the city, perhaps she *is* wondering why the city looks this way. On some level is she, in fact, contemplating why the buildings do look Phallic? And by what process has this phallitecture become so sharp, so angled, so cold? Is it just a matter of real estate, that the only way you can go is UP? That every square inch must count? Even if that is true, does she wonder, even if true, why the colors and textures are so incredibly insensitive? But does that line of thinking have something to do with how the forces of this cityscape see her and her place as a woman in this world? Does that count toward that pouty, somewhat weary look on her face? Does that belie a deeper truth that she maybe knows too well, but tries like hell to keep away from her—that, in order to survive, she can't be herself; she must survive by how others perceive her.

That must be Tiring.

4. *Very* Tiring.

"Sweetheart, sweetheart—a little more thigh, raise the dress a little higher, turn this way—"

—Click—

"Got it, honey, okay, okay uh, sweetcakes, smile, *smile*, yeah, I know it's been a long shoot, honey, but smile, even if you don't mean it, smile, that's right, bend a little more, a little more cleavage, oh, honey, that's right, yeah, now, like you're laughing—"

—Click—

"Good, that's good, that's very good. Okay, turn a little and let's have that sweet and sorta sultry look, you know, no, no, a little more smile—raise your right leg a little, like you're ready to take a step, turn, let's see a little more flesh up there—oh, *dyn-o-mite*—"

—Click—

Very Tiring indeed. But you'd never know that by the way she smiles and smiles and smiles...

5. But in the picture, she's not smiling. She saves that for the pin-ups, the centerfold, the director's cue and she saves the innocent/shock-smile for the scene where the air blast is blowing her dress up and she saves the giggle for *that* scene too. Everyone knows she enjoys that scene. Does she know she enjoys it? Or does it *look* like she's enjoying it because she's getting paid a lot

of money to *look* like she enjoying it? Maybe that's why she's smiling. It's worth a lot to her. A *lot*.

But if she's so happy, if she's got it all, why the dour look? Why the sadness? The Tiredness?

6. She's disappointed again. The Martians were supposed to be there at noon; it's four o'clock, and they aren't there. They were supposed to come and take her on the tour of the Grand Canal and then they were to have dinner before the High Priestess in the City of Syrtis Major. After dinner, a tour of the vast lichen fields was planned. Marilyn feels very disappointed. She really wanted to be with the Martians. She really wanted to be with those whom she thought — cared.

She looks down to the streets. It's a long way down. It would be so easy, so easy. But she decides against it. Maybe tomorrow will be a better day.

Maybe the Martians will come — to take her away.

Chapter 2

Cellular Temporal Collapse

Maybe Marilyn Monroe, with that weary expression, could be contemplating the Beatles. But of course, she wouldn't know about them since they came along after she died. But had they been her contemporaries, maybe she would be contemptuous of them because it seemed they were singing their hearts out and just Being Themselves.

Ah, geeze, maybe she'd be thinking, *ah, geeze, to get somewhere, I gotta show my tits and thigh and butt and sound breezy and brainless and these guys, they just sing songs and they take over the world. Ah, geeze.*

Then she'd take that cigarette, puff on it long, blow it out and look down to those streets in New York, a long, long way down.

And if we all had control over the Space/Time Continuum, Elvis might pick up on her silent despair, maneuver his Space/Time dimension next to hers and say, "Hey, honey, it's a game, you know? It's jus' a game. Treat me mean an' cruel, treat me like a fool, but it's a game just the same, ya know what I mean?"

"Oh, Elvie, I know, I know," she might respond, "but why is it I can't get anywhere except by being who I'm not?"

"Hey," Elvis might say, "I didn't get nowhere till I started moving my hips and my *whang* and then people noticed, holy houn' dawg, did they *notice*."

"But," Marilyn might say, "what about the Beatles, the group that's gonna be famous after I'm gone?"

"Well, hey, Honey," Elvis might say in his deepest, velvet voice, "maybe they didn't wave their *whangs* around enough but there was plenty of 'stuff' in their songs."

"I don' wanna be a *whang* object." Marilyn might don her famous pouty look, that innocent appeal. "Even though no one really won't know what that means until many years from now, on some level I already know how I'm seen."

Elvis might smile, his Space/Time dimension moving a bit closer. "Being a *whang* object has its ups and downs," he might smile, "an' its ins and outs, sometimes, but honey, being a *whang* object is tough but the world revolves on it. Not money, but *whang*."

"Is it supposed to be this way?" Marilyn might ask. "I just can't believe it's supposed to be this way."

Abruptly, a stronger Space/Time Continuum shift occurs, and Lenin might replace Elvis. "Revolution," he might whisper. "It's not about sex my little petty bourgeoisie urchin, it's about revolution."

"No," and Marilyn might sigh, "no, your problem is that your *whang* and your heart are miles apart."

"You little Kulak," Lenin might whisper, "you deserve to be hung." And his Space/Time image retreats so quickly that the red shift is pronounced and the color of blood.

And Thomas Jefferson's image might then appear.

Marilyn might look at him with disdain. "At the time this picture is taken," she might say, "I'm being portrayed as long on *whang* but short on brains. But, Mr. Jefferson sir, I think Time is gonna diminish your image and you're gonna no longer be seen as the *whangless* guy I learned about in school."

But none of this is really happening. Marilyn is not getting solace from Elvis, the Beatles or anyone else. No shift along the Space/Time Continuum occurs except in her sub-subconscious, an ancient part of the brain clobbered by alcohol and pills and where the concept of time doesn't exist anyway but is somehow in touch with—? And she knows it and the Martians have yet to appear to take her away. She continues to look over the balcony, to the streets, far, far below.

Chapter 3

A Kringle In Time

So, Marilyn Monroe continues to look over that railing and not even Elvis could give her a hand.

"Ahem."

Hearing this, Marilyn turns slowly around, to see Kris Kringle standing in his red suit and a bag slung over his shoulders.

With great effort he plops the bag down. "Oof," he says, "guess I'd better enjoy being Kris Kringle now."

Marilyn eyes him warily, takes a drag off her cigarette. She doesn't say anything.

"You know," he says, pulling out an hourglass-shaped bottle of Coke from his heavy Santa suit, "I'm a mythic figure, I've got a list, been checking it twice, figuring out who's naughty and nice, and Santy Claus has come to town."

Rudolph, the Red Nosed Reindeer turns and says to Marilyn, "You know why Santa ain't got no kids?"

Kris, looking warily at Rudolph, stops in the middle of raising his arm for another swig of Coke.

"Because he only comes once a year and when he does it's down the chimney."

Santa's eyes, how they twinkle, his nose like a cherry, and when he laughs, it's like a bowl full of jelly. "Oh, ho, ho, ho," he roars and smacking Rudolph on his side, says, "Oh, ho, ho, ho. My wife has been wondering all these years what has been wrong. Now I know! Oh, ho, ho, ho." Then he begins coughing. After that passes, he wheezes. "Just came from Youngstown, Ohio," he says to Marilyn, "right now, in the late fifties, no one really thinks about the shit being pumped out into the atmosphere but I can tell you, being the mythic figure that I am, I am God-like and I know the future and I'm getting my stats all together here for a future class-action suit because I get emphysema from breathing all this fine particle crap I have to fly through once a year. The damage is cumulative, you know."

Marilyn puffs on her cigarette, saying nothing.

"And you know something else, my little kitten?" He takes another swig of Coke, "Boy that's good stuff, even though years from now, it will be common knowledge that this stuff not only cleans out drains but removes paint from cars—another class action suit coming up—but that also years from now, I'm going to be suing a guy named Bill Gates because of all the back injuries I'm gonna be getting from delivering computers on Christmas

Eve. Boy, even *another* suit. I'm gonna be rich. But," and he takes a long drink of Coke, "that is neither here nor there. The question is, What have I got in my bag for you?"

Marilyn drops the cigarette. "I'm not your little kitten," she says. With much energy, she grinds the cigarette out.

"Figure of speech," he says, "but don't forget, this is the fifties and sexual harassment is years away so you can't get me on anything yet. But, hey, I do have something for you."

Marilyn lights another cigarette. "Why?" she says. "It's not Christmas, that's months away."

Kris Kringle nods, finishes the Coke and tosses it over the balcony. Then putting a finger aside his nose, he ponders her question. Distantly, the sound of breaking glass and a scream drifts up from the streets below. "But last year you refused to see me—so I was just flying over, running errands, and saw you standing here, so I thought I'd drop in and give you a gift. I can't give you anything politically or gender correct or appropriate or enlightening because that type of thinking is at least ten years off in the future, so the only thing I can give you—and I hope you'll see it as a compliment—is this." And from his bag, he pulls out—

"—a *doll*? A Goddamn doll? What are you giving me a *doll* for?"

Kris Kringle shrugs. "I dunno," he says, "guess the sentiment is that everyone sees you as a 'doll' in a complimentary sense, of course; given the time and place, it seems appropriate."

Marilyn nods. She puts the cigarette back in her mouth and accepts the blond-haired doll with the blue eyes and pretty, fluffy blue dress that comes down to her knees. The arms are out-stretched; it's made of that late forties/early fifties hard plastic. She holds it stiffly and doesn't say anything.

"Ho, ho, ho," says Kris Kringle. Marilyn notices Kris climb up to the balcony, sees the reindeer pawing the air as Kris gets in his sleigh. "I like this era," he says. "I can stay parked for relatively long periods of time. If I were to stay this long in the nineties, my sleigh and reindeer would be shot to hamburger by now from the AK-47's. It's rough in the future."

Marilyn stares. "You've been there?" she asks. "What has happened to me? How did my life turn out?"

But Kris Kringle shakes his head. "Can't tell you that. I know, and I guess that was another reason why I wanted to stop by when I saw you here. But no, I can't tell you that." He whistles. The reindeer tense. "On Comet, on Cupid, on Donner, on Vixen—" and with that, the sleigh surges, is off and away.

Marilyn holds the doll, she watches Santa disappear into the smoggy haze of the afternoon. Then she looks at the doll and after some minutes, she goes to the bedroom, takes the doll and puts it in a box filled with tissue paper. Putting the lid on, she says, "It's just better this way now, to put you away, to hide you. It's not safe for you to be here right now. But some day, but some day..." and kneeling in front of the closet, she hides the box under blankets and other things of Yesterday.

Chapter 4

The Flapper

Marilyn goes back to the balcony; she goes to the railing and suddenly feels dizzy. She can't remember how many uppers she took this morning. Or was it downers? Abruptly, Humphrey Bogart appears to her—as an Archangel. He flutters pale blue wings and wears a silvery garment, a harp is cradled lovingly in the crook of his left arm; it is gold, and the sunlight reflecting off it is so bright that Marilyn has to look away.

"Sorry kid," says Humphrey, "didn't mean to blind you."

Marilyn looks up at him. "Why are you an angel?" she asks, "Have you died?"

Humphrey strums his harp. "Didn't you know?" He coughs. "Throat cancer."

"I'm sorry," Marilyn says, "but the booze and the pills... I'm sorry—I—I've lost track of time—why are you parading as an angel?"

Humphrey looks at Marilyn then gently flutters over and sits on the railing of the balcony. He smiles benignly. "Even if I weren't dead, you don't necessarily have to *be* dead to be an angel," he says.

"Oh," Marilyn looks startled. "I never thought of that. So why didn't you just pay me a call like a real live person instead of coming to me as an angel?"

Flutter, flutter, go the wings; they shimmer in the sunlight and Marilyn can see minute rainbows dance across the delicate feathers.

Humphrey Bogart thinks for a minute. "You know, kid, that's a good question and I suppose maybe I should, though, in all these years, I've never figured too much into your life—maybe coming to you as an angel is what I need to do. Or," he shrugs, "maybe I'm appearing to you as an angel to remind you that no matter what happens, you, too, are an angel. Maybe I just wanna make sure you know that. Do you?"

Marilyn giggles. "Gee, I never thought of that. Ya really think so?"

Humphrey sighs. "Ya know," he says, *flutter, flutter,* "it's too bad that you can't be the bright girl that you are. Wouldn't sell, ya know? It's a bad business, ya know? This trying to be something that you're not, just like I gotta be the tough guy with a marshmallow heart."

Marilyn looks at him somewhat askance, uncomprehending.

"Acting," says Humphrey, "acting. It's so easy to forget not to act. So easy to become—to become—" He looks away, looks toward the sun. From his gown, he produces a cigarette. "Got a light, honey?"

"Oh, yeah, sure, sure. Here ya go." Marilyn produces a lighter, flicks it on, reaches over and lights Humphrey's cigarette but in the lighting, ash breaks off and lands on Humphrey's robe. Instantly, it begins to smoke and flame.

"Oh, no—" Marilyn says, and she tries to pat out the flames.

"Shit—" yells Humphrey and the cigarette drops from his mouth, falling away from him like a comet and *he* tries to pat out the flames but it's too late. The flames spread to his wings. He loses his balance but yells, "Don't worry, kid, it's a dream—" and he flutters awkwardly up and away, still swatting at the flames and some distance away, he falls from the sky and *poof* explodes in blue-white light.

Marilyn shakes her head and looks around. No smoke. No trace of anything. She shakes her head again, "My goodness," she says, "my goodness. *What* was *that*? A bit unnerved she continues to look around not sure what to make of it all." Then she laughs, "My, my, I do have a good imagination or else I gotta be more careful about what I take—"

She moves closer to the balcony. *Clink.* She looks down. At her feet—a lighter.

Chapter 5

Lighter Memories

Marilyn stoops, picks up the lighter. She looks off to the distance then back to the lighter. It is silver, squarish and not at all "feminine" looking. Raised letters, initials on one side: "R.F.K." She studies the lighter. "R.F.K.", she whispers out loud. "Who is 'R.F.K.'?" *It's funny*, she thinks, *all the people you run into. All the things that come your way and you are left with these little things, and at the time you get them, they sure seemed meaningful and now, you know, the thing is, I can't remember when I got this much less who gave it to me.*

She holds the lighter, then looks up, over the cityscape of New York, off into the haze of the distance. *It's nineteen fifty-seven*, she thinks, *and I'm what, thirty-one?*

She studies the lighter. *R.F.K.* she muses, *R.F.K. — Who...*

She opens the lighter, flicks the wheel; a spark, barely discernible in the daylight, then a flame, exploding up then becoming still, quiet, almost invisible except for the blue soul of the flame. Somehow—somehow—*religious*... muses Marilyn in wordless wonder, the shape of the flame like two hands in prayer...

She continues to look into the flame, and with that little flame, for whatever reason, memories surface, memories of an ancient void, then memories of going from foster home to foster home, of being raped when she was six, eight, eleven, twelve—then—of being careful, so careful, of hiding inside, so deep inside that no one knew who Norma Jean Baker really was, for even Norma Jean Baker did not know, but she always knew the void, the hunger, the ache. Marilyn stares into the flame, the words gone now, but a deep sense of wonderment, of curiosity that, if put into words, would be a moving testimonial to survival at all costs, no matter what, no matter what the circumstances; her wordless wonder: that flame, that flame, is that my hope? Is that my drive? Is that my promise to myself of the future of what I could be? Or could become? Is that what I held onto? Or is that the light in the darkness? Is that light the burning urge to shine, in spite of the darkness, the pain, to shine, to shine with my own light, for in the end, my own light is all that I had, all that I was left with. A long stillness: all that I have now or ever will have. Is that it?

Marilyn stares even deeper into the flame. The wordless wonderment continues, the eerie sense of all of this surfaces: or is it the darkness and the fear of the dark that makes this light so bright? Is that what fuels it? The fear of being left again, the fear of not being seen? Is that what makes me burn so bright? But just as someday the fuel that makes this lighter burn must be spent, what fuel do I have that will be spent? Or will it be spent? Or will it take me to places where it will be spent whether I want that or not? At what cost this flame? At what cost this flame? She snaps shut the cap to the lighter. Oxygen gone. Flame is out. Smothered.

And for an instant, Marilyn Monroe, aka Norma Jean Baker is cold, cold, so terribly, *terribly* cold.

Chapter 6

Lighter Memories Too

Marilyn holds the lighter, feels its warmth and doesn't really know what to think about it all. Finally she just looks out to where Humphrey Bogart disappeared and thinks, *Poor Humphrey. What was he trying to say to me?*

She glances down and starts. There, just a few inches away from her on the balcony, a cockroach. In her mind, she hears, "Maybe he was trying to tell you that you were an angel because you don't realize it."

Marilyn stares at the cockroach. "What—" she says.

"Kafka," says the cockroach, "Kafka's the name. What a metamorphosis, eh?"

In horror, Marilyn backs away, "I *hate* cockroaches," she seethes.

"Eh," says the cockroach in her mind, "everybody hates us. But you know why that is? I mean, you *do* know why that is, right?"

Marilyn stands back, horrified, but listening.

"Because," the cockroach continues, "deep down inside, everyone thinks they're a cockroach. Even you, my dear, even you."

"How *dare* you—"

"Just an observation," says Kafka, "But look at the people who have come by to talk to you—Elvis, The Beatles—who are just getting it together about the time you die—"

Marilyn gasps. "Die? Die? I'm going to die—?"

The cockroach doesn't say anything for a minute. "Oy," it finally says, "Oy, I blew it. I gave you information that you couldn't, shouldn't have known about. Oh, what a loathsome creature I am, lowest of the low—"

"I'm going to die?" says Marilyn, "How am I going to die?"

"Oy," says the cockroach, "Oy, oy, should have kept my insectial thoughts to myself. Oy, tampering with the future, oy, oy, oy, oy—"

"Answer my question!" says Marilyn.

"That's what you get for being a weird writer—"

Marilyn slaps her hand on the balcony near Kafka. "Answer my question!"

"Well, look," says the cockroach, "we all have to die, even me although my books will probably live forever—what'd you think of *The Trial* by the way?"

"Never mind that," says Marilyn, "I want to know if you know how I'll die."

The cockroach backs up, its antenna twitching. "Oy," it finally says, "oy, musta been those crumbs I ate last night—made my chitin itch—isn't it dreadful what they do to food these days—you don't know—"

"How will I die!" yells Marilyn.

"Alright, alright, you needn't get all insectial about this—I can't tell you but I will say that your love was well-intentioned but—um—just not very much appreciated."

Marilyn is fuming. "What does *that* mean?"

In her mind she hears the cockroach sigh, "Just be careful whom you love, O.K.? Just be careful."

Marilyn takes off her shoe and holds it threateningly above the cockroach. "That's a lousy answer."

"But that's all I can tell you," says Kafka. "If I tell you any more, history will be totally altered and just because I know a lot doesn't mean I have to tell people anything—"

"Darn you!"

Smack, and Marilyn's shoe comes down just inches form the cockroach.

"*Oy!*" says Kafka, scuttling backwards, "God, we artists always suffer so—"

Smack! and Marilyn's shoe comes down again.

"Such a trial this is," says the cockroach. It falls off the balcony, on to the balcony floor.

"You have it coming," says Marilyn, getting ready to smack at the cockroach again.

"Just know how many people really do love you, Marilyn," says the cockroach. And as it scuttles off into a dark place, "Just make sure you love yourself enough to make the right decisions—" Marilyn, now ready to throw the shoe, stops, and looks puzzled. "What?" she says.

But silence is her only answer.

Chapter 7

What If...?

... what if? she thinks, *what if this is all a mistake? What if everything is a mistake? Maybe I should have stayed married to James... but something, but something led me on...*

Flutter, flutter, flutter, and it's Humphrey Bogart again, descending from the heavens, looking somewhat doleful, and gently playing his harp. He stops just a ways from and above her.

"Bogie—" she says.

He nods. "Know what you're thinking, Kid, I know what you're thinking. God knows why we end up doing what we do. I don't have an answer."

Marilyn looks down to her feet. "I was happy with James," she said, "I guess I shoulda stayed married to him—or to Joe..."

Thrum, thrum, thrum, goes the harp and Bogie looks disdainful. "Too bad it's not a violin," he says, "what you're saying is sad. Yeah, it needs a violin."

Marilyn looks up, somewhat abashed, "Are you happy? Were you happy with the way your life turned out?"

Bogie stops playing the harp, moves closer and sits on the edge of the balcony. Putting the harp in his lap, he just looks at Marilyn. "God," he says, "who knows? Is anyone ever satisfied? Is anyone ever really happy? Content?"

Abruptly, there is a tear in the space-time continuum and Isaac Asimov falls through, pauses near Marilyn and Bogie and says, "I died in 1995 after writing over 500 books and I'm still not happy."

And he continues to fall, then slips through another opening in the continuum.

"Who was that?" asks Marilyn.

"Don't know," says Bogie, "but it's hard to believe someone wouldn't feel okay about writing so many books. Probably didn't break the world's record. And even if he had, would he have been happy?"

The space-time continuum opens again and Gustave Flaubert falls though and slows. "I wrote the world's greatest novel, *Madame Bovary,* and a woman who loved me—died—I was so busy I couldn't love—I died miserably alone and unhappy."

And he continues to fall, then is swallowed up in another tear in the continuum.

Thrum, thrum, thrum goes the harp and Bogie says, "God, now I really *do* wish I had a violin. That was *really* sad."

Marilyn considers all of this. "I was happy with James Dougherty," she says, "but I was unhappy, I wanted something more."

A beautiful light shines down from above. An ethereal voice drifts down from above. "Beware the fame and fortune addiction. Page 120, *The Artist's Way.*"

The light fades. Both Marilyn and Bogie look up and then to each other. "What was that?"

"I don't know," says Marilyn. "I didn't understand it."

"I didn't either," says Bogie. "But let me tell you this. No point in wondering about the past. Day by day, you gotta go on. You gotta do your best and go for it no matter where it takes you. 'Cause where it takes you is where you gotta go because if you don't go, you won't really be happy—"

Again, the space-time continuum opens and Oedipus tumbles out, eyes bloodied and blinded, screaming, "Why didn't I listen? Why didn't I listen?" and he vanishes into the air.

"What did he say?" asks Marilyn.

Bogie shakes his head. "Greek to me. Anyway, you gotta go on and see where your life goes—forget the past—"

Suddenly in the sky, letters form and the message flashes on and off: "BAD ADVICE. BAD ADVICE. BAD ADVICE."

"Hum," Bogie says, "weird weather we're having. Anyway, kid, you just keep on goin' and you'll be just fine."

Marilyn looks at Bogie. "You have a reputation for being a boozer, and having terrible fights with your wives. Is this what you want?"

Bogie looks startled. "Uh—well, Kiddo, you have a reputation for being a pill-popper, boozer and sleeping around with just about anyone. Is that what *you* want?"

"Well, gee, Bogie, what's wrong with sex?"

Bogie grins, "Well, it's not so much that—" he shakes his head, "God, look at us. Who knows why we do what we do."

Again, letters in the sky appear. "RIGHT QUESTION. RIGHT QUES-TION. RIGHT QUESTION."

They both laugh. "Oh, the weather is so strange here in New York," Marilyn giggles. "But maybe it is just the way it is and it's dumb to think much about it."

Again, letters appear high above them. "WRONG ANSWER. WRONG ANSWER. WRONG ANSWER."

Bogie looks annoyed at the sky. *Thrum, thrum, thrum.* "I gotta go see the man upstairs about the weather," he says, "whatever the sky is doing, it's real distracting."

"Yeah," says Marilyn, "fix it. And when you do, come back? But—um—"

"Yeah, Kiddo?"

"—um—could you leave the harp behind? I don't know why it just—bothers me—"

"Sure," says Humphrey, "I'm not real big on them anyway. How about if I bring back some booze?"

"That'd be okay," says Marilyn.

"I'll be back." He flutters away, thrumming his harp, *pink-plum, pink-plum, plum-pum.*

Marilyn looks up at him, drifting away and then she hears a familiar voice, "Oy, oy, 'the mills of fate grind slowly, but they grind exceedingly well'."

Marilyn whirls about, takes off her shoes ready to hit the cockroach—except she can't see him. "Where are—"

"Oy," says the cockroach, "you'll never find me; but little matter that—just remember Oedipus—"

"What are you talking about, you nasty bug—"

"Please, the name is Kafka," says the cockroach. "But you know," and he sighs, "maybe we know exactly what is going to happen to us and we just can't help it even though we know it. Maybe we just can't help it after all."

Marilyn whirls about looking for Kafka. "Where are you?" she whispers fervently, "what do you mean?"

But after some minutes, she realizes—Kafka isn't answering.

Chapter 8

The Mind/Body Rag

Marilyn stares off into the distance. Is it the alcohol she had this morning? Is it the Nembutal? Or is the universe doing something strange again, for suddenly the sky is filled with stars which abruptly blur to a blinding light and, surrounded by this light, she shakes her head: "It's 1953, I'm twenty-seven again and I—" Suddenly, she sees the scene in *The Seven Year Itch* when the street vent is blowing her dress up. She has several pairs of panties on, but her pubic hair shows through anyway.

"But," she whispers to herself, "I haven't made this movie yet—this is the only thing I know about it—yet is it something yet to be? It must be—but how can I know of something yet to be? What do I make of it?" she wonders. "Is this a dream or do I have foresight of a reality yet to be? Since it seems so exact, it has to be real, but is it possible to have a dream such that it parades as reality?"

Suddenly before her, the sky turns an intense, cobalt blue and she sees a heart suspended in mid-air on the left, but a voice comes to her from the right. It speaks in excellent English: "Beware of dreams."

"Why?" says Marilyn, "A proverb says, 'To not respond to a dream is like not answering a letter'."

"Beware of dreams," comes the voice again, "since they cannot be sensed by the senses, they cannot be real."

"Well, they sorta feel real enough to me," says Marilyn. "—uh—who *are* you, anyway?"

"Rene Descartes," comes the voice, "I'm a philosopher."

"What do you philosophize?" asks Marilyn.

"The separation of the mind and body. They are not the same. The only way that one knows that one exists is by thinking: *cogito, ergo sum*. I think, therefore, I am."

"Gee," says Marilyn, "sure sounds complicated—guess I don't understand why mind and body aren't the same. Why can't you also say, 'I feel, therefore I am'?"

"Feelings are subjective; they always change and that way, they are the same as dreams. Thinking is the only proof of existence. Trust me."

Marilyn thinks for a minute, shakes her head. "I don't wanna be a dumb blond," she says, "but maybe I am — I just don't get it. Your voice is over there, but your heart is over here. So, who do I trust? *What* do I trust?"

"The voice. The voice is the product of thought and thinking proves my existence."

"But without your heart, how can you talk to me? Or think?" She giggles. "Gee, maybe I'm not so dumb after all. Me! Arguing with a philosopher! Gee!"

Long pause.

"Trust me," comes the voice, a little less pedantic, "trust me that dreams are not reality."

"I dunno," says Marilyn, "I'm standing on a balcony and I'm pretty sure this conversation isn't really happening in, you know, reality, just in my head, like a dream, and this 'inside talk' really is like a dream and as far as I'm concerned it is, therefore if the dream isn't really reality, then neither are you." She grins. "Hey, I'm pretty good at this."

A *very* long pause. "So — what do you know for certain?" Descartes finally asks.

"Only what I feel and that is really all I know and I also know I feel strange about the future as well as what you're talking about."

For whatever reason, the heart begins to beat erratically, then abruptly drops.

"I think," comes the bold voice, "therefore — "

Splat.

Marilyn looks over the edge of the balcony to another balcony that juts out just a foot or so more. A red mass quivers on the balcony and a white poodle trots over to sniff it, then begins to piddle on it.

He tried, Marilyn nods to herself. *He truly tried. Separating mind and body, guess that's one way not to feel pain. But I think mind and body are the same — one influences the other, back and forth and right now, I feel strange 'cause I'm seeing something about the future and Mr. Rene Descartes, you didn't really help much. All I know is what I feel and I feel strange for there is no way I can explore the future or explain it and whatever it is, it is up to me to deal with it.*

Again, she sees the wind blowing her skirt, the stage hands looking, smiling, some smirking, some leering and Marilyn wonders, wonders, wonders, and then thinks, *A dream of a future yet to be? Can this be changeable? Maybe I really want this? Is it reality a dream? If it feels like a dream is it a dream? What if it feels like reality? This is a reality yet to be, never unchangeable? Is it that I imagine a future I see and I help create it hence it is unchangeable? That no matter what I do, it is to be this way and the act of trying to change it invariably brings it about?*

"There is only way out of this, Mr. Descartes, Marilyn says to herself, *I do not think, therefore I am not*. But it doesn't work, Mr. Descartes, because even if I don't think, I *still* am. The only way out is to die—and—" she shudders, "I don't want to do that right now, maybe in the future; maybe I did in the past, but right now—no, therefore, my future is cast for me and no matter what I do, I can't know if I will change it because any change I make might be the *exact* change to bring it about. So, therefore..."

She wonders if she could somehow do something to have the scene filmed with her wearing long pants.

But, somehow... she doubts it.

Chapter 9

Of Ids and Beasts and Marilyn

Marilyn continues to ponder these questions. Looking about, the blue around her fades to a burning, searing white. *What age am I now?* she wonders. Some part of her answers; "Older than you want to be, younger than you can possibly imagine." Another memory appears. But this one is of the past. It is a memory of her as a little girl in an orphanage. She remembers what it was like. *I dreamed*, she thinks, *of being glamorous and famous, and here I am. Famous. But I never had a dream of me leaning over a balcony looking back to when I was a little girl.*

She remembers what it was like, the fantasizing about glamour, the movies. She would be a movie star someday. Someday. Why? How? She does not know. Cannot know. It's all a flow of images, a blur of faces and time and... men.

If this were taking place in the 90's, if she were exposed to therapy as it is practiced in the 90's, to Inner Child work, to imagine her as her adult self, sitting in a chair, talking to the child self and the child self talking to her, what would *that* be like?

"Are you happy, Little Marilyn?"

"I don't know. I'm sad, I think, Big Marilyn."

"Why, Little Marilyn?"

"I think all this man stuff and being naked is kinda scary—"

"May I offer why you might feel that way? Little Marilyn? Maybe it's because we've grown to depend on sexuality as a way to find the love and affection you never got as a child and no matter how much we try, it's never enough and will never be enough—oh, the anxiety, Little Marilyn, I feel so much anxiety—"

And at that point, the therapist might break in and say, "The anxiety is a signal of something—go with it—what do you suppose—"

And Little Marilyn might begin to sob uncontrollably—But this isn't the 90's; it's the mid to late fifties and the only real thing available to the General Public as far as insight and self-esteem is Dale Carnegie's *How To Win Friends and Influence People*, *The Power of Positive Thinking* by Norman Vincent Peale, and to some extent, A.A.

It is hardly enough. But it's the only thing out there in a society so preoccupied with maintaining unconsciousness: look this far but no further. Let's not *really* look at the impact of rape or sexual abuse. It didn't really happen. And we all know that women *really* ask for it, they *really* want it, even at age six. Of course.

So Marilyn just looks out, remembers the fantasies of the little girl and just knows, just *knows* that if she keeps going, she'll be fine, she'll be happy. She smiles at the thought, but is aware that in someway, somehow, it just doesn't feel quite right but doesn't quite know why. She only knows that somehow, someway, she'll really be happy. Someday. If she just does this show, gets this shot, this part, it will be fine. It will be all right.

She smiles, but the smile fades and Marilyn continues to look out at the distance, on the roof tops, to New York, to the grey marble and granite, somehow everything a prison in a century and a country not particularly known for its ability, much less willingness, to be insightful.

Chapter 10

What's It All About, Marilyn?

Marilyn blinks her eyes. *What year is it now?* she wonders. Then she hears a labored flapping and, looking to her right, sees Humphrey Bogart flutter up. His wings are singed but he has obviously grown a few new feathers.

"Hey, kiddo, how are you?" He sips a drink. "In answer to your unspoken question, we're back in 1957. In answer to your next question about how I can figure out what you're thinking, just take it as a given. I can do that. One of the fringe benefits of afterlife."

Marilyn studies him. "You don't die easily do you?"

"Hey, kid, I was in eighty-three films, made a mint and had plenty of F.Y. money so I could do what I wanted to do. You think I'm gonna fade away so easy?" He downs his drink and reaching into a secret place in his gown, pulls out a full bottle of Scotch. He flutters over to Marilyn, puts the glass on the balcony edge and pours a drink. "Want some?"

"Sure. Thanks," says Marilyn demurely.

"Good stuff," says Humphrey, pulling out another glass from his gown. He smiles. "Always in the mood for a sociable drink. Keeps ya going. Never did like food much, but this stuff is a life line."

Marilyn regards him for a long time, then goes inside, and returns with a pill.

"Upper? Downer?" asks Bogie.

Marilyn shrugs. "I dunno." She giggles. "I kinda forget at times." She pops the pill and takes a long drink, draining the glass.

"Risky taking pills with booze," says Bogie.

Marilyn shrugs again. "Maybe. Makes me feel good, though." She looks at Bogie for a minute. "You an alcoholic?"

"Nah," says Bogie, "I can hold my liquor just fine and I can stop drinking whenever I want to."

"What's the longest you've ever been dry?"

Bogie looks at her squarely. "Wanna 'nother drink?"

Marilyn nods her head. "You didn't answer my question."

Bogie refills her glass and takes another drink. "Good stuff." He then downs it, fills the glass again and puts the cap on the bottle.

"You're still dead, aren't you?" asks Marilyn.

Bogie smiles. "Yup. Nothing's changed but also, no, I'm not dead. Ya know, in 1950, I first thought about this business, when I was still alive. But like I said before, I do die in 1957, this year, so I guess all along, I, my spirit, was the spirit of the Bogie-to-be." He smiles. "—which, as you notice, isn't all that different than the Bogie that was—"

"Or un-was, as the case may be," says Marilyn.

Bogie shrugs. "Well, hell—"

"So what do you think about, now that you have all that time to think in heaven?"

Bogie laughs. "Eh, who has time for thinking. I just like to fly around and needle people like I did in real life." He smiles again. "Gotta continue the family tradition."

Marilyn shakes her head. "Death hasn't really changed you?"

"Well, my third wife Mayo is up there along with the other two, and we still battle, but because we're spiritual, physical objects don't do us much damage and if she tries to hit me, or if I hit her—she still sets me up to do that and I really can't help it—well, being spiritual, you can kinda control your atoms—pull them apart, reappear, disappear, so it really is kind of fun up there."

"Golly," says Marilyn, "you can do all that?"

Bogie nods. "We have a lot of control of matter and the time flow, so I can keep myself in an endless supply of Scotch and cigarettes and can appear whenever I want to."

"Doesn't it bother you being dead?"

"Not too much," says Bogie. "We don't make films, though. With everyone disappearing and reappearing up there, it's hard to create an audience."

"Oh," says Marilyn, "so if I gotta do something, I gotta do it here and now."

"Right, kiddo. In this form, in this place—yeah."

"So is that why you're visiting me? To tell me this?"

"No," says Bogie, "I've always had a crush on you and just wanted to come back to see how you were doing."

"What about Lauren? Isn't she gonna be jealous?"

Bogie takes another drink. "I visit her all the time. She knows I'm around. But Lauren Bacall isn't Marilyn Monroe. You're gonna be famous honey, and when I was alive—" he says, "—I am alive now but in another form for—uh—eternity, I guess—well—you're already famous. I just wanna know what you were like when you were young and maybe give you some advice along the way—"

"Sweet of you," says Marilyn.

Bogie holds his glass out to her. "Lookin' at 'cha, kid." He drinks.

"Can you tell me one thing, though?"

"What?"

"Do you know how I die?"

Bogie frowns. "Whether I know or not—either way, I can't tell you."

"Why."

"Just can't. I'm sure there's an ordinance or a law somewhere that says that but I can't tell you one way or the other."

Marilyn ponders this. Then, "If you are the Bogie-to-be, did you visit Bogie when he was alive? Before he physically died?"

"Nope, kiddo, can't do that either. Just like the Marilyn-to-be can't come back and visit you before you die."

"Why not?"

"Game would be up."

"Game?"

"See, kiddo, it's like this. It's not the knowing that makes life worthwhile. It's the not knowing and it's the knowing that we die that gives life meaning. Since we never know what is going to happen to us or when, means we gotta live life like the dickens right now and make the most of what we got—like what you're doing. Got it? And that's all you need to know."

"So your spiritual side will never meet the you that dies?"

"Of course," says Bogie, "when the life-essence of the real me dies or leaves, then we both flutter off together."

"Is *this* what you've come to tell me, then?" asks Marilyn.

"No," says Bogie.

"Then *what?*"

Bogie pours himself another drink. He looks at Marilyn. "Lookin' at 'cha, kid." He downs the drink, puts the bottle away and gently fluttering his wings, ascends to heaven.

Chapter 11

What It's All About, Marilyn

The booze, the pills, do their deadly dance and suddenly Marilyn is enraged. *Damn literature class*, thinks Marilyn. *If I hadn't taken that course at UCLA, I wouldn't have known or cared about Emerson, Greek Mythology, Rilke, Hemingway, Wolfe or Joyce or Tolstoy. My imagination is running away with me. There are plenty of things I should be — could be — doing.* Yet, she stands on the balcony. And she is about to make a gesture, take a breath, when she freezes —

— and the writers she speaks of form an apparition, the Ghost of Literature Past — the face — old, sad, is that of the Ages, it looks upon her with sympathy and it whispers, "What she doesn't realize is that she knows too much but she doesn't *know* that she knows too much. She knows too much on an unconscious level. No words for it. Just a hunch just a 'gnawing knowing,' a raw, pre-verbal sense that she is Out Of Time. She is Out Of Time yet what do you do when there is only one game in town to play? What do you do when you have a history of suicide attempts that utterly belie the public persona? What do you do?"

The apparition moves toward her. "Look at her," it whispers, "She is thirty-one, born in 1926. So many people she meets are ten, fifteen, twenty years or more older than she is, born in the last quarter of the 19th century and the first part of the twentieth century, a time when Victorian ideals are changing, a time of a world war, the establishment of a future enemy of the U.S., the depression. Too busy to survive to know how to talk, to introspect. Too busy, too busy, too busy and everyone and the society operates on unconscious automatic assumptions and there is no luxury of thought, no models, save the books, the books, and even then, mirrors of the times. Brave mirrors, but, nonetheless, only mirrors for the vast unconscious, too distorted, too trapped to realize the power of the mirrors, or seeing the power, unable to access it, hence in pain, sometimes obvious, sometimes not so obvious."

The Ghost, with insubstantial hands, touches Marilyn Monroe's face, her hair, her hands. It is a very loving, caring touch and the ghost caresses her. "Pity, pity, pity. For this is the way it has been, this is the way it is. She cannot know what she does not know. She cannot access what she cannot access because there may well *be* no access. And she is Just Like Everyone Else, but she just has the beauty and the vulnerability that no one else thinks they have—but in reality—do. So Marilyn can only wonder, 'I wonder how people see me?' But deeper, it is the Eternal Question, 'Just how do I see myself?' But more than that, 'How much of myself do I see?' But even more than *that*: 'How much of myself do I *accurately* see?'" The Ghost of Literature Past sits on the edge of the balcony and considers Marilyn, "But what about those attempted suicides? And why, even with all the psychiatric help, why the booze? Why the pills? How much can you know, but still *not* know? How much pain can you be aware of, and yet not be aware of at all? How many times can you hear the ideas of others? Yet not hear at all? How many times can you say 'Aha!' and a few minutes later, forget what it was? Even in 1962, when she is thirty-six, how much she knows, how much more she knows, yet how pathetically little."

The Ghost drifts off the balcony and the scene around the ghost turns black. "Oh, Gods!" screeches the Ghost in shrieking pain, "Oh, Gods, oh, Oedipus and we sons and daughters of Oedipus, the hideous blinding paradox: damned by the torment of not knowing and cursed by coming to know—oh, Gods! Oh, Oedipus, Oedipus and we sons and daughters of Oedipus, our will to know is our courage to face the pain of what we have done, what we have become! Oh, Gods! the torment unbearable yet it is in this hideous darkness that the courage to come to know—it is our tragic brilliance—oh, God and Fates and Destiny: thou names art Oedipus! And we are all burned in thy image."

The Ghost sobs. "To be released from darkness only to be released to darkness; oh, Fate, oh, Gods, oh, Oedipus, is the only pain worse is that of not knowing at all?" The Ghost turns to Marilyn and with infinite compassion, touches her face again. "Not knowing at all?" And after a pause, "Or is there even a greater pain? Can there be a greater pain than not knowing at all? If so, it would have to be knowing and remaining utterly unable to alter the path that Fate has predestined—be it for her or for us—like moths, knowing of candle's flame, feeling the heat but unable to pull back, unable to stop—knowing but unable—what the greater pain? What, oh Gods, oh, Oedipus, what greater pain than this?"

The Ghost changes and becomes Dr. Greerson. "You never got over your loneliness, your abandonment, and you keep hoping you'll find love; your desperation drives you to be appreciated, but how much do you, can you really appreciate yourself?"

But Marilyn remains frozen, unable to hear him. He is but an apparition, a Ghost of Future Insight that, even though she may someday hear it, it can't touch her core now. And *now* is when it needs to touch. But cannot.

"And you've told me," Dr. Greerson continues, "that you have a memory of your grandmother trying to suffocate you with a pillow when you were one year old. Think, Marilyn, think—"

The ghost of Dr. Greerson changes to Joe DiMaggio. "You'll never know how much I love you," he says, "and you can't hear any of this because it's too ghostly, too strange for you to grasp. You can't know any of this. So much won't be figured out until long after you die. But you always want to be public, wanting to show yourself off all the time, your incessant need for attention—if anybody had a pillow jammed over their face when they were one year of age, how would that play out through life?"

Marilyn continues as a statue, to look off into the distance. Joe sighs. "I know you're looking through me. I am a mist, a vapor and what I say has no connection with you because you can't connect with how your past plays out in the present. Oh, my beloved Marilyn, my Marilyn, no love from anyone can give the love we must give ourselves when we choose that dark journey to the midnight of our souls."

The ghost of Joe fades away and is replaced by Henry Miller. He, too, drifts about her. "Incessant," he says, "never ending starving for attention. Never enough. Never enough. Whatever attention, you had, never enough. Never enough. Never *ever* enough." And Arthur Miller fades away.

Marilyn stands there, tired-looking, weary, at thirty-one. She suddenly comes back to life, looks startled at the darkness around her, steps back from the railing, unaware that little Norma Jean Baker is still crying, crying inside.

Chapter 12

... and The Truth Shall Set Ye Free (?)

Marilyn stumbles inside, pours herself some gin and takes a white pill and then pauses. *What was it I took?* she wonders. In a daze, she finishes her drink, and wanders back onto the balcony. She shakes her head; her vision blurs and she hears a ringing in her ears. She leans on the balcony, her eyes closed. Her head spins and in her mind, she sees an apparition approach. He's a tall man, thin, dark hair, and he has a pillow.

"Stay away from my brother," he whispers.

"Who — what — "

"Stay away from him. I don't care how you do it or what you do — stay away from Jack."

"I don't know who you are — "

The man takes the pillow and bringing it up over his head, brings it down full force on the railing; the pillow case bursts open; the feathers fly out, over Marilyn and for a minute she can't breathe — — a memory from the past vomits up from the depths of her mind, her grandmother trying to suffocate her with a pillow —

" — what — ?" Marilyn says, " — what — "

She is able to open her eyes, but sees no one there. She stumbles back, back against the sliding glass door and she closes her eyes again.

When she tries to open them, everything is a blur, but she thinks she sees someone else standing there.

"Hello, Marilyn — "

" — what — "

"For I am the Ghost of Future Literature. Much will be written about you. You will indeed be famous — for many reasons — "

" — maybe I took a chloral hydrate by mistake — " she says to herself.

"You will be remembered for your great beauty, but also your vulnerability and your search for your father. All the men, never satisfied, constant attention — that tells you nothing — ?"

" — uh — " whispers Marilyn.

"But no one can replace the father you never knew. Not even the President — "

Marilyn leans forward, she wants to vomit but cannot for what she *needs* to *desperately* vomit — she cannot.

The Ghost of Future Literature hovers near. "If you could only know what drives you. If you could only hear what the future says about you. You are, as everyone, a child of Oedipus. It cannot be helped. It cannot be helped for no one is a God and no one has perfect knowledge. That is the lesson of Oedipus. Be it killing your father and marrying your mother, or searching for your father in every man you have sex with — ultimately, we pay and we pay *dearly* for knowing the truth to which our quest has led us. And that is the price of knowledge: to have the courage to face where our quest has led. For this, we die in pain, but we die courageous and noble."

Marilyn starts slipping down the sliding glass door, but with effort, remains standing.

"And what," whispers the Ghost of Future Literature, "and what the Greater Pain? In the end, what the Greater Pain? Where the greater sorrow, the greater courage? To go forward in life and not be aware of why we do what we do? Or to go forward, knowing what drives us, but unable to stop it and we still end in the same place? What the greater pain? What the greater courage?"

Marilyn struggles to open her eyes; when she finally can, she thinks she sees an apparition, a ghost, fading, fading, fading away.

Chapter 13

"In Dreams Begin Responsibilities" —Delmore Shwartz

Marilyn leans against the sliding door of the balcony. *Shit,* she thinks, *I thought I took an upper*— Abruptly, she slides down the glass door to end up sitting on the floor of the balcony. She clasps her arms around her knees, lowers her head until her face rests against her knees. *Shit*— she thinks, *I*—

Bogie flutters down from above, even more feathers have appeared to replace the burned ones. Gently, he sits on the balcony railing, pulls out a bottle and a glass and quietly fills the glass. He looks to Marilyn.

Abruptly, a flying saucer appears, cruises up to the balcony and hovers there. The opaque dome slides back and three little blue aliens look at Bogie.

One, with very large pointed ears which are dark blue on the inner surface, looks to Bogie. He points to the sky. "We from Mars. We come to take Marilyn Monroe to Mars to show her the deserts and Syrtis Major. We told she be here."

Bogie takes a drink. "She is." He points to her.

"Where?" the Martians ask. "We don't see her. We want to take her away to some place wonderful. Where she is?"

Again, Bogie points down.

The Martians tilt the ship and lean so they can look at her.

"Oh, so sad," says a small one. "We too late."

Bogie shakes his head. "No, no, she's not dead. But I don't think she can go anywhere."

The one with the pointed ears with the deep blue inner surfaces shakes his head. "When she be okay?"

"When will she be awake?"

"Does that mean she'll be okay?" another one asks; he has not spoken before but looks genuinely distressed. His eyes are large and turquoise.

Bogie takes a drink. "No. Just means she'll be awake. Will she be okay? Probably."

The three Martians look relieved. "That good," says the one with the big ears. "We can't come back for long time. But we be back in five years. How you say it?"

"Don't tell me," says Bogie, "it comes out to August 4, 1962."

The Martians produce a little flat handheld device that they tap on repeatedly and babble among themselves. Finally, the small one says, "That right. That right. That right date. We be back then. She be okay to go to Mars then?"

Bogie smiles. "Probably."

The Martians clap their hands. The small one speaks. "Marilyn like Mars. We know she want to visit and we come to take her away. Her father also there and he want to be with her and be the father he never was. He say he make it all up to her."

"He a neat man," says the tall one, "when he first meet us, he give us all Mars Bars."

With that, they wave to Bogie, the translucent dome slides forward to close and their little silver ship shoots straight up—then horizontally scoots across the sky.

Bogie looks to Marilyn, slumped against the sliding glass door.

"'She be okay to go to Mars then?'" he laughs. "Probably not. But we're all rootin' for ya anyway, kiddo. And I lied 'cause I *do* know how you die. And I *hate* how you die. But I can't tell you because you wouldn't believe it because this is all a dream, an alcohol-upper-downer-Nembutal-Barbiturate dream, honey, and because it makes no sense, you won't and can't see any of it as a warning." He sips his drink. "Old Descartes might as well be right—but somehow when you slipped Out Of Time—we thought, I thought—" But he shakes his head. "Nope, can't change nothin' after all. The world loves ya, honey—" He picks up the cigarette lighter off the balcony railing. He looks at it. "R.F.K." he sniffs. "When the world loves you, why did you pick guys who couldn't? Wouldn't? So wanting to be smothered with love but you end up getting smothered by something else." Bogie takes the lighter and flings it toward the skyline. "Son of a bitch." He notices movement on the railing.

"Oy," says a cockroach, "Oy, oy, oy. I knew it was to come to this, I just knew it was to come to this, my mother, God rest her soul, oh, she could be nasty, you know, with all us little ones to take care of, but you know—"

"What?" says Bogie, "What?"

"Life," she said, "life, it takes courage, oh, much courage and Marilyn, she had courage, she had more guts and man, how many cockroaches do I know that go to bed with the prez—I mean, knowingly, you know? I mean, sure, we could be in the mattress or maybe crawling in his dirty socks or underwear you know, but oy, oh, she had the guts—she wanted to know how she dies—guts to want to know that—"

"Indeed," comes another voice; Bogie turns and it is the Ghost of Past Literature. "It is the question forever asked, for we are mortal and afraid, for we know life must end." And the ghost changes to become Oedipus, "And the question becomes the Quest, to know the truth at any price—"

"No matter what the outcome," says Bogie. He finishes his glass, pours another. "How'd I know I'd end up with throat cancer?"

"Oy," says Kafka, the cockroach, "I could be squished tomorrow; oy, what a miserable fate, to be crunched under a shoe. Oy, or to choke on Raid. What miserable fates await."

"Yet, you live," says Bogie.

"Oy, yes, I live. I live."

"In spite of it all," says Bogie.

"In spite of it all," says Kafka.

"One can do no less," says Oedipus. "And therein lies the courage."

Bogie lifts his glass to Oedipus, then to the cockroach and finally to Marilyn, still sitting, stuporous, on the balcony floor. "Lookin' at 'cha."

For a long moment it is quiet. Then Kafka, the cockroach, says, "Oy, is there something—"

Overhead, the sound of bells. They look up to see a sleigh. "Oh, ho, ho," comes a distant voice, *"No problema* as they say in the nineties. The Doll's okay. She had one. She'll just think—"

Bogie nods.

Marilyn stirs.

Kafka scuttles away. Oedipus vanishes.

Marilyn wakes up then starts, thinking that she hears the flutter of wings; woozy, she stands, but looking out, sees nothing. Looking down near her feet, she sees a doll and picking it up, she shakes her head. *I thought I—* but she stops, then gently cradles it—beneath a dark and haunting sky.

End

...and Other Strange Tales

All The Stars In The Sky

Now William, at age eight, had a very favorite saying. He liked to sit out in his backyard, look to the sky whenever it was clear and say to himself, as every child usually does in some form or other:

"Twinkle, twinkle little star,
How I wonder what you are.
Wish I may and wish I might,
Grant the wish I wish tonight."

And he would wish. And the wish was pretty much the same wish as everyone wishes: Oh, how I would like a good, close friend. And at age eight, that's what everyone wants—someone to climb trees with. Or, if a girl, someone to help serve breakfast to dolls of blue eyes and happy, but fixed expressions that, with the help of a little imagination, have a way of changing. Someone to help look for salamanders under logs, someone to do something with. That's what friends are for—someone to tell your troubles to, someone to tell about what a nasty person your older sister is—or your brother. And William was no exception. He wanted a close friend to play with and also to share his interest in astronomy. Astronomy! His father had given him a picture book about planets and stars and galaxies and William didn't read too much of the text—it was the pictures that were wonderful. William tried to pronounce the artist's name "-Bons-Bonstell-Bo-nstell-Bonstell-" and he stared for hours at those pictures; but oh, to have a good friend to share that fascination. Someone who was as interested in astronomy as he was.

Now it has to be said that William was very likable. He was as energetic as any eight year old: he had lots of freckles, brown hair, brown eyes—and wore glasses. He hated the glasses. So, even though he actually looked fine, he thought he looked horrible with the glasses and he had worn them ever since he could remember. It was the glasses... that was why he didn't have any close friends. It was the glasses. He was ugly and people thought he was ugly even though he wasn't but he thought he was and that's what matters here.

So, even in his classes at school, Sammy Jackson, who always smiled and said "Hi," well, since William wore glasses, Sammy was just being nice.

And there was Deborah, but she was a girl, and even though she smiled at him a lot—that didn't count.

And there was Edward who was shy and who cried a lot and who always seemed happy when William talked to him—but he knew that Edward, deep down inside, probably didn't like the fact that he, William, wore glasses. Even when they got into a discussion about astronomy—and Edward was obviously enthusiastic about the subject—well, you know, William just knew—just *knew*—and was utterly convinced that because he wore glasses, the friendship would probably not go very far and wouldn't last long.

So, there you go. William was without a friend in the world. Except for his parents and his older brother, Robert, and his sister, Kathy, but they're your family and they don't count and besides, his brother and sister teased him about the glasses and if your very own family teases you, then everyone else in the world will also. Just stands to reason. To get close to people is to get teased. That hurts.

So. What was William to do? When school ended for the year in June, well, for an eight year old without any friends, it sure looked like a long summer.

But William was resourceful. He had a library card. And the library wasn't very far away. And it had a big section on astronomy and also had a big section for science fiction. And going to the library turned into almost an every day venture. Every day that William went, he became more and more fascinated by what he found—that somehow the stars in the sky weren't only just little suns—but every one was different—red dwarfs, novas, neutron stars and the list almost seems endless—almost as endless as the night sky.

And William began to see the world a bit differently—the cocoa in his cup, when stirred and milk added—well, what do you know! A spiral galaxy whirls about. And the next time he went hiking with his father and brother, the trail led to a lookout point and thousands of feet below, a valley, green with trees, stretched out below and before them and William asked his father, "How many trees are in that valley?"

And his father, a little perplexed at the question, said, "Well, that is a good question—I'd say there are as many trees in that valley—" and he thought for a minute, "No, I bet there are as many trees all over the earth as there are stars in the sky."

"That's a lot of trees," said William, nodding.

"And you know," said his father, "I've heard that there are as many sand grains on all the ocean beaches as there are stars in the sky."

William, looking out over that valley, to the mountains beyond and knowing of all the beaches in the world beyond the mountains certainly meant for a lot of sand, realized something else. "In one of my books," he said, "it says that the universe never ends —"

Then it was time for his father to look a bit startled, "Oh," he said, "that's right. So in spite of all the trees and sand grains — and insects, and animals and blades of grass — in spite of all that — it is still far, far fewer — than —" and he paused " — all the stars in the sky —"

William sat on a rock and looked out over the world — all that he was seeing — still less — infinitely less, because the world is finite — less, much, much less than all the stars.

Right then, he wished he had a close friend that he could tell that to. Not that his father wasn't his friend — he was — but that was different.

And when he went home that night after a long day of hiking and thinking about infinity, he was indeed exhausted. Physically, that is. Emotionally, there were a lot of issues going on and of course, that often leads to dreaming. Ah, such dreams! Such imagination! He dreamed he was in the library and he had opened a book to a two-page, full color painting by his favorite artist, Bonstell. It was a picture of the moon of Saturn, Titan, with a snowy foreground, deep blue sky and Saturn hanging in the sky — an incredible silver crescent with the rings seen edgewise, slicing across the planet, out into space and curving like a sickle back around the planet. And as he stared at the picture, the picture got larger and larger and — just like that — he was there, standing in the snow, looking up at the exquisite ringed planet. And then he looked straight up — my, how the stars were sharp and clear and so many of them — more than all the glittering snowflakes around him? More than that. He looked back to Saturn. And are there other Saturns in the universe? Other Titans? William sighed. There must be. And in the dream, William experienced two feelings: one of utter astonishment and wonderment at the idea of that which is utterly incomprehensible: infinity. And he also felt very, very small, very insignificant, utterly tiny and right then, he wished he had a friend.

"I'll be your friend," came a voice.

William turned. It was Edward. Edward. The shy kid who cried a lot in school yet who loved astronomy. But William turned away. Edward looked hurt and William noticed that and said, "What's wrong?"

Edward said, "What'd I do? Don't you like me?"

William felt puzzled. "Yeah — but —" he stammered.

"Then why can't I be your friend?"

"Because—" began William, "because—"

Edward looked even more hurt. "Because I'm a crybaby?" William stood there, stood there on Titan, with Saturn huge and white overhead, just as Bonstell painted it in the fifties, and something began to dawn on William. He shook his head and looked down. "No," he whispered with mighty shame, "I wear glasses."

Edward ceased to look hurt and instead looked puzzled. "Huh?"

William could barely look up. "I wear glasses," he said, louder.

Edward shook his head—then smiled. "I still want to be your friend," he said. And then it was his turn to look shameful and uncomfortable. "I guess I understand if you don't want to be my friend. Nobody wants to hang around with a crybaby." He looked down. And William saw tears roll down his cheek and freeze there. Edward turned to leave.

William, without understanding quite why, or what changed, said something he never thought he'd say. "Don't go! Wait! I want to be friends with you—I thought no one wanted to be friends with me because I wore—" he gulped, "glasses."

Edward shook his head. "Uh-uh. I don't mind your glasses. I always thought you didn't want to be friends with me because I was—" and Edward sighed, "a crybaby."

"Nope," said William, "I like you fine." And he smiled. Then grinned. As did Edward. Of course both of them realized that something very strange and wonderful had just happened and they shook hands and then clapped each other around the shoulders and William said, "Hey, you like astronomy, right?"

"Yeah," said Edward.

"Did you know that space went on forever and ever?"

Edward nodded.

"So," said William, "are there as many sand grains and snowflakes as there are stars in the sky—or less?"

"Gee," said Edward, looking at the sparkling snow around them, then looking up to the sky. "Gee," he said again, "that's an awful lot of snowflakes and sand grains—there would have to be as many—" and he thought and then he looked surprised, dazed and then dumbfounded. "Space goes on forever—" he said, "but the earth is a ball—there would have to be more stars than all the sand on all the beaches in the world—" And he looked at William for a long, long time. "Wow," he finally said, "Wow. That's really—" and he stopped and looked to the sky, to Saturn, the snow, and simply said, "Wow."

"Feel real small, doncha?" said William.

Edward nodded. "Feel like nothing," said Edward.

"Yeah."

And they looked up and Saturn became a mirror in which William and Edward saw themselves and there was a voice: "Twinkle, twinkle little stars; small but special stars you are." And the image on Saturn changed and they were looking at Earth, the oceans, the clouds, the land and then that changed into a mirror on which they saw little red starfish, a rose, birds, a weeping willow, an octopus. And the voice again, "Twinkle, twinkle all that lives," and the image then changed to an immense spiral galaxy, "Twinkle, twinkle all that is."

And sometime later, William woke up, feeling rather different. He remembered bits of the dream—enough—so that when he got up and went to the bathroom, he looked in the mirror—and for the first time in a long time—he smiled. Maybe the glasses weren't so bad after all. Maybe he'd better use his glasses to see that the person behind the glasses was his best friend first. He smiled again. Then: a breakfast of Cheerios, a poached egg on toast (he ate with energy and his mother said, "Well, looks like you're ready to conquer the world today. Maybe later, with all that energy, you can conquer the lawn." To which William replied, "Aw, gee," then shrugging, "Okay," to which his mother said, "My, you not only have energy but a different attitude. My. What a nice change. More toast?")

And after breakfast, William went to the library to take back some books and who do you think he should meet there? Sitting at a table, with a big astronomy book opened to the scene of snowy Titan with the huge crescent of Saturn in the sky—was Edward. And Edward was absorbed in the picture of Bonstell. William took a deep breath, went up to Edward and said, "I dreamed about that last night."

Edward, very startled, startled enough to forget his shyness, looked up. "Yeah?"

William grinned. "Yeah. And you wanna hear something neat?"

Enthusiastically, Edward nodded.

"Are there more stars in the sky than sand grains on all the beaches in the world—or less—?"

And while Edward pondered, William smiled and thought to himself, Twinkle, twinkle little star, yes indeed, how right you are. Wished I did, wished with might, I granted me my wish last night.

Nightscape II

Numbly-bumbly Frogged Man
Wanders heartland of the night;
See his eyes shining bright
Like that of wild cat,

Wild dog, hungry bear
And this and so much strangeness
More—the Frogged man with moist skin
And memory like stretched membrane,

Frogged Man is of the night, of the
Stuff of rotting logs and leaf-mold blight
Of some wicked forest floor
That you see in nightmare scene,

Sharp and clear as if honed and cut
By saber bright and tempered by
Blood of creatures of the Other Realm;
Such the nature of this Frogged Man

Scuttling though the earthen night,
Slopping though the slime of fear,
Waking you from deepest sleep,
Making you not want to hear

The Sounds Out There;
Frogged Man carries a dark sack
And in it all the broken sighs
And shattered screams

Of things you'd like to forget,

Of the darkside of the soul
Of the dread of haunting past—
Like beast slobbering 'neath your bed.

And Frogged Man chitters past your window,
Makes you grab the covers tight,
Makes you fear and wonder at just how
Long is this horror of a night.

The Eyes of Little Juan

In the village of M there was a boy, age six. His name was Little Juan, but sometimes he went by the nickname of Big Eyes. Large and brown were his eyes. Oh, so very large and brown. It seemed his brown eyes could never see enough of the world. That was what people noticed about Little Juan. And Little Juan had an eager smile. When he smiled, his face looked like sunshine. People liked to look at Little Juan's face when he smiled. It made them happy.

Little Juan's father was a teacher, and he never smiled. He was a good teacher, but he had never learned to smile. He walked slowly and carried a brown briefcase that was filled with lots of papers from his students. And when he walked, he always looked down at the ground. So where did Little Juan get his smile from?

That is hard to say.

Did he get his smile from his mother?

Little Juan's mother was a large woman and had many things to say about many things. Her hair was dark and so were her eyes. They were the same color as Little Juan's eyes. And she huffed and panted as she did her chores each day.

She didn't smile much, but she was kind and always had a cookie and a glass of milk or juice for Little Juan. Perhaps her face didn't smile, but her heart did. And oh, she worked so hard.

So where on earth did Little Juan get so much energy to always be just beyond his parents' tired reach?

It is hard to say.

As little Juan grew up, he was all over the neighborhood and would come home to tell his mother what discoveries he had made.

"Oh, down the street," he'd say with his eyes so w-i-d-e.

"Oh, there are lovely roses, Mama. Oh, you must see how big the petals, how red the color. And the smell... oh, Mama, it smells like the most wonderful smell there is and..."

To which his mother might interrupt and say, "Well, my little one, I'm glad you have the energy to smell the roses. Now wash your hands and get ready for supper. Hurry... hurry!"

Sometimes, Little Juan would wait for his father to come home after school. His father bending and walking slowly, carrying his briefcase stuffed with papers and books and the remains of lunch in a piece of bright foil.

And Little Juan would say, "Oh Papa, Papa, did you see the sunset last night? What a sight. It was grand, the gold color over the mountains became light yellow-green and then it faded to deep red and blue and oh, Papa, such colors...."

And Little Juan would wash his hands and eat his dinner and then, he'd be off again. And in half an hour or so, he'd return with yet another tale.

"Oh Mama. Oh Papa. In the vacant lot I saw a salamander scamper. It was dark on top and its belly was burnt yellow. In the bushes I saw spiders spinning webs and a huge, blue dragonfly circled around my head."

His father wouldn't answer, because he was always busy reading or grading school papers.

"Oh dear," Juan's mother would sigh. "What you see and the places you go. Oh dear, oh dear." And she would sigh again and say, "Did you say your prayers today, Little Juan? Did you thank Aunt Lila for the new sweater she sent you for your birthday?"

And his father might find a little extra energy to ruffle Little Juan's hair. "Ah, what pleasure that you use your eyes so well and see so much. Good for you. The only glory I see is an occasional long word a student has spelled correctly." And Little Juan's father would return to his book.

Now, no one knows why, but not too long after Little Juan turned seven, he seemed to disappear more often. He would always return with reports about someplace new that he had been. And oh, the sights that he had seen. And his mother and father would sometimes pay attention to him but most of the time they didn't.

One evening in December, when the air was crisp and cold as ice, Little Juan asked his mother, "Where does Santa Claus live?"

His mother, baking little muffins covered with poppy seeds, opened the oven door. She pulled out the pan and gave Juan a muffin and said, "Well, I'm too busy to think about THAT right now, but your father might know. So run along."

And she put another tray of muffins in the oven and *chump* went the door as it closed.

Little Juan, munching on the muffin, went into the living room and looked out the window and smiled because there was snow everyplace.

After dinner, he put his heavy red jacket, the one with the hood, and he wore his thick blue gloves that he got from his Aunt Lila and his good, warm shoes and said to his parents, "I'm going out for a little while."

And he didn't return.

Some hours later, his mother sat on the sofa and wringing her hands, and said, "Oh where can he be? I hope nothing bad has happened to him."

Little Juan's father, pacing, pacing and pacing about, said, "We must call the police, tell the neighbors, Little Juan has never been gone this long before."

A policeman came and asked so many questions... "What color is his coat?"

"Red," said Little Juan's mother, dabbing her eyes with a handkerchief. "Red, and he wore blue gloves and jeans and brown shoes."

"Well," said the policeman, a very tall fellow with a helpful smile, "this is a little unusual since nothing bad ever happens in this small town. I'm sure your boy is all right. Perhaps, he got lost for a while. But we'll do everything we can to find Little Juan, I do promise you that."

But three more days went by and NO Little Juan. Oh, that such a thing could happen. Particularly at this time of the year. Right at Christmas time, the loveliest season of the year. Where oh where was Little Juan. What had happened to him?

"Oh, oh," said Little Juan's mother. By now, she was either sitting or suddenly standing and walking about and then sitting again. "I cannot stand this."

And Little Juan's father sighed frequently and sipped coffee out of a bright, yellow mug all day. "I know he must be all right," he said.

"I know he must be fine..."

The phone rang, and it was the policeman. Juan's father spoke to him and said, "Yes, yes, I know, well, yes, yes, no, no, and thank you very much." And he sighed. "No word yet. Oh, what could have happened to Little Juan?"

Clump, clump, clump.

The sound of heavy boots outside the front door and a, "Oh, ho, ho, ho, now here you go, little one."

Little Juan's parents hurried into the living room and there... coming in through the front door, was Little Juan with a smile so wide and eyes so bright and large.

"Juan," cried his mother. She dropped to her knees and hugged Little Juan.

"Where have you been? Why didn't you let us know where you were?"

"I'm sorry," answered Little Juan, hugging his mother and then his father.

"I saw the snow and took my sled and went for a walk. But I didn't mean to scare you. I walked and walked and finally I came to a hill. And I climbed to the top and sledded down. There was a little house at the bottom. And I knocked on the door. Oh, Mama, oh Papa, you should have seen what I've seen... and been where I've been...."

"We're glad you're back," said his father. "That's all that matters."

"But I saw..." said Little Juan. "Such wonderful things..."

And finally, his parents looked into his eyes, because they thought he might be sick from being gone so long in the snow and the cold and might need some medicine.

Inside Little Juan's large brown eyes, they saw everything he had seen, the aurora borealis all blue and white against the northern skies, and the moon and the stars and a figure dressed in red, waving and laughing. And they heard a voice, as though from a great distance, call, "Merry Christmas, Merry Christmas, Merry Christmas to all!"

In Thy Name, Revenge

"T'was brillig—" Lewis Carroll

The princess wakens and lovelooks to her prince, sleeping stilly near. "Sha-ta, sha-ta," chimes the princess to her prince. "Sha-ta, sha-ta," and toyily she dances fingers across his dawn smooth brow, her fingers foresting through his hair, the curls licking around about like a bamblecat's, curly as the hair in a hooloboot's ear.

But the prince wakens not and trambles on within his dream—oh, the paindream once again—the explosion, then a long and dumbfoondious darkness. A vision: the princess looking tendcarely upon him; and all before that vision? Obliterased. And try as he will, he cannot rememcall past the intensearing heat and light.

And in his dream, he feels frusasperated as he again seeks yet cannot find the answers of what was before.

Then quite sudbruptly, a vision new. He sees himself riding a vast and heat-eyed Sayerbeast. They drakraggle over the mummel of the marthdale, through the forest dark and dwill. "Ah, sweet and nasty beast," says the prince with grin darsk and feverbright, "how you carry your meanhead high, high as lifepride gathering form before the sun!"

"Ska-toe! Ska-toe!" yabbles Sayerbeast, yaddling heaftily to and fro, the marthdale passing drakly-swort beneath paggling, haggled hoof.

"As sure as the invaders swet their breath on damsy-erbs, as sure as the moons banter yes and banter no in their wamsy-wurvy light, we shall quassle, we shall work for the death of the invaders!"

"Ska-toe!" says the Sayerbeast; oh, the nostrils yorst and beige in Sayerbeasts's clawhate of the evil from the sky. "Ska-toe! Ska-toe!"

The prince hangs on, tight as malintent, clinging like hurt to a heart, clinging like madness; riding, riding the huge and mulky Sayerbeast, it with head so borst and bost, it with body lodoriously vord and vast and vill!

"These invaders, whoever they might be," says the prince, "I shall destroy them—for my pride, for my princess and the kingdom! Revenge-god Gal-Trosto! I come to you as strong as pulse-burst of blood, bulding, durking in my veins! Yes and yes; the ancient wrongs to be revengectified!"

And the prince whispfervents in fierce sleep, "Gal-Trosto!" and his hands are claws as though grabbing truth.

The princess is swuptly startled; her eyes go ohsoround. "My prince," she whispers, "what searthought burns in your mind?"

She sits, her head alert, the sweetlight of rising double sun whimms doftly, doftly, through the glass, illuminating her hair browndly-long and curling like shyness transtendled with openness and therefore strong.

But the prince wakens not and in the dream hears mindvoice swive and strong: "I am Shastau, humilumble creature-servant of this revenge-god Gal-Trosto! Gal-Trosto wakens, wakens. It is time. Long enough has he slept in his kravven anger. I, Shastau, mindgive his message to sons, to daughters of the ancient blaspucklid horror of the invasion which drove our spirit down until the hurt-anger of the race fused, melted with the rock itself and gave Gal-Trosto birth. And he who responds first shall carry us again to the magnigrand peak of the greatness we once knew. Now I mindgive to you the ancient horror that is Gal-Trosto."

And in the dream, Shastau's voice fadims, and the Prince sees that across the yroopitous ghast of space came the hot-stone minds, all hwuff and basst, to scrash and kwham the surface of calm star-system; oh, the ret and holrooing of mindmouths not knowing of what to do as when the sky is enemied with creatures pok, with skaggling weapons wheeling, whissing, white and burndeath blasglaring forth.

In a second divided half, it is done. Oh, oh, it is done! The kingdoms, like gentlefaces knowing the slice of sudden pain, crumble, crumble. The once highpride needletowers sapsur into sucking earth; high heart, eyesbright traditions fall under muggling truff and trump of greedlust strangeness from some ballfalden damn drearworld too damncradden to be concerned with anything but their own ezorforous glut.

Oh, the will! Oh, the rak, prestosnian will: we the shattered, we the mulplorsted, we who sadly yet pridely recall our gretan cities, we who lived with no malcauseness toward summel sky nor double sun, nor swuff of dawn nor ploss of dusk: we remember, we remember, and by the arced claws of time, even if done bisk by bisk, oh, listen invaders, so trulled and bluck, this wasped anger high, oh, yes, we give it to our children and our children's children, by vorkid sperm, by voslid mouth speaking of your orsal, issil, vipid deeds until they feel the rage we know. Oh, no. Oh, no. We may be trumsudden now, but beware, beware; our prosclid rage is hiding

now, within us, and deep, deep within our world, the rage melds with oozing white of liquid stone, and so thus in form, the god Gal-Trosto, he is born.

And the prince again whispfervents, "Gal-Trosto! I serve!" And he awakens, kashakes his head and sits with backled look; his breath is stot and quick
and klee. "It is time," he shuspers, "Gal-Trosto calls me. I hear him calling in
my mind. Over and over; from swarth sleep does he waken, vurklid anger
glowing in his gortonlian eyes."

The princess looks a little waggle. A fidge of smile upon her oh, solocious
lips. Running shoot soft fingers through the prince's bamblecat-like hair, she
says, "I think the depth of dream has you a bit askag."

But the prince foresqorly shakes his head. "No. Something wakens, wakens. I know it like I know the moon, Askoro, that wings and wambles overhead. The intricible god Gal-Trosto wakens and seeks revenge. He with
claws a planet wide, with voice that silences a star's heart, he with mouth
that swallows light of a galaxy in just a gulp."

Intivitibly, the princess knows that the prince speaks of something
chaturse and klee. She knows that something must slurk about because the
prince is so noyield.

Astrutely, the prince does stand; his dlusk eyes so sharp and brilst. He
looks strong and bandytrust, his mission clear as the light of Kwissul's sun
burning noonhigh at dawn with light oh, so unshamenaked bright.

The princess' eyes are mellycholliedloss; she knows, she knows as sure as
stars keekle in the dawn that her prince, her strong and wufflepostern prince,
oh, so soon shall he be gone. Oh, dooloors, dooloors, her heart does famble in
her breast, for in the going, in this ulfrut decision is the possibility that he
may come not again. Oh, fidious finality! Realization so sad and drurk. She
wants him to stay; her mouth forms a tolouruous line; her eyes wide and
drask and dark; their message is that of implortaking, and he knows, oh, he
knows and withstands the heartslaught of the moment for he too knows the
possibility — oh, betratsorous fate — that he may die in this doing. And yet, to
not golstanter forth, is that too, not a death? Is that not diaboldidnious cow-
ardice to not go forth and release the good from the uldurterous fangs of
bad?

The prince knows. Oh, the deethle dream so real! Gal-Trosto calls. The
balskordian god who slept a sleep somotovious, he awakens with revenge so
slaring in his eyes. Revenge! Revenge! Revenge so long overdue that even
stones skree and cry in plathnos rage. The plockrod enemy must be destroyed. They who came from sky far from here, whose only sklur to righteousness is the viciousness of the trulplid attack and therefore their implum-
dium might makes them right.

He goes to the princess and arms go 'round each other.

"You must go," the princess whispers, "Oh, I know that you must go — but why? But why?"

The prince implorsadly shakes his head. "I am called. Why or how this is, I do not know. But what I do is for me, for us, for the empire. A vuskid invasion has occurred and must be fought and I am called."

The princess shakes her head. "But I've heard of nothing; there is no invasion! Surely your dream must be errbased."

The prince sighs. "Then of this I shall soon learn." He kisses her, oh, so long, and then, "I go." He strides away with a senseaura of action that is as definite as a planet swinging about its sun.

The prince brists along his way, mindpurpose clear. He finds the feped stables; the Sayerbeast sits dultly dozing yet awake; hearing the quick and steply footfall of the prince, it opens vum and oply eyes to regard the prince with credulosity; it rimbles slowly to its feet. "Ska-toe?" it orkly asks.

The prince tosses on beast's back the saddlehome for days to come and he says to beast, "Do not question this now, oh, rambitious beast who, with me, shall ride to fame or despair. Our journey will take us over marthdale, through hill-mountaneous landfall and rise, through the forests icklydwill."

"Ska-toe. Ska-toe," and lightly, the beast yaddles, yaddles to and fro. It's morovorious hooves pawpit the ground; its breathing comes labbed and fast in anticipation. Ortoomly it backs out of the stall and waits impatermanbly while the prince loads oslovorious fruit and dense crumbcake into the saddlepouches deep that attach to the saddlehome like afterthoughts.

"Ska-toe?" the voice of beast bomble-bambles in its throat.

The prince hops and lands squardroitly on beast's back. "The time is here," says the prince. "Oh, the long foresought time is here. Gal-Trosto calls me in my dream. Gal-Trosto calls in voice long and implormanding and it is the call to revenge."

Sayerbeast's eyes grow wide in wonderstun. The beast comprestands all too well. It is an opaque moment that translutely clears into a sharpness vorklud, stark. Oh, the moment of the nova truth when all you see is water-clear: the double sun shining brilradiantly in the calm and remandren sky, the bright, sweet yellow crescent of the planet Orclas dipping down to horizon line, the green and rumply grass, still and quilst in morning light. Just a mimsly step beyond, the isolated clumps of throket trees grow with withered and trorsted arms reached up-sky and beyond, still further, the hills arch and humple into mountains granite and so sharp.

"Hee-hi!" The prince thumps knees into beast's scale-thick sides. The muscles of Sayerbeast abstutely tense and then as suddenly as light breaks forth from just born sun, they move, oh, like the dream: the marthdale passing drakly-swort beneath the paggling haggled hooves.

And as the prince rides in silence dolst and deep, he thinks thoughts ran-
dombout: *Is it wise or ordolforous pride that we follow our sometimes jamble
dreams, even though the dreams seem so right, so clear? Or do they intoolimately
lead us to despair? Do I follow indeed my mind? Such volsorvorous fortune I leave
behind – for a dream, a dream, a phligment of mind and heart that leuds me to slart
upon this voyage – is not a dream but a mauvely thing? Sometimes as mythly as
bistbeast's love or about as sweet as fart from bamblecat. I leave behind so much, so
much – and who am I to take upon myself this responsibility of revenge? And yet the
dream, the dream, this thing I condamn, yet such urgency, such urgency.* A long
and heartsolorious sigh. *I go. I go. On the morthly basis of a dream I go.*

In the marmmist of the dream, prince imagines Gal-Trosto, vagueform
shining in the fog; he feels Gal-Trosto; how simmel, kind, angerproud and
strong. The god's sense is righteousness, vindicaring, patience sworf and
long, purposenoble clear, clear like the Swibird's song.

The dreamind slips, dissolves into sudden mist and the prince gently (but
oh, so dwortly) opens his right eye. The Sayerbeast has stopped. The prince
makes not a fingertwitch.

The prince looks down into the eyes, dorst, sharp and green of Shastau
who mumblefubs away, "Ickle, ickle, eekle, rort!" In grobotuous hand,
Shastau holds the Sayerbeast's mouthreins tight.

Confissuredly, the prince leans and looks down. "Shastau," he whispers,
"keeper of the furvile forests, spirit of the darkwell lands, unchant your
chant, unchant your spell. We mean no harm; we are but passing through the
greatorious land in which you dwell."

Shastau holds the mouthreins tight; the prince sees his dark and ookle
eyes stedroitly examining him so well. The prince glastares at Shastau, at his
gloss and pinrickled body, dressed in rags so drab and gree. The creature's
back is humbuckled and Shastau looks up with effort forced and dreed. The
thin and minkle lips pull back. A grin? A sneer? "Oh, prince," it finally utters
ootly, "go back, go back."

"Gal-Trosto calls me," the prince issolutely asserts.

"Let him haunt you with his call. Better that than with the truth."

The Sayerbeast was quiet, still, bound by magic, round and round. "You
cannot stop me," says the prince, "I must go on. This is the moment of revenge."

"Do not go!" Shastau says.

The prince is palled and gasps at Shastau's words; Shastau, servant and
will-fulfiller of Gal-Trosto! Shastau, dwuerk and dwelty valet of the god Gal-
Trosto! The prince lets his eyes surveymeasure all the scene; the nightness,
whitened by two folopolous moons; the hill on which they stand above the
forest and in the distance, the mumble of a mountain range, much nearer,

louder than in the morning and now bluewhite in moons' light. Nearby, the dark of forest, and then the dworty Shastau, his eyes shingleaming in the light and the Sayerbeast moving not a hoof; asleep, awake and utterly ens-woffed by the spell.

Finevitably, the prince looks back to Shastau and simply says, "I must go on."

Shastau shakes his monstororious head. "I urge you not to go. But I will stop you not. If some things are better left unsaid, then some truths are better left unknown."

"You marsky Shastau! Imturpurable messenger of Gal-Trost—why will not you tell me?"

"The only thing Gal-Trosto hears are his secrets and only he can say them. Were I to say the performious truth, I would die. But I can warn you and warn you I must and so do."

"Unspell my Sayerbeast, Shastau, I must go on. Gal-Trosto has called me."

" —as he has called *everyone!* Whoever arrives first shall ride with him—"

"And it shall be me!" The prince straightens. "If there has been an invasion of the empire, then I step forward, for myself, for the princess, for the empire! Wherever this invasion, whenever the invasion! I go! I serve!"

"Perfundering fool!" husses Shastau. "Impertenable arsk! Let someone else be a hero! If you go on, I must surlander forth tell him you are coming."

"Then surlander forth, oh, masky messenger! Tell him I come to help him bring anhilvestation upon the invaders!"

Shastau hoffs his head this way, that. "Your courage is both bold and sad. It is eloquent yet despair. Truth! Truth! At any price, as if it always makes one free! Ha! Oh, someone else! Someone else! Not you!"

"Enough of this, you labryntod! You banstankerous cutswill, you petty god! Gal-Trosto, he with name that of Revenge, he and I will avenge our ancestor's humiliation!"

"You do not have to go! You may refuse!"

"Damsky spirit! I choose yes!"

And Shastau screams, "Ah-yee!" and spreading wide his valpid hands, explodes to smoke and disperserpates into the night.

"Ska-toe?" The Sayerbeast shackles his head, as though confused. It looks about, garfumps a bit to itself, and then, "Onward!" shouts the prince; knee-jab in the osibrious flanks.

"Ska-toe!" Hooves up and out and down and through the darkness, bleached by moons, beast and prince scullunder forth to a most insiprious fate. What it is, the prince knows not; all he knows is the challenge, the challenge to resolve the ovoplundrium weight of two centuries of unwanted rule by the invaders. *Revenge! Revenge! Surely the skineverous beast, Shastau, must have a bemuckled head! Ungurply spirit!* And thinking such thoughts, along with the yaddling to and from of Sayerbeast, the prince dufts down to swunzy sleep.

Stillness. Stillness like the heart of a stone, as profound as the color jade. Stillness: a moment uninhindered by before, by after.

Eyes open! The prince looks warily about. The Sayerbeast, again with the stillness of a glacial sculpture. The prince finds himself unbenerved. He looks about, this way, that, the saddle squeereeking as he moves. Bedown from him, the ground is sand, the surface is ovomumulated in little ridges. On one side, a stretch of tumblehills, low and roundrock. The other side, the horizon rim, pale with birth of double sun but a breath away. The sky above is a tri-bold blue. It is the stillness of bewaiting, of a something about to be. The horizon becomes brightwhite, brightwhite; the double sun's light burstploding across the world; the loworn ridges in the sand cast wee shadows drot and dark.

What's this? The prince looks ahead. A line beforms in the sand, longer, longer, all without a mimsk of sound. Then the line widens. Smoke. Smoke denseavy, ablack, aboiling, churls and churns about and then two smolten, redorange clawhands grilps at, then clutches the edge of the rift. A redorange, volcoscus face, shwavering in bultroturous heat; the eyes, the mouth: it is as though the light of suns pourpulses forth.

The prince blinks, then shutters his eyes with tolomulous hand. He wants to scrampable away but is as fearfrozen to the saddle as the Sayerbeast is to the ground.

"And so," comes the protundious voice, "you are the first to have come to help."

"Yes," and the prince realizes how swiffle his voice sounds and says boldoudly, "Yes, Gal-Trosto, I safelt you call me in my dream."

"And many I called and you are the first. Why? Why have you answered my call for revenge?"

The light from the eyes is brilintense. Gal-Trosto stands, his smolten feet melting sand, burnfire fists on his lavian hips, clouds of dark and chokethick smoke upboil, upboil to the blue and serenquil sky.

The prince, remembering well the dreams, takes in a deep and shambering breath and speaks. "Gal-Trosto, oh, mighty god Gal-Trosto, whose name is Revenge, Gal-Trosto, oh, rage of our ancestors, damned and shattered and plutundered by invaders, ah, mighty vindustrious Gal-Trosto, whose time has arrived for avenging like a sun arrives for the day, I fight with you, I the flesh, I the blood of my ancestors, I their will that the insiferous invasion will be avenged. You, Gal-Trosto, the power of rage not resolved, I the power of this flesh now that the diebodinous deed *be* resolved."

Gal-Trosto kneels. "Little kunnel of blood and bone, your valrageous words give me lifeswelling pride. Your words will make our masters shuster, make them erggle in their sleep, make them falsestep when they walk, make them despair as they laugh, give them cause to stop and weep. For now their vuspid reign shall end!"

The prince spreads his hands. "Gal-Trosto, I stand with you."

"Know well your words! To not stand with me after I share that which I know —"

"I hear, Gal-Trosto! I hear! My will is starsong strong!"

Gal-Trosto stands and raises his burnglowing arms in prayersupplication to double-sun. "As your warm and osphosphorous light brings out this new day from night, so now our long and dursky darkness of our ancestral wrath shall be avenged so that, too, our new day may begin!"

Gal-Trosto glows, glows, glows with uncredievable brilliance bright. The prince shutters his eyes with hands against the whiteblast. Then he hears: "Hold out your hand."

Dutibediently, the prince does. Something drops into his hand; something small and ohsoround. Slowly and askancidly, the prince looks. In his mid-palm is a sphere, circumsmooth and creamyshine. It is warm. And in his mind, he hears a voice, "Close your hand about me. Hold me close, oh, hold me fast. For now we travel to avenge the past!"

"Where do we travel to, magnifonderous Gal-Trosto?"

"To the invaders' mark upon this planet; to their fortress that they think so strong and dweur."

The prince finds himself feeling capuzzleprecious. "I did not know they had an outpost here."

A long, forbohensive silence.

"You did not?" comes the voice.

"I did not."

Another long and glooding silence. Then, "You are unaware that this planet, Issedera, is the main defense—you did not know?"

"No, my most plondorious Gal-Trosto."

"Are you not of this homeworld?"

"I—forgive me, mighty Gal-Trosto—I am not sure. So long ago, I was in a blast—so much I do not recall—"

"It matters little," says Gal-Trosto. "If you have heard my call, you are indeed a victim of the ancient gissly attack. For the invaders cannot hear me. We are joined, then, in this holmoric journey. Let us go then to the post."

The Sayerbeast, suddenly released from yet another troublemsome trance, has time enough to say "Ska-toe?" and shakes its head in contusion and looks about somewhat betraxed and then, oh, suns! Light so intensearing! Slowly the light fades and fades to show a scene that the prince knows all too well: the fortress Moondeux. His breath catchalts in his throat; he screams, "No! No! This cannot be! This is an error! It cannot be what I see!"

And the mindvoice, stoot and clear, "It is indeed as it seems."

Sayerbeast fabbles and squnts about; wanting to leave but it cannot.

The prince's look is skag and blust; he shakes his head in disbelief. "Oh, sky! Oh, suns! Tell me that this cannot be! Shastau, Shastau, why did I not believe you? Your voice so hissle, which I hated, yet what you said was blut and true."

And Gal-Trosto's mindvoice: "You have little choice; if you had doubthoughts, you'd been better not to have come. What is it that hollanders you?"

"The fortress Moondeux! The princess—my lover—she is there."

Silence. Silence of the shock, the break, the presupposing sheared away until the snerile, blost truth remains. Wearincholia fills the prince's head, both from himself and Gal-Trosto. When Gal-Trosto speaks again, the voice is that of lead, heavy, dense. "You've been making love to the murderers of our ancestors!?"

"I did not know! I did not know! How could I know? They told me nothing! They saved my life! They found me naked, dazed and wandering—"

Silence again. Silence as the second before a star brilliant's to flashdeath in explosion and sends chaosclysmic lightvoice far and wide.

Gal-Trosto, mindvoice kloss and strong. "It is as I said. You obey or you're destroyed."

After a moment, the prince responds with sadness great. "I obey."

The Sayerbeast says, "Ska-toe, ska-toe," and with great and ortly eyes, looks down.

"What must I do?" asks the prince.

"Toss me over the fortress walls."

The prince looks upon the fortress. "Oh, my princess," he shuspers, "that I should learn that I slept with you when it was your kind, your ancestors who oblivitroyed the worlds and a world upon which I was born! That you saved me, my burned, shattered, nonmemoric form and now I must turn on you. And there is no other way."

Gal-Trosto, mindvoice soft, "And there is no other way."

"The ancient, ossiferous wrongs must be righted."

"And," the mindvoice, "there is no other way."

"Malsolvent fate, had I only done this or that—but as it is—"

"There is no other way."

For a long and dwissle moment, the prince looks upon the scene: to the klasson fortress, high walled and looking so indismitable, in those grounds he had walked with the princess, so marse and fair, who, she said, had found him, nursed him to health — that all of it, all of it would soon become trunderous blast and blekked smoke.

"And," he thinks, "there is no other way."

And that evening, when the moons had set, the prince whispers to Sayerbeast, "Ya-hi! We go!"

"Ska-toe," and the creature slowly pandangles forth, moving like shadows within shadows until they are outside the wall. And where the prince gathers courage — even he cannot say how — only what with ofundious will can he raise his hand to let Gal-Trosto out, to pitch him up and over the high wall and soon thereafter, the prince, hiding in the forest dwill, watches the walls burstbillow out, watches Gal-Trosto, burnrage tall and screaming, screaming as with feet smolten and beclawed, he stumples down the fortress walls.

Sayerbeast is still as sky and lowers head: that this should all be so.

"Eeekle, eekle, ickle, swort."

Stunumbly, the prince looks about and sees a cloud of vorsy smoke condensetract into Shastau. "Ah," says Shastau, "my friend, did I not yell you so? Why did you not listen?" Shastau looks with eyes of implorsadness.

"I don't know," says the prince.

"Does the truth set you free? Are you glad you know the truth?"

The prince does not speak for a time. Fintivitably, he says, "I do not know." His breath shambers in his throat. "I do not know." With his hand, he slowly bossles the scales on Sayerbeast's neck. "Perhaps I'm wise, perhaps I'm more foolish than a bamblecat which hunts during the doublebright of day. Perhaps being like the Sayerbeast is the tranquilst way to be. But in the end, what do I really know that is certain? Only uncertainty is certain, only change is unchanging. I now know that — and also that I must go on."

Before the prince, a creamygloss sphere appears. Then, the mindvoice, "We go on. We will snarapture a ship behind the fortress; the liberation has begun!"

The sphere of Gal-Trosto droplops into the prince's hand. The prince kneejabs the beast; the malovrious hooves pass quickly over marthdale, yes, past the burning fortress, the broken jagged stones belittering the land like shattered teeth — and to the ship beyond — Gal-Trosto and the prince, like double-sun, rising, pushing back a dlusk and desperate night with the promise yes, that the dark be gone as they bring forth the light from the swale of dawn.

No Matter Where, Perhaps the Same

Beneath Andromeda (rich and star-swirled sky!)
Tentacles intertwined in love and
Amber eyes a-glow, the lovers love.
Gliding along pseudopodnous way

The lovers love. Beneath strange, starry
Sky where moons of silver and dusky
Rose loom like dreamscape of
A child who still knows how

Wonderful it truly is, the lovers
Glide, in their language maybe saying
Words such as, "Forever," "Cherished One"
"Oh, say 'yes,'" And "Forever, ever."

The lovers glide silently perhaps
To grass-like glen while something
Somehow birdshapable swoops through
Warm evening air and screams

"Skeeee!" The lovers glow in pale
Blue love as is right for them
Given their biology and psychology
And physiology

And the type of world they're of and
On and how they evolved, so forth,
So on — it's magic to them anyway.
Their tentacles find a firmer hold

For each; they make love as lovers do
The way they do, having orgasm as they might
Or are prone to do and afterwards lay soft
And glowing the way they do,

Looking up at that glowing sky,
The several moons, and at that moment
Perhaps they are as children
Seeing their world as for the

First time — new —
And renewed in faith, hope, the future
too — then gazing into each others eyes
And loving love... as lovers do.

Jack of the Lantern

This is how Edward came to know about Jack, who lived in this clutch of a house surrounded by big fists of laurel and beyond that, grey green pines that speared high into the heavens. Edward and Roy, they walked past that house regularly and somehow it always looked the same. Fall, winter, spring, summer, on nice sunny days it looked dark, foreboding, sinister. When Edward and Roy, all of 13, passed by that house, they slowed their pace, glanced up the walkway that had a high grass arching over but not touching, no, but leaving a narrow strip of concrete walk wide enough for a leg to pass.

On this particular day, the day before Halloween, a day of slanting yellow sunlight and orange leaves cackling up the street from a heavy, dust-laden wind, Edward and Roy stopped and looked up the walk, past the curving grass, to the dull green painted and faded concrete steps to the screen door with the brown screen torn and the door behind, forest green. The windows on each side had brown shades drawn. Edward looked to Roy and asked, "Does anyone live there?"

Roy, pulling his new white pile blue denim jacket close, said, "Yeah, Jack."

"Jack? Jack who?"

"I dunno."

"What's he look like?" Edward looked back at the house, peering past the laurel bush, vaguely noticing the shininess of the leaves which reminded him of a sowbug's skin.

"Um," Roy said, shifting his *Modern Biology* textbook from its perilous position on his loose leaf binder, "Well, I saw him a long time ago... you know, he's real fat and wears those grey pants and a green plaid shirt and he's got white hair and his face is puffy and he's got pink ears like a rabbit."

"Oh," Edward said, "how come I've never seen him."

Roy shrugged. "Maybe you ain't been using your eyes..."

"Huh," Edward said. Then, "Hey, let's stop by here tomorrow night and see if he'll give us some treats."

"Huh," Roy said, "you just wanna see what he looks like. I don't wanna bug the old guy."

"Whattaya mean?" Edward said, sticking his hands deep in the pockets of his large maroon coat while pinning his loose leaf between his arm and side. "If he hasn't been seen for a while, maybe we should look, what harm is there in that?"

"Come on, come on, let's go...

"Wait," Edward said, "let's stop by...."

They pushed and they fought and they tugged and they laughed and the afternoon and evening passed and before either realized it, it was 6 p.m. Oct. 31st. The rap on the door announced it.

Edward opened the door. "Boo," said Roy. He was dressed in a white sheet.

Edward laughed, "Good try, grape nuts."

From the living room, Edward's father yelled, "Edward, you apologize to Roy."

"Sorry, grape nuts."

Edward's father's stern voice boomed, "Edward!"

"Come on in," Edward said.

"You ready?"

"Yeah."

"So where's your costume?"

"Right here," Edward said, unrolling a huge burlap bag and pulling it over himself.

Roy stared, "You're going as a bag of potatoes?"

"Naw, you dope. I'm going as a paper bag."

"Yeah?" Roy said. "Well, sure is a good costume for you."

"Huh?" Edward said.

"Just air inside."

"Ho, ho," Edward said, wishing he could think of a clever response. He grabbed his shopping bag, "Let's go get some goodies."

They stepped out into a blustery, billowy Halloween night with a thin crescent moon that gave the sky a sly smile. Their first stop was the Henderson's party. Two big baleful pumpkins squatted on the front stoop and the carved images were sinister indeed-faces of a cat, a bat, Edward guessed. "We should make a haul here," he said.

Martha Henderson answered the door and said, "Eeek, a ghost and a sack of potatoes!" as she slapped her hands on the sides of her jowly cheeks. Someone peered over her shoulder, a tall guy with bleary red eyes and mumbled, "Eh, looks like ghost stew, heh, heh, now if that ain't all...." The man whispered to Martha in a voice Edward and Roy weren't supposed to hear, "You the meat, my love?" Mrs. Henderson dropped her arms suddenly down and back, which told Edward and Roy that the gentleman had a little trick of his own in mind.

"Here you go," she said, depositing in the empty accounts of Roy's and Edward's bags, popcorn balls.

And after the door was shut, Edward looked at Roy and exclaimed, "Popcorn balls!"

Both broke into fits of laughter, snickered and ran, throwing the popcorn balls at each other.

Mrs. Smith, who was dressed like a black cat with red whiskers, also had a party going when she opened her door and purred, "Meooow, my children, what are you going to do?"

"Say 'trick or treat'," a dumbfounded Edward said.

"Meow," Mrs. Smith said and into the bags fell handfuls of Hershey's Miniatures.

"Thank you," Roy said.

The ritual continued. Children and adults playing with the spirits and the forces creative and always the laughter, gleeful screams. The laughter subsided when Edward and Roy reached Jack's house, which sat in the dark with light creeping out from behind drawn shades.

"Um—do you still want to..."

Roy said, "I dunno. Looks pretty spooky."

"Are you sure you know this guy?"

"I think I did. Maybe it was somebody else."

In the darkness they continued looking at the house. They heard distant sounds of laughter, the voices of children, ghostly, audio phantoms of the night. And Edward and Roy stood, staring, with bulging sacks.

"Let's," Edward said. "I will if you will."

"Naw," Roy said, "I don't think we should."

"Scared?"

"Uh, no. No. But you know he might have a big guard dog..."

"Hee, hee, hee," Edward said, "maybe a big guard spider."

They both gulped. "Are those eyes over there near the porch?" Roy asked.

"How many do you see?"

"... um... three..."

They shifted.

"Still wanna go?" Roy asked.

"Gee, um... you don't really see three eyes do you?"

"No."

"Whew!"

"Now I see five, still wanna go?"

"... um..." Edward said.

"Chicken."

"Am not."

"Are too," Roy said.

"Dare you."

"Double-dare *you*."

And before they knew it, they were daring and bluffing right up the walk.

"Something moved," Roy whispered.

"Did not!"

"Werewolf?"

"Shut up," Edward said.

They crept closer.

"Do you hear breathing?" Roy asked.

"Yeah. Yours."

"Do you remember the scene from *Frankenstein* where the monster —"

"Would you shut up?" Edward hissed.

Movement in the laurel.

"Wind," Edward said.

"I dunno," Roy said.

They moved closer to the house until they were on the front porch.

"You really want to do a trick-or-treat here?" Roy asked.

"I dunno," Edward said. "Don't know what will happen if he opens that door."

"How do you know that it's even a he that will open it?" Roy whispered.

Edward felt the hairs rise on his neck, felt his scalp tingle. "Let's see if we can peek through the window," he said.

They put their bags on the ground and carefully crouched by the nearest window.

Snap. Edward stepped on a twig.

"Shhh," Roy said. "Whoever or whatever inside can hear that... be careful."

"Okay, okay."

Quietly, stealthily... there... a place where the shade did not come down all the way and Edward looked into that room on that Halloween night, a night when the wind haunted the brush and sent leaves cackling up the street. A night where the silver moon shone thin light on ghosts and other costumed horrors, where evil lurked disguised and ready. Edward and Roy looked into the room and saw him. And they stared. Jack was standing, shirt undone, drinking from a tall, green bottle; abruptly, it slipped from his hands and fell to the floor. He looked down at it, swayed, caught himself by grasping the top of an overstuffed chair, then looked up, to the ceiling, to a bare light burning there and sobbed, "Oh, God!" He staggered forward, stumbled, fell over a table crowded with beer cans and bottles and *crash* and *clatter,* they cascaded to the floor and, finally, he made his way to the over-stuffed chair and collapsed into it and then closing his eyes, he appeared to slip into sleep.

Edward and Roy continued staring and after a while, they stopped look-ing and grabbed their bags and who knows why but they sat on the porch, and into Roy's plastic bag, they placed an orange, an apple, some Oreo cook-ies, a few Fig Newton bars, some Hershey Miniatures and a Milky Way too, and tied it to the doorknob with a long thread from Edward's costume. They knocked on the door, hard... and then ran — out of sight, and into the dark heart of that Halloween night.

Sledder

Do you like my new sled? It's all shiny and new. See? The runners are steel and the top is painted black. I like my new sled and I hope you do too. My sled is special and it takes me to places where I must go. It takes me over mountains of bodies; the runners crunch over the bones.

It's a wonderful sled and I can ride it year around, over the frosted lands and under the pale and starless sky. Oh, but it's a nice little sled. And often when I'm going, I can visit places without anyone really knowing just how close I am. Why, just the other day, I came sledding to a party. Oh, this really was different, a little pocket of gaiety in this cold, dark world. But I could see it all. Oh, such things draw me, draw me draw me close and draw me fast. And I could feel that pocket of goodness why, way far away and I drew close and runners on my sled going *swiss-swiss* down the stinking run, *swiss-swiss* over the decay and rot, riding my little sled, yes, I could see it then, a family, a little pocket of a street and houses and I drew near and there was a party with the mother there and maybe five or six children, and there was a cake and everybody loved the party and I did too and I hit a perfect hill and flew up way over head so I could look on it down below. Yes, her name was Susie, it was her birthday, oh, yes, I remember her pink little dress and her hair tied up in a pony tail with red ribbon there, and she was seven and she cut the cake, and I waited and I circled about, *whissssh* went my little sled, climbing up high going up to where the air was cold, and circling, circling about and down again, and her hands went for her throat and it is not me to question why, but I swooped down and scooped her up and asked her, "Do you like my little sled? It's so much better than what I had before. This is quiet and brand new." But she said nothing, nothing at all and I held her body in my great arms and my other arms held fast to my sled and after I devoured her soul, I let go of her body, I just let her go and again I was on my way. And before long, I felt the warmth once again, and I turned my sled about and went down hill over the mountains of bleached white bone and skulls and *whish*, again airborne and there oh, yes, a big Saint Bernard, laying on his side breathing hard, unable to stand, and a car was stopped and a man standing there saying, to his wife, "Fucking dogs. If people don't keep them locked up, what do they expect? Jesus H. Christ."

And the wife, she was a frightened sort and looking around, this way and that, said, "Don't you think we should make an effort to find out where it belongs?"

The man, dressed in dark clothes, a business man perhaps, said, "Martha, this is the middle of nowhere! God knows where this mongrel belongs."

And the woman wringing, wringing her hands, said, "But we really should make an effort."

And the man said, "Oh, all right, We'll stop at the nearest place we can. But if people don't want their fucking mutts killed, they oughta keep 'em on a leash."

And they drove off in their enclosed sled, and slid off down that road and I swooped down, oh, like the gods, and scooped him up, and couldn't feed off that sort of soul but flew away from here out of the pocket of the green and the blue and dumped the animal right there along with everything else once their body's through and I moved on, moved on, oh, my sled is so much fun, and it's such a pleasant task I do and there, yes, again I see, another place for me to be and this time it's a hospital, and in a patient's room I hear the doctors talking to a young man and the doctors say, "Looks like the smoking and drinking has finally caught up."

And the young man has the sheets clutched in his hands. "But surely I'll have enough lung left—"

The doctor frowned. "We don't know exactly how far it's spread but we'll see what we can do once we get inside—"

And I laugh to myself, oh, this is so wonderful indeed. I like these once robust ones, their souls to me are like meat and I can eat for such a long time. Then I think, you know it's too bad that some people do this to themselves and I turn my sled around and by the time I aim it down, the man is in the operating room and I waste no time, there is no suspense here and I slide into the room and scoop up the man oh just like that, clutched in my chitinous arms, and I say to him, "Do you like my sled? It's awfully fast and new. I do hope you like my sled, for I've a long, long ride for you." And I am so hungry now, and I eat his soul just like that, very tasty, a delicate snack, and I drop his used form on the pile far below and oh, this sled is oh, so quick, and I keep thinking I ought to name it but I smile and with my other hands grip the sled and make a tight turn beneath that starless sky, over that land of bleak bones, I fly, I fly, I pass over other pockets, see what there is to see, but not many today seem ready for me, to seek my new sled, coming to give them a ride but I know there are others who don't suspect me close by and it's that element of surprise that I always enjoy—it's almost like a toy that is so much fun until you abruptly turn it a certain way, and then I come from the sky and you cannot stop my ride — in spite of all that you try to do — I'm gliding down and I'm coming — I'm coming — for *you*.

Blue Dinosaur

Now, it must be known that we all have our passions and Nicholas had his; oh, don't we all? For you know, that's just the way it is; passion upon passion and we all have quite a few: perhaps it's Lawrence Welk or Mozart and/or old films of the *Creature From the Black Lagoon*. We all have our passions and Nicholas had his: dinosaurs. Oh, those lovely, bulky creatures of the Cretaceous Period. Those poor beasts, never realizing that they, along with their supper of weeds and their vast green environment, would eventually end up as coal some millions of years hence and then end up as someone's fuel in a fireplace. And who, tossing a lump of coal on a fire, would stop and consider that what they were burning was in part the flesh of some poor Brontosaurus? And while this was all very sad, nonetheless, Nicholas knew that dinosaurs had feelings, too.

If those dinosaurs knew what their fate would be many millions of years hence, they'd be sad; they'd be blue dinosaurs. Blue as the water in which they wallowed, blue as the sky, blue as the dawn and blue as the dusk.

But what was to done? Nicholas considered this as he bought another plastic authentic replica of yet another dinosaur that was supposed to be an authentic real life replica of the way they were really supposed to appear. You name it and the neighborhood McKesson's store, run by old Mr. Archer, (who, himself, seemed to be somehow wallowing in the drying swamp of time), had it. Mr. Archer said (as Nicholas brought a Tyrannosaurus Rex, king of the dinosaurs, with mean little reptilian eyes, and a heart probably just as trite and cold as the lump of coal that even he — or it — was to become), old Mr. Archer said (as Nicholas plopped down a dollar-five largely made up of nickels and dimes from trade-ins of pop bottles), old Mr. Archer said, (in a voice incredibly soft, seemingly in spite of his walrus-like mass from years of living well from a profitable business which yielded steaks and puddings and other high cholesterol goodies that Mr. Archer, as a pharmacist, should know better not to eat, but as a human, could hardly resist), Mr. Archer said, "Well, young man, your collection must be nearly complete. I've sold you one of everything that I have — what are you doing with all of them?

Starting a zoo? Trying to bring back the period of lizards?" Then he laughed, "Keeping me in business?" He rang up the sale and gave him a receipt with a note at the bottom (faded by want of a new cash register ribbon), "We appreciate your patronage." Somewhat embarrassed and not quite knowing why, Nicholas simply said, "Dinosaurs are neat."

Old Mr. Archer smiled. "Indeed?" he said. Then, as though more to himself, "Indeed." He picked up the dinosaur and looked at it closely. "Surprisingly realistic," he murmured. "Yes, indeed. You must have the whole set now—"

Nicholas nodded, "I think I do."

"Well, good for you; I hope you enjoy them. They've turned out to be quite a big hit. And I'm not sure why. What do you do with these? Play soldier or what? Be an interesting war if you did."

Nicholas, still not quite knowing what to say, simply said once again, "They're neat."

Mr. Archer laughed. And in the laugh, Nicholas saw humor, humaneness, sadness and memories all rolled into one. Mr. Archer said, "Gads, I wish I'd had this stuff when I was a lad. But nonetheless, we still had great fun; grew up in Florida and had this rope swing—"

And Tyrannosaurus Rex sat on the counter between Nicholas and Mr. Archer. The dinosaur stood, authentically mean with painted white bared teeth, small beady eyes, and little arms raised, ready, like a praying mantis to seize anything near. Mr. Archer talked "... and there was Sammy Tarron and one day he swung out on that rope swing and the darn thing broke and off he went sailing into the swamp; oh, covered with mud head to toe, oh, yes, what a mess—"

He was about to go on when old Mrs. Haggar, age seventy or so, came up to the counter with her weekly supply of *National Enquirer*, *Hollywood Secrets Revealed* and *The National Gossip*, and she typically frowned as she flopped down her papers. She looked at Nicholas and said, pointing to the plastic beast, "Shame on you, throwing your money away like that."

Nicholas, somewhat abashed, didn't know what to say: he never liked Mrs. Haggar and the more he saw of her, the more he disliked her. He placed his hand on the model and Mr. Archer looked at Mrs. Haggar and, pointing to her papers, said, "Shame on you for throwing your money away like that."

Mrs. Haggar, what with her hair all done up like a tight knot on her head and her small eyes flashing with indignant rage at being confronted with her cruel little plot, said "Well, Mr. Archer, I suppose if you were his age, you'd be throwing your money away like that, too."

Mr. Archer grinned and simply said, "You betcha."

"Well," said Mrs. Haggar, "maybe someday you'll grow up to set a better example for young folks who come in here."

Mr. Archer smiled, "Well, I would certainly hope the imagination I encourage is better than the imagination that you would encourage."

Mrs. Haggar, tossing down the three ninety-five that her reading material cost, said, "What's wrong with the imagination I encourage?"

Mr. Archer smiling, then laughing, took the plastic authentic-looking dinosaur, pounced it on the papers, and said, "Grrrr! Snort! Snort! Grrrr!"

Nicholas laughed while Mrs. Haggar looked just dumbfounded and stunned and beside herself and shocked and finally said, "I'll never, but *never* come in here again! I'll report you to the Better Business Bureau!"

"Please do," said Mr. Archer.

Mrs. Haggar, totally enraged, grabbed her precious papers and in so doing, Mr. Archer lost his grip on the genuine mean-looking beast. It jumped up, danced across the counter, landed and broke right at her feet and she, with seeming hatred unbounded, kicked at the pieces, scattering them across the floor. Utterly outraged, she quickly left the store, obviously resolved to never return.

Nicholas looked at the dinosaur; some of it here, some of it there, some of it most likely lost to the ages, gone to the places of dropped old candy and smelling of drugstore dust.

"Well," said Mr. Archer, leaning over the counter and surveying the broken symbol of a lost age, "as soon as I get more in, I'll save one for you—or, you can have your money back now—"

Nicholas, though sad at the loss, smiled and said, "It's okay. Just save one—"

"I'm really sorry—" said Mr. Archer, and he sighed and smiled, "except that oh, it was *so* worth it. Oh, how I've wanted to do that—whether she ever comes back means nothing to me. And as soon as another dinosaur comes in," and he thought, and pulled out one dollar-five—"it's on me. You can have that dinosaur—have it for free."

"Gee, Mr Archer," said Nicholas, all smiles, "that's really neat!"

Mr. Archer just grinned. "My pleasure, young man, oh, my pleasure indeed." He went to the back to put stock away and Nicholas, smiling, went to magazine aisle and read *Tarzan* comics for the rest of the day.

The Loving Deed

Furry lover, flapping quickly, sailing in
Through window open to the dawn.
Eyes a-glittering, lover settles slowly down
On sleeping one; slowly down then

Nuzzling almost as if affectionate
Between her arm and her breast —
Victim at rest and with the touch
Of the creature, goes deeper, deeper

Into sleep, "Promises to keep", the victim
Dreams of Sandburg's line which is fine
As furry lover goes; doesn't mind
What the rhyme as his fangs deeply into

Her breast goes; not exactly the milk
Of human kindness is what the creature wants,
And of blood only incidental here as
Furry lover drains carcinoma.

Such a dear this little beast, lover
Doctor, who knows what, but furry lover
Having had his fill of tumor juice,
Yawns to reveal those oh, sharp teeth

And nestles down for deep deep sleep.
Little lover, monster, savior, slides
Into dreamless, sated sleep, unconscious
Of promises to keep.

Nightmare 32.6

Whistling bravely, young boy walking
Midnight streets, hears behind him
Sounds of strange feet,
Dragging, clicking not far away

And young boy walking hastens pace,
Looks for doors unlocked with welcome
Light beyond, but this city is as dark
As the night behind your closed

Eyes and even REM won't pry them
Open; young man walking city streets hears
The quickening of the feet, hears
Laughter of something familiar

But as alien as can be; weird laugh:
The scream of tortured cat and a maniacal
Cry, perfect to make pursuer
Delight in the wicked game.

Young boy running, running into the night,
To be embraced by the pustule arms of
Fear, into the dead breath of the
Nightmares that haunt the streets on which

We walk, all followed by the demons in our
Souls; young boy running, screaming into the
Night, and close on his heels,
His Nightbeast fright.

Fishin' Off The Starry Stream

I belong to the Amalgamated Dimension Sliders Union, Local Group 386 and I get paid good wages plus six Standard Time Frames of vacation a year which is enough time to visit my sweetie in the inter-dimensional district of Yoodoob.

Now, it's not easy work I do, shifting and sliding dimensions back and forth. With all the universes, all the galaxies that abound, there's gonna be friction and the way you ease the friction — well you have to slide dimensions but no matter how careful you are, a little White Space slops over into Red Space, a little globular cluster from the Purple Universe slips into the blue galaxy and makes for tremendous fireworks. But, that's okay. It's pretty and no real damage is done.

So, I got a good job and it's interesting and full of responsibility — as if I don't have enough already. Got a child to take care of, but he's growing up fast. And that's sad but it has to be. We went on — I guess — our last fishing trip a Standard Time Frame back. He came up to me — I had just eased the sixty-seventh dimension between a negative universe and a positive one (now this is risky — and I get paid triple time for this, you don't slide a dimension right and you're gonna blow out the negative universe with the positive one and vice versa; nasty business but certainly spectacular when a little negative comes in contact with the positive: explosions, brilliant light and strange colors and sparks go flying and the other Dimension Sliders are yelling, "Slide it! Damn it! Move it! Too much contact! Slide it or work overtime! Get a move on!" And we slide the dimensions in and about and the two universes touch, spark, but they're protected now and they slowly stabilize) and anyway, we sat there on break and my son drifts up to me. It's amazing how fast he's expanding; he used to be so small and white; an intense little pulsing sphere of energy and now he's growing yellower, older, larger, as he becomes diffused with more experience. Soon, he'll become like me, large and red. He comes up to me. "Can we go fishing at the Starry Stream?"

"Why," I chuckle, "thought you'd never ask." I call, "Hey, GC N 45!"

GC N 45, the supervisor, comes drifting over. He's older, a bit on the purple side. He's always flashing red with irritation. "Yes?"

"Gonna knock off early. Things are quiet right now. Going fishin' with my son on the Starry Stream."

GC N 45 thinks for a minute.

"Problems?" I ask.

"No, it's okay," says GC N 45. "Just trying to remember how tight the universe is with the Starry Stream. It's still expanding and has a ways to go—you and your son's matter shouldn't upset it unless, of course, a new universe starts pushing from someplace—but that's unlikely right now. Yeah, should be safe. Go ahead."

"Thank you," I say.

"Good-bye, GC N 45," says my boy.

"Good-bye, little LG L 37."

We drift in silence for a ways. And I keep marveling at my son. Have so many Standard Time Frames gone by? So much more expanded he seems than last time I remember. Also so much quieter. We finally come to the place of Maximum Contact between our inter-dimensional world and the Universe with the Starry Stream. Actually, the Starry Stream Universe is just like any other one, except that, for some reason, there aren't many like it: only two basic—if you will—colors: black, which is cool and white which is very warm. My son always has asked how it was possible that such coolness could, as he put it, "pull itself together and get hot and bright." And I confess: I do not know. It is the same process that occurs in every universe, but here, it's the contrast that makes it so obvious: that some of the blackness turns warm and brilliant. Amazing.

We stand on the threshold of the universe. "Well," I say, "this is it. As soon as the universe ripples and the dimensions part, we can slip in."

He nods. And almost as soon as he does, we can feel the universe ripple; slow, heavy ripples. The dimensions slowly pull apart, some blackness spills out. We grab it and flow in with it when the ripple retreats. And before we know it, we are standing on the black banks of the Starry Stream.

I sit, extend my filaments into the river to feel the stars, all sizes and colors roll and turn through me; ah, the warmth, the flames!

How they tingle, excite! Lovely, lovely. In the immense system of things, this has to be my favorite place. I withdraw my filaments and sigh; something calm, soothing about being here. Old SC K 452 likes the violent Yellow Universe. Gets a thrill out of holding stars and having them go novae. Says the heat helps warm up the colder parts of himself. LM M 34, still young and learning the trade, likes the Red Universe—a very energetic place. All sorts of things go on that he loves to watch or experience. But here, yes, here on the banks of the Starry Stream — ah. Serenity. To watch those suns slowly moving by. Don't know from where they come, don't know to where they go.

Little LG L 37 lays down and extends a filament into the stream. He fishes out a huge yellow star, almost as big as he is.

"Nice catch," I say. "Beautiful."

"It is, isn't it?" he muses. "Gotta do something with it."

The star keeps wanting to drop down and flow with the stream again and little L GL 37 says, "No, no, not yet. I'll let you go in a minute. But I'm not gonna let you go alone."

He reaches in again into the stream and pulls out some, as yet, unformed, glowing starstuff. He makes little dark balls of it. "Here," he says, "a close one. A hot little world." And he sends it scurrying about the star.

"Nice," I say.

"This next one's gonna be neat," he says. "It's gonna be a little larger, have a shiny atmosphere, but be terribly hot." He makes the world, and sends that one spinning about the star.

LG L 37 is happy. Happy as I remember him all the times before: he is lost in his own magic. He creates yet a third little world, a stunning jewel of blue water, rock, and swirling cloud patterns.

For some time I watch him. Such an imagination. Large worlds with bands of swirling clouds. A world with a splendid wide band of rings. Then pale green-blue worlds and an icy final world. How happy LG L 37 is. Finally, he gently pushes the sun away and it drifts about the Star Stream.

"Well done," I say, "that was quite well done."

After a long while, he says, "You know, I've been thinking about The Breaking."

I am at once proud of little LG L 37. I am also sad. Expanding and expanding away. And that's the way it is and yet it is difficult.

"Yes," I say, "I know that has been with you."

"And you know what I most enjoy."

"Just as you were doing."

"Yes," he says, "yes, that is what I want to do forever."

His enthusiasm sends me feeling, dreaming of an earlier warmth, a brighter color.

"You will not be upset with me for not wanting to be a Dimension Slider?"

I sigh. "How it is you know me better than I know myself? I want so much to say, 'No, no, it bothers me not in the least.' But it does. And here I've been trying so hard to appear that it does not, that I can let go so easily and yet it is so hard." And I touch him with a filament. "I must remember that you may be of me, but you are not me. Just understand how hard it is to let go."

He touches me with a filament and light and warmth flows into me. And I give him my light and warmth of time, patience, endurance and respect for himself hence for others. "Thank you for your honesty," he says, "I suspected that I might be disappointing you—it is difficult for me too. But, I must do this."

"Yes," I say, "and I am glad you have the courage. I am envious that you are doing something that I never did—for I did not want to be a Dimension Slider—but did not have the courage—" And I stop. "But that matters little now. It matters little." And for a small time space, there is a silence between us. And then I sense his restlessness. "I think it is time," I finally say.

"Yes," my son says, "it is time. I must go."

Little LG L 37 now is no longer little; before me he has expanded more, become brighter still. Behind him flows the stream of stars.

"Yes," I say, "yes, it is time."

Again, we flow warmth and light into each other. Then he says, "We shall meet before long."

"I know," I say. "Carry my warmth with you."

"Thank you," says LG L 37. "Goodbye."

"Good-bye," I reply.

With that, he leaps into the Starry Stream, joining the slow and ever moving brightness and I sit and watch for a long time until my joy, my sadness blurs the Stream, the Stream, the Starry, Starry Stream.

Stardance

Now in the days before the days, Dark One could be found standing in his shop, standing behind a long, glass-topped counter. The shelves in the case were covered in black velvet and crowded with little diamond bright and burning figurines, sparkling, sparkling and making the shop oh, so bright indeed. And Dark One smiled.

He enjoyed looking upon the brilliance, but the little burning diamond figurines kept calling out, "Release us, Dark One, release us, release us one and all—it is not right for you to keep us here, in your store on these shelves, in this counter."

But Dark One smiled and simply said, "Be grateful to me. You are safe here. I am protecting you."

But the little figures reached up with shining hands and spoke with despair, "No, no, this is wrong. You must let us be free."

And Dark One smiled again and said, "Freedom is a dangerous thing and it is so, oh, so easy to misuse and so much bad can befall its use. No, no, be grateful my little ones, I am here, you are there, and I protect you."

And forlornly, all those little shining hands fell like little wilting crystal petals and the heads of the little diamond figures bowed in sadness.

Of course, there came the new ones, the new diamonds yet to be: they appeared on the counter top and Dark One would smile and simply say, "Welcome."

And the new ones, of course always frightened, be they animals or people just transformed from the flesh, knew not what to do. And the job of Dark One was simply to say, "Welcome; you are safe here. I will protect you. You shall move on but only when I am ready to let you go."

And the new ones, even if they were once insects or little gentle furry things, they knew that this was wrong—and cried—and instantly transformed into beautiful diamonds, such beautiful, radiant diamonds of themselves—and then would appear on those infinite shelves beneath the counter.

And in the days before the days, this went on for a long, long time, until, of course, it happened. No more new ones came. At first, Dark One was undisturbed, so fascinated he by the glow, the light from the shelves in the counter. But as time moved on, Dark One became aware that, somehow, somewhere, something was not right. But he did not know what to do—if anything, and therefore put the doubts aside and let the dark shop glow with the light of uncountable figures.

More time passed and Dark One became more aware of something wrong, a feeling that would not leave so easily. He then realized that the little diamond beings no longer pleaded—they sat and were very still.

Dark One looked down the counter, this way, that, and whispered, "What is wrong? Where is your voice? Why does no one speak?"

No response.

Dark One tried again. "You should all be happy: you are with each other: beingness should be wonderful and trouble-free. Are you all asleep?"

Again, no answer.

And then—in the wonderful glow of the infinity of figures—Dark One realized something disturbing indeed. Since no new ones were coming, then all of this was not infinite. Which meant that things could end. Which meant that he was not infinite which meant that *he* might end. Already, his power to transform, by there being no new ones—had ended.

As if a cue... perhaps a clue... *flicker.*

"What is the meaning of this?" whispered Dark One. He was abruptly aware of his fear welling up to become anger and wanting to control, "What *is* all this?"

Flicker. Then, again: *Flicker.*

In consternation, Dark One leaned over the counter and stared at the small figures. Dark One leaned, his black robes spread out about him and he whispered, "I do not understand."

A few figures slowly raised their crystal hands, as though shining petals reaching for the warmth of a seemingly warm sun but expecting to get back false heat and searing cold. "We told you," they whispered, "we told you."

Dark One shook his head and said, "Don't you know you are safe here? Don't you realize such a favor I am doing for you? The protection?"

Flicker. Flicker. The crystal hands dropped again and from each end of the counter, darkness spread, coming like two waves and rushing toward the center where Dark One stood. Stunned, he watched, then shouted, "No! No! You cannot do this! You are ungrateful!"

The darkness continued on, continued on. "No!" said Dark One, "Stop! You cannot do this—if you all die—"

"Yes," came a gentle voice, "then what are you?"

Dark One looked down. A solitary shining figurine remained—a butterfly.

"I order you not to die!" said Dark One.

Flicker, went the butterfly and the butterfly looked up. "For what is there to live? Being kept here is dying. Good-bye."

"No!" said Dark One, "Please—"

"I am the last," said the butterfly. "Everything that is here—everything that was here—is within me. If I die, all dies, *you* die."

"No," said Dark One, "that must not happen!"

"Then break open this case so that I may be free—"

"I cannot do that—"

"You are afraid, Dark One, you are afraid. Why are you afraid—?" *Flicker*.

Dark One could not answer.

Flicker. Flicker.

"Why should I be afraid?" whispered Dark One. "Why?"

"Why does anyone try to possess and keep anyone?"

Again, Dark One could not answer.

Flicker went the butterfly and then in a voice, soft, despairing, "Oh, Dark One, can it be that you are not aware of your fear of being alone? Of your presumed worthlessness? Of your fear that if you let us go, that you are so terrible, we would never come back? Is it possible you cannot see this?" *Flicker, flicker, flicker.*

"No!" whispered Dark one and, as though burned, he jumped back and stunned, he found himself whispering, "Oh, yes—" And with a mighty fist, he struck the case. The counter split open and the butterfly glowed, grew— and suddenly, a vast explosion of light and when Dark One finally opened his eyes—he was amazed—for all through his dark body, the figures glowed and danced and then each transformed into stars and dumbfounded, Dark One whispered, "I had no idea—" and inside himself, close to his heart, he saw the butterfly and it whispered, "Be not afraid of yourself, Dark One," and the butterfly turned into a warm star, and the star whispered, "Be not afraid to be loved."

Dreamscape I

Wiley, slyly, creeping stilly
Past the twilight, past the dawn,
Creature nightmare, fangs a-glowing
In sun rising it comes near.

Flowing, moving mist-hued being,
Hair as soft as spider's silk,
Multi-eyed and many legged
It comes creeping

In his dreams?
Silly, thinks he, still in sleep,
That this dreamscape should be
Threatening, if at all.

Yet his breath catches in
Pale morning; swiftly, stilly
Creature stalking, comes
Through the misty, wispy yard

Out there with moon
Newly silver, whitely shining,
Now pewter dullness in the day,
He stirs beside the open

Window; shhh — he hears a brush of
Something — something now
So near his bed —
Something, something

Multi-eyed with eyes

A-shining in morning light—
Something bulbous, bloated,
And hissing—in insectial delight.

Horrorscape IV

Waltzing, dancing, it comes to me
Eyes filled with what I cannot
Fathom, abdomen throbbing with what
Purpose I cannot guess

But she/it comes to me,
Creature of my nightmare fever dreams,
Arms encompassing —
Does she need to dance?

Terrified I want to leave
Yet fascinated stay and couldn't leave
If I dared; I'm snared and smell
The sickly sweet of something I

Cannot guess; trancing smell and I can
Fancy she or it is beautiful,
Wasp-like creature, tall as I,
Body banded red and black;

Of this earth? Of Somewhere else?
Of their intent? I cannot know and
Feel not quick slash of
Razor appendage

In my gut — she/it yanks me close;
Something shoved into the gash
Creature is in ecstasy I guess — it hums
And something green foams on

The mandibles and then it leaves,

Yanking free, flutters wings of
Crushed rainbow; moves, then flies, circles
About then leaves; is gone.

I look down, the gash is sealed
Abruptly—tired—cannot stand on my feet
And fall, knowing suddenly something
In me waking, hungry—as I drift to sleep.

The Christmas of Eddie McGrew

Now this is the story of Eddie McGrew who had one Christmas—oh, let me tell you—it was a Christmas he would never forget, what with his Uncle Jack there, fat as a plum and with raisin-like eyes, the image of a man who was all dessert from head to foot, in contrast to candle-thin Eddie with a complexion that seemed waxy at times. And there was his mother, Mrs. McGrew who fluttered about on that Christmas eve, like a nervous young hen, bustling here and there and once in a while putting her hands on her hips as she watched the rest of the family rough and tumble about the living room. In the background the radio might be playing *Jingle Bells* or blurting out a commercial for antacid; Mrs. McGrew might chirp out a word or two then hop back in the kitchen to stir the corn or check on the mince pie sweating and sizzling in the hot oven. And there was Mr. McGrew, a dark, fiendish-looking man who this day, brought home the Christmas tree and set it in the middle of the living room floor and said, "There, if ever there was a great tree, now there it is." Eddie's father bounced the tree two times against the forest floor-colored rug and said with pride, "Twenty-two fifty, a good deal if I ever saw! Jack, take that friggen' cookie out of yer mouth and get over here."

Jack, sort of molasses-oozed over and managed to say "Ooomph," as he helped hold the tree.

Eddie said, "Gee, what a great tree!"

His mother came out of the kitchen, clucked her approval and dashed back into the kitchen again.

"Ooomph," said Uncle Jack.

Eddie's father, though he looked sinister, maybe because of his bituminous eyes, maybe because of his bony neck and hawk nose, smiled and said, "Yes, yes, a good tree this is, worth every penny in these inflationary times, a good buy." And he stood back, turned up the music and it was *White Christmas* sung by some choir. It was Eddie's favorite song.

There was a *tok, tok,* on the door and Eddie knew it was his cousin Justine. Justine, a guy a year or so older than Eddie, entered the room and sniffed the air and said, "Urk. Who burned the formica?" like this was the most clever remark ever made in the history of the planet or at least in the last minute or so and he stood there, in his red shirt with the Levi tag sticking out horizontally like a strange, minute, cloth erection and said, "Jesus H. Christ. Since when was the dump selling used Christmas trees?"

Eddie's dad, who was beginning to string the lights on the tree, stopped and said. "Justine, can't you put your orneriness away for a few days of the year? An hour or so? At least when you visit us?"

Uncle Jack stared at his son and said "Ooomph."

Eddie who, at sixteen, had the simultaneous understanding of a child and an adult, but didn't know how to put it into words, stared and looked perplexed. His father turned away and said, "You're welcome to stay for dinner, but Justine, you better ditch all that venom of yours."

"Well, hey," Justine said, his eyes focusing in like a wolf, or wolverine, "if you were raised with a name like Justine—"

Uncle Jack, snacking on an Oreo, waved his arm, and said "Ooomph."

Justine glared around, his hands fists, his mouth firm like his lips were steel and his face cement.

"Joy to the World" the radio blared and in the kitchen, *skreeeeee—!* screamed the kettle. Justine finally sat down and his mother, Aunt Justine, who had been taking a nap in the back bedroom entered the room, tall and robust with baseball-like eyes and tiny signature of pupils—she stared at her son with a look somewhere between affection and scorn, shook her head and said, "Can't you be civil this one day of the year? Christmas eve, for goodness sake, be civil, please."

Justine, looking to the ceiling as if the answer might be written there by Santa Claus or maybe the tooth fairy, answered, "God, I just can't wait to change my name—"

"You'll do no such thing," Aunt Justine said, "oh, if you'd just been a girl—"

"Shit," said Justine, "I come to Christmas dinner for this crap? God, let me have some turkey and get out of here."

"Ooomph," said Uncle Jack.

Eddie wondered just what kind of dinner it was going to be, though he already had some idea.

"Oh, night divine—" the radio promised in choirly voice. "We'll decorate after dinner," Eddie's father said.

"Hamms, the beer refreshing," the radio sang.

"Ooomph," said Uncle Jack.

"Dinner's ready," shouted Eddie's mother flouncing back and forth between kitchen and table with candied yams, cranberry, turkey dressing and pumpkin pie. Aunt Justine sat stiffly down, like a two-by-four-was nailed to her back. Eddie's dad sat at the head of the table and finally, finally, finally Justine came to the table.

"Goodyear tires griiiiip the road," the radio observed. And Eddie's mother, she then sat down too, and while she said grace, Eddie smiled at his own secret grace, "Good bread, good meat, good God, let's eat."

Dinner passed in snowy silence with the icy clinking of silverware and everyone but everyone grateful for the radio, grateful for *White Christmas*, for selections from the *Nutcracker*, for commercials about Anacin, acne cream and Plymouths and Fords and the weather forecast brought to you by Preparation H, and the occasional "Ooomph," from Uncle Jack. Eddie ate silent as frost, avoiding the contemptuous eyes of Justine.

After dinner, everyone gathered in the living room to listen to Christmas music. Eddie and his father decorated the tree; Eddie could feel Justine's stare at his back, eyes drilling, drilling into his soul but Eddie smiled anyway and before long, the tall tree was bejeweled, shimmering, sparkling, magical. "Oh, Holy night," the radio mused as Eddie and his father stood back and marveled at the magic and Justine yawned, bored as a resigned fly on a no-pest strip.

"Mighty nice," said Mr. McGrew.

"Yeah," said Eddie, the lights of the tree reflected in his eyes. He put a red ball on the end of a branch.

"Vicks Formula 44," said the radio.

"My," said Mrs. McGrew, in a nesting tone, "the tree looks better every year."

"Ooomph," replied Uncle Jack.

"Very nice," Aunt Justine clinically observed. She looked at her son. "Isn't it?"

"Merry baseball," he sneered.

"Any time is Taco Time," said the radio.

Eddie found himself thinking, something weird—happening. *Scrape!* Something—in the chimney—?

Eddie saw his father frozen in the act of putting tinsel on the tree, looking thoughtful, as if thinking, yes, it does need more tinsel here.

Strange, thought Eddie, he's not moving. He looked at his uncle, in the middle of chewing pale Christmas cookie—only Uncle Jack wasn't chewing...

"T'was the night before Christmas—" said the radio.

"Heh, heh, heh."

Scrape, scrape.

Eddie looked around again, and saw Justine, mouth open, eyes staring at the fireplace.

The fire burned brightly, little yellow dancing, sharp devils of burning light, spearing about the logs.

Something coming down the chimney — ?

" — and all through the house — "

Eddie looked to the fireplace again. Black boots, two legs. Two arms.

Heh, heh, hiss.

Four arms.

" — so lively and quick — "

Six arms.

"Heh, hiss, hiss."

Eddie gulped, backed up, saw Justine frozen, screaming, screaming in silence.

The figure, dressed in red, with hat, white beard and holding an empty bag, had the face of a spider. Burning, it crouched in the fireplace, then bounded over to Justine, picked him up like an ornamental fallen angel and tossed him into the sack, and then looking back at Eddie said, "Hiss, hiss, hiss, I just *have* to have one to witness *my* spirit of Christmas."

" — then up the chimney he rose..."

All was movement once again, and Mr. McGrew stood back and said, "Now, that's a tree if I ever saw a tree — what do you think Eddie?"

No answer.

Mr. McGrew looked irritated and said, "Something the matter? Too much Christmas cheer?"

Eddie shook his head.

"These are beautiful memories you're getting now," said Mr. McGrew, "this is what Christmas is all about." He turned to Uncle Jack, finishing off a square of fudge and said, "Now, hey, don't you wish you woulda had kids?"

Uncle Jack wrinkled his nose and said, "Ooomph."

For a minute, Eddie thought he heard a raspy voice, mean, quiet and tight, say "Merry Christmas, Merry Christmas — "

" — aiiiiiieeeeeeeee — "

"And to all, *heh, heh, heh,* a good night."

The Proverb Man

Tootsie-Roll, the dragon, and his sidekick gremlin, Corrugate, sat on a rather lush world: they sat on a mossy bank of a lake, dabbling their feet in the water. It was a lazy day: Tootsie-Roll, with finely controlled laser-like jets of flame from his mouth, occasionally vaporized insects—he didn't kill the butterflies, just the biting little monsters.

Corrugate simply sat on the bank, infrequently scratching his iridescent blue stomach scales and ruffling his white face feathers in contentment.

"Ah," sighed Tootsie-Roll, "a fine day. A fine day indeed. We haven't been in trouble with the Inter-Galactic Council of Mangled and Mismanaged Magic for some time now. We must be doing something right."

Corrugate laid an egg. It hatched, revealing a blue and tranquil sphere of water.

"Yes," said Tootsie-Roll, "our life has been that calm. To be truthful, it's actually been a bit boring."

Corrugate took the sphere of water, opened his beak and popped it in his mouth. He splashed his duck-like feet in delight.

Tootsie-Roll sighed, shot a jet of flame and brought down a smoking ember of a fly that meant to chew on Tootsie-Roll's more sensitive parts.

It was then that he heard whistling. Tootsie-Roll glanced down the path that serpentined through the forest and wandered beside the lake.

"Company," murmured Tootsie-Roll. He listened to the tune. It had the quality somehow of something being whistled backwards.

"*Strange* company," said Tootsie-Roll. He frowned and dark smoke eddied out of his nose. He scratched his jaw a bit nervously. Corrugate sniffed the air.

And soon enough, where the path came out of the forest, there emerged a small, warty gentleman, very much red-faced and dressed in clashing red, blue, orange and purple plaids. He was very overweight and moved with a waddle. He had a paisley bow tie and his forehead was hummocked with minute beads of sweat, his red hair stuck damply to his temples. When he saw Tootsie-Roll and Corrugate, he smiled and stopped. "Fribblin' in the fishprah, eh?"

Tootsie-Roll looked at the visitor. "Beg pardon?"

"Ho-ho-ho," said the stranger. "Let me introduce myself. My name is Peter Proverb. I go from planet to planet, adding colorful expressions and richness to language." Out of a breast pocket, he produced a little calling card which read, "Peter J. Proverb. Language Enricher. Fulluptulize your language today."

Tootsie-Roll looked at the card then handed it back. "Interesting occupation."

"Furjingobingoso. Does your language need enriching?"

"I don't think so," said Tootsie-Roll. "Our language is already as rich as—" He thought for a minute.

"As rich as—" asked Peter Proverb.

"Um—" said Tootsie-Roll.

"See?" said Peter Proverb, "that proves it. Your language is totally empty. That—or—"

"Or *what?*" said Tootsie-Roll, his eyes narrowing down.

"Well, suffice to say, your language needs enriching so that it can be as full and resonant as a bumdong in scattering."

"As a what?"

Corrugate looked skeptical, dropped an egg and, picking it up, it hatched. Inside was a plaid worm. He flicked it into the water where it was promptly devoured by something dark and tentacled.

"What?" said Tootsie-Roll, "that doesn't make any sense."

"Your problem," said Peter Proverb. "You don't know what a 'bumdong' is, right?"

Tootsie-Roll nodded.

"Therefore," said Peter Proverb, "you can't know what a bumdong does when it scatters."

"No," said Tootsie-Roll, the smoke getting a bit thicker in his nostrils, "I can't. Am I missing something? I frankly don't think I am."

"Yakfurtz!" exclaimed Peter, "what a perfectly perforklytod remark."

Corrugate's yellow eyes began to burn a darker hue. He laid another egg. It hatched. Inside was a plaid rock, which Corrugate promptly dropped into the water.

Tootsie-Roll noticed the webbing in his wings growing taut. "'Perforklytod' means what?" said Tootsie-Roll.

Peter Proverb stood there shaking his head. "Tsk. You don't know what that word means either? Behitzoopreedle!"

Little blue flames began to dance in Tootsie-Roll's nostrils. "Stranger," he asked, "what *do* you want?"

Corrugate hatched yet another egg. Inside this one, a plaid toadstool. As before, he threw it in the water where it floated with seeming direction— then just drifted.

"Oh," said Peter Proverb, suddenly realizing something, "I think I'm making you angry."

"Very much so," said Tootsie-Roll.

"Oh, my goodness," said Peter Proverb, abruptly ingratiating, "oh, dear Lukus Lupjohns, oh, my, it's what my bofoodranous mother always said, 'Anger in the cup curdles the mind'. Oh, my, I'm so sorry, gentle dragon and gentle gremlin oh, dear, please, please don't be angry at me, oh, please!" And Peter appeared very distraught and stood wringing his hands, "It's just like they always say, 'A close friend will scrub the sky and a distant one will scrub your toes.' Oh, my, my most dipthroputlitoid apology, dear dragon and dear gremlin. I am prathosootly apologetic clear down to my ramshackle knees." And he wrung his hands some more and looked utterly pathetic and despairing.

Tootsie-Roll looked to Corrugate. Corrugate looked to Tootsie-Roll. Corrugate laid another egg. Inside was a clear sphere and inside that was a little plaid insect running frantically about.

Corrugate shook his head and let the little sphere drift in the wind.

"Really," said Tootsie-Roll to Peter Proverb, "I think you're taking this—"

"Icklypazerdroid!" said Peter Proverb, getting even more frantic and worrisome. "'A quest in gold is a brass misstatement'! Oh, fortrissydid vandanbum—"

"Look," said Tootsie-Roll, becoming alarmed. "I'm not really mad at you—well, not now—but you really are getting far too upset over this—"

But Peter Proverb stood and put his arm over his brow in a dramatic manner. "Bedwazzle fac!" he moaned, "'A scorpion's headlight outshines the rock—', 'A rolling vinegar gathers no soak!,' 'Don't milk over a spilled cry', and I must remember that, 'A vanquished army eats dishrags not'!"

Tootsie-Roll was now *very* alarmed. Corrugate stood and chirped in fear and dropped an egg. Inside was the image of something plaid, screaming, and bashing headfirst into a brick wall.

By this time, Peter Proverb was ranting. "Zhe vyt scar veratti sbot—e plurabus unum nada en our lifetime skiz for torbunalcuz pissorium great end of tunnel light—" Peter Proverb hopped about, flailing his arms, his little face shiny with sweat and very red and suddenly, a black explosion—*Fwum!* and there, before Tootsie-Roll and Corrugate—was a black little tornado spinning furiously about. *Guzzzzzzzzz!*, it roared. *Ghzzzzzzzzgiizzzzzzzgrummmmmmmm!*

And howling and buzzing with the sound of a vast swarm of angry bees, it skipped and zigzagged down the path.

Tootsie-Roll stared. "What was *that!*" He shook his vast and scaly head in wonder. "What *was* that!"

But Corrugate shed a tear and gave an egg to Tootsie-Roll. It hatched and inside, a sphere. Inside that was a little dark beast, lonely-looking and forlornly looking out. Then it ran about the sphere, shrieked incoherently, then stood, little dark hands against the side of the sphere and looked sad.

"Ah," sighed Tootsie-Roll, and after a minute he said, "let me guess: wanting so much to be understood, so angry at not feeling understood, feeling so lonely and so anxious to please and so angry at self for not feeling good enough."

Corrugate looked down the pathway where Peter Proverb—now Peter tornado—had gone.

"Well," sighed Tootsie-Roll, placing a paw with carefully filed and blunted nails on Corrugate's shoulder, "it's sad. But we all have to keep on trying. And he does too. And maybe he'll find a form and a way of expression that will make sense. Running around, an angry tornado, certainly won't help."

Corrugate nontheless sighed again and dropped an egg. It hatched in Tootsie-Roll's paw and a deep blue coolness oozed out.

"Yes," said Tootsie-Roll, "it is very, very sad. But after all, you've learned to communicate and sometimes what Peter said made more sense than you."

Corrugate snorted indignantly and went back to sit on the bank, splashing his feet in the water while Tootsie-Roll did the same and as before, with careful jets of flame, brought down the biting insects, letting the butterflies flit about, and, presently, a very pretty one indeed landed on his paw. Tootsie-Roll looked at it—and was startled to see that the head was not that of an insect.

"Bahoodrenpood!" said the butterfly brightly, "'you can lead a horse to kitchen but you can't make him fudge'!"

Darkscape V

Monsters! Monsters! Yours
Leap about in the nightscape
Of your eyes; I draw close
And your Monsters! come alive.

Monsters! Monsters! You draw
Close and I can feel my Alien,
My Dracula, my Creature from the
Black Lagoon yell and screech and writhe.

Monsters! Monsters! How are we to
Ever talk
Between the Monsters! the Shriek and
Howl that exists within us?

Monsters! Monsters! Shall my Dracula
Sign an agreement, a non-aggression pact
With the Jekyll/Hyde within you?
So that, at least, we may have a starting place?

Monsters! Monsters! Will the Blob within
You sign a trade agreement with my Creature
From the Black Lagoon? Will some sort of
Barter lead to trust?

How shall we do this, my dear?
What must we do to keep our monsters
From attacking the monsters in each
Other? What shall we do?

It's tough enough being of different

Sexes and sorting out all the lies,
Without having to fight the monsters!
We see in each other's eyes.

The Master Goes Whacko!

Now in the beginning before the beginning, before the night and before the day, in the time before gray and the vast permanence, in the days before changeless change and McDonald's hamburger stands and pet rocks, the Master sat—the Lord of Darkness on His right, the Lord of Light on His left and the Master sat, looking over His infinite empire and said, "Nothing is working! This is the pits!" He promptly dissolved everything and...

... in the beginning before the beginning, before life and before death, in the time before water could turn stone hard, before moon followed sun, before death became life, before Coca-Cola, hula hoops and senior proms, the Master sat and this time sat with the Lord of Darkness on His left and the Lord of Light on His right and said, "Okay, let's get all this razz-ma-tazz going! Gods! I'm rotting before my very own eternal and infinite eyes!"

And He waited. And still nothing happened. And the Master waited some more. He glanced at His watch and discovered that it read "zero." He pulled from His neutral-colored gowns an hour- glass. The sands did not move. The Master stood up, pulled up an opaque cushion from his elegant throne and located a thin manual entitled *Operational Instructions for the Functioning and Care of It, The All, The Everything, The World, The Infinity, Etc.* It was, of course, written by the Master and, just as He thought, He had forgotten to put in anything about how to start It up. He sighed. He said, "Oh, damn!" and again He dissolved everything and...

... in the beginning, before water became fish, in the beginning before land transformed and walked about, in the beginning before the beginning, before Seven-Up, Anacin, and the Brooklyn Bridge, in the time before time, before the dark transformed to light and the light transformed to dark, the Master sat, the Lord of Darkness sitting in front of Him, the Lord of Light sitting in front of the Lord of Darkness. The Master smiled. "Now," He said, "this will do it." And He waited. And He waited. And as before, His watch read "zero" and in the hourglass, there moved not a grain. The Master scowled. "What the shit?" He muttered. He brought out a notepad, and discovered a notation on the back page: "What to do in case of emergency."

There were two phone numbers. But, the Master realized, there were no phones. Yet. So He created one. One right on the left arm on His immense throne. He dialed the number. No answer. "Of course." He said, "I need another phone!" So, on His right there appeared another phone. Again, the Master dialed the number. The phone on the right rang. The Master picked it up. "Hello?"

No answer. Abruptly, He realized the foolishness of this and said, "Oh, dammit anyway!" And once again everything dissolved....

... and in the beginning before the beginning, in the beginning before gasses condensed and congealed into spheres, before comets slashed the heavens, in the beginning before the earth knew how to lift itself to become birds, in the beginning before Edsels and Zenith televisions and lo-cal beer, the Master sat and before Him, the Lord of Light sat *upon* the Lord of the Dark and the Master said, "Now maybe this time. The light should flow into the dark and..." And He waited. And waited. Abruptly, He smiled and snapped His fingers. "Oh, how obvious!" He laughed and...

... in the beginning, before water and sunlight knew how to make rainbows, in the beginning before darkness knew how to ignite itself to make stars, in the beginning before Dick Tracy, Little Lulu and Ronald Reagan, the Master sat with the Lord of the Dark on *top* of the Lord of Light and the Master said to Himself, "Darkness is heavy; it will flow into the light and finally —"

But the finally never came. The Lord of Darkness sat on top of the Lord of Light — and nothing happened.

"Ye gods!" raved the Master, "What must I do?" Scowling, He snapped His fingers and...

... in the beginning, before lava froze to become land, in the days before the days, before soil did the impossible and transformed itself into plants and plants did the impossible and transformed sunlight into energy, the Master sat, the Lord of Dark on His right, the Lord of Light on His left. The Master was getting very weary of all of this. And in the beginning before Jacqueline Onassis, Great Leaps Forward and Soviet Five Year Plans, the Master simply sat, not knowing what to do. He was at a total loss as to how to get the Whole Thing going. And who knows why; perhaps out of immense frustration, perhaps out of keen intuition, the Master reached over to the Lord of the Dark and, scooping out a handful of darkness, smacked the Lord of Light right in her heart. Aghast, the Lord of Light looked inside herself and seeing the darkness, screamed, "Who did that?"

The Master smiled. "I cannot tell a lie," he said truthfully, and he pointed to the Lord of the Dark. "He did it!"

The Lord of Darkness was shocked and pointed to the Master. "No! He did it!"

And the Master looked hurt. "What? I'm a peaceful sort! I wouldn't do anything like that! Besides, where in heaven's name — just look in yourself — that's *darkness* in there and it can only come from one source." And the Master pointed at the Lord of Darkness. "*Him!*"

"But wait —" said the Lord of Darkness.

Too late. Already the Lord of Light grabbed some of her own whiteness and threw it at the Lord of the Dark. *Wham!* Right in his heart!

Enraged, the Lord of the Dark screamed and leaped on the Lord of Light and they fought and rolled like a wheel, Light chasing Dark, Dark chasing Light. And the Master sat back, sighed and then grinned as he watched the cosmos *finally* begin.

Fidine Knows

Fidine is a dog of few words—barks, rather. She's an amber-colored pooch, almost looks like a Labrador, but she's not. At least, I don't think she is. She just kind of wandered into my life one day while I was out planting a cherry tree. She looked into the hole I was digging and looked up at me and said, "Wuff." Nothing fancy. Just "Wuff." Then looked back into the hole. I was just about ready to plop the cherry tree in, and lament the cost of the damn thing given that I had just lost my job and was hurting for cash, but when an unknown dog wanders into your yard, looks into a hole you are digging and says, "Wuff," well, I hung on to the cherry tree a minute more and then, for what reason I cannot comprehend, dug a few more shovelfuls. *Chunk.* "What the—" I muttered, "What—" I dug around some more and it turned out to be a quart Mason jar and what was inside the jar? I couldn't believe it. *Money*; "Migod!" I said to the dog, "Migod! How *could*—how *did*—you—" Opening up the jar was difficult—given that it had been there for a while—but the rolled money demanded to be counted and 8,483 dollars and forty-six cents later, I looked at the dog sitting in the doorway to the basement and I said, "You know, if you're looking for a place to stay—"

The dog just sort of cocked her head to one side.

"You're a dog of few words. What'll I call you? 'Wuff'?"

The dog looked away. Disdainful?

"You're making this hard. Fido? But you're a female. Fidine?" The dog got up and padded softly over to me and sat looking up at me with those golden brown eyes. Now, I've never been an animal fancier and actually, come from a long line of cat-loving ancestors whose idea of a good pet was one that just kind of draped over everything and purred; I did have an uncle who was obsessively in love with a cocker spaniel that peed whenever it could or sat there looking at you and you could tell that there wasn't an awful lot going on inside that canine cranium. But Fidine here, oh, hell, I guess all animal lovers say it don't they? *My* dog, cat, turtle, canary, hamster, etc. etc. etc. is *different*. I'll say it anyway. Fidine *was* different. I mean Fidine was *very* different. Not so much in behavior, but somehow she had the knack of either coincidentally knowing what I needed or somehow being in the right place at the right time. When I lost my wallet, she padded off to God knows where in the house and somehow found it and, with minimum drool, dropped it at my feet. When I lost my new screwdriver, she went to the sofa, said, "Wuff," and there it was beneath one of the cushions. The list goes on, but needless to say, Fidine was spooky, especially the thing about the money. There was that, and her watching T.V., and sitting at a certain part of the basement staring for long minutes at a particular point of the wall. But there was something else, a more about her, that was somehow a bit unsettling. Others picked up on it. My sexy neighbor, Sally (she liked to be called Sal), who once in a while leaned over the back fence to chat and, on a particular day, (after Fidine had been a guest for about a week), dressed in her blue OshKosh overalls and with her dark hair under a wide-brimmed straw hat and a trowel in one hand, when she saw Fidine, she shook her head. "Stanley. I *never* thought I'd see you with a pet—much less a dog. What kind is it?"

I shrugged. "I don't know, Sal. She just kind of wandered into my yard one day and somehow," I was careful, of course, not to mention the money or Fidine's other 'gifts,' "we sort of took to each other."

"Will wonders never cease," she said. She leaned over the fence a bit, held her hand down and said, "Here, girl, come here, girl," obviously expecting the dog to docilely and dumbly sprint on over, tail a-wagging, mouth a-drooling, manner aching with that aura of "OH, Gawd, *petmepetmepetme!*" But Fidine didn't. She just sat there, near the cherry tree, looking off into the distance.

"Huh," Sal said, "you sure you don't have a cat in a dog's bod?"

"Nope."

And we talked a bit—about this, that. And Sal looked over to Fidine. "You know, I got this really weird feeling about that dog—like she's not only *listening* to us, but she understands more than she ought to—"

I smiled, "You mean for a dog?"

"No, I mean for *any* animal." I looked over with a smile and then was aware that I felt that tug in my gut—that what I saw wasn't quite as it seemed. Fidine was looking directly at us and I met her gaze—there was something else in there. And it wasn't dog. I don't know what it was—but it *sure* as hell *wasn't* dog. Immediately Fidine broke eye contact, snuffed, got up on her feet and slowly wagging her tail, headed around the side of house.

"Strange pet you got yourself. Hope it's okay."

I smiled but it didn't feel as self-confident as I'd hoped.

"She's been fine. She really has. I just let her stay in the basement."

"Hm," she said. "Well, my petunias are calling me. See you later."

A little uncertain, I went back to the house, and went into the basement. There was Fidine, sitting, looking at that particular area of the concrete wall. I squatted beside her. I looked at the wall, but all I saw was the rough concrete unevenly painted over in white. "Boy," I said out loud, "sure wish I knew what you saw there."

Abruptly, I turned to look at Fidine, and there it was again, that intelligence, that deep, penetrating look; it was as though I was being scrutinized and it was *really* unnerving and I remember thinking how cats look intelligent but on the I.Q. scale, they aren't really all that bright. This has gotta be the same thing. But then, the money, the screwdriver... I swallowed. What *was* this I was dealing with? It was like she could read my mind. Then I felt something else—a presence, a calmness and—a warmth. Fidine scooted a little closer to me; unconsciously? Out of habit? I put my arm around her and again she looked at me and the look again was that of not only a profound intelligence—but, coming from anybody else, what I saw sure looked a lot like love—not devotion or mindless whatever—but a deep, abiding, intelligent love. Strangely embarrassed and thinking I was going a little nuts, I looked away, stroked Fidine and then stood and said something, like, "Good doggie—uh—yeah." I backed away while Fidine resumed looking at the wall. I went up, had dinner, put on some rock music and thought about leaving to visit my friends Alice and Jack for the evening. Fidine was just too strange even though I knew that she or whatever she was—was harmless and sure liked my basement wall. But a little later, distracted, and gorged with steak, potatoes, ice cream, and a diet soda, I had fallen asleep on the sofa.

"Wuff!"

—crazy dream of my Grandmother chained to a wall and I was yelling at her, "You'll never make me eat rhubarb again and this is for all the grief—" and I was smooshing her face again and again in banana cream pie—and then Fidine appeared, gently grabbed me by the sleeve and led me to a hill and the sky was filled with bright stars—which was lovely except for one thing—the three moons—*Tug, tug, tug.*

"Wuff, wuff, *Wuff!*"

Startled, I awoke, "Wha—? Hu—?"

Fidine had me by the sleeve of my shirt, gently tugging on me. "What, Fidine? What? What is it?"

She went over to the clock; it was ten p.m. "Wuff," she said to the clock. Then she turned to look at me, and I guessed she wanted me to follow her. Groggily, I did so; down the steps into the dimly-lit basement. She went to her favorite part of the basement—the wall. And she watched. Then I felt her lean against my leg; I looked down and looked into sadness. "Fidine," I whispered, putting my hand on her head, "What—" Before I could say anything else, the wall before us blazed into colors; then it cleared to show images, a starfield, three moons, around a planet, a vast city of spires, and subtle shifting blues and amber and there was a crowd of beings—without a sound, Fidine leaped into the image; and somehow she changed—still the amber color, but now she was standing tall, lithe; her face canine-like but something else very, *very* different—*alien* but the eyes dark and the face handsome and again, that intense, intelligent and loving look. She held something in her four-fingered hand and she put it forward and let go—and the scene abruptly collapsed in colors and then—*bink*—was gone.

Dazed, I stared; then on the floor, a rectangular card, shimmering. I picked it up and saw individual strands of darker silver moving about; abruptly, it was like they somehow "arranged" themselves and there was a message spelling itself out word by word: "Thank... you... for... helping... me... while... I... was... waiting. I... wish... you... could... come... with... me— but... it... cannot... be. I... never... forget. But... good... fortune. Sal... is... in... love... with... you. Farewell."

And suddenly, the card simply "evaporated"—became a sparkling mist, and dissipated. I think I ended up sitting on the floor and finally, still unable to grasp exactly *what* in God's name this was all about, was able to figure out one thing that *was* certain: I wanted to talk to Sal about things other than— petunias.

A Little Spider Shop Talk

Now, I remember talking to my neighborhood spider, you know, she lives right next door and spends all her time in her apartment weaving those webs that others would not care to admit to weaving but she does it right in her living room and doesn't seem to mind that people walk by and scream at her frankness.

Me, it never bothers me. No sir. We became good friends. I always admired how hard she worked as she anchored one end of the web here and the other end there. If I worked as hard as she did, I'd be sweating in a second.

"Really," she said one day as I was visiting her, "it isn't really all that difficult to build webs, it really isn't at all." She regarded me casually with a few of her eyes.

"Huh, do tell," I replied. "It certainly seems like a task."

"Care for some coffee?" she asked. (I know she had a very complicated latin name, so I just called her Mrs. Webb and she said that was fine.)

"Yes," I replied.

"Well, you know how to do it. Excuse me while I lay a batch of eggs."

"Certainly," I replied. And shoving a few silk strands aside, and being careful which burner to turn on (a part of her web was anchored to the refrigerator near by and I didn't want to burn the silk) I put on a pot. "I take it you'd like some?"

"Uh-huh," she said; she really didn't seem all that interested; laying eggs and all does take some concentration. So, I brewed some coffee up, ducked some silk strands and put her cup in a fairly level area of silk where she often sat, sometimes splayed like a black flower in a delicate silk setting. And when she was through with her onerous task, she came up the web and sat right down and with her front legs, she held the cup and drank. "My, that's good," she said.

"Is that the last of the Maxwell House?"

"I didn't see it," I said. "This is the Brim."

"Nice," she replied.

"How many eggs do you lay all at once?" I asked politely, not knowing if she'd be offended by such a question.

"I don't know," she said, and I think she might have glanced to the corner, to the eggs, with all her eyes, but I wasn't too awfully sure. "A few, I suppose."

And she sipped her coffee. And I sipped mine.

"I really do admire you," she said, "for being my friend. So many who walk by would like to pretend that I don't exist, but I know they are frightened. I wonder why."

"People are afraid of spiders," I simply said.

I suspected Mrs. Webb was amused but looking at her, she appeared expressionless.

"Spiders outside of themselves or the kind that dwell inside?" she asked.

"Oh, hell," I said, "maybe it's both—maybe there's a part of ourselves that so reminds us of insects that we can't stand the knowledge. Or maybe it's a fear of being ensnared in something and having no way out, or being overwhelmed by something symbolic that catches us with so many legs that we can't escape—"

And Mrs. Webb did laugh. "Oh, the fear. It's the fear, isn't it? Of being overtaken, of being unable to escape, of being held powerless by the incomprehensible."

"Maybe," I said, as I drank my coffee. "But maybe people are specifically frightened of you—"

"By my webs?" And she lowered her coffee cup. "By my silk?"

I laughed. "'Oh, the tangled webs we weave'—uh, Shakespeare, I think."

"So, I remind people of the webs they weave and they see themselves more like spiders than they want to admit?"

"Possibly. But with you, something else—"

"And that is—"

"Your name—isn't it latin for Black Widow—"

"Oh!" And she was definitely upset, "all that folklore about how deadly I am? That I eat my mate?"

"Well, you do—you have done that—"

"Well," she said, "is it that act that I do or is it the fear people have that, if they get involved with one another, they will somehow be devoured? The sense of themselves lost to another because people will do just about anything for love? Or be slowly drained of the essence of themselves until just a shell of one remains?"

I almost choked. "That's rather good," I said, "matter of fact, your insight into the human condition is awfully astute."

"Thank you," she said, "our species has been around long enough to have quite a folklore about humans. Actually, probably more accurate than your folklore about us. But tell me, is there anything else about me — specifically — that may bother people?"

I thought for a minute and then said, "Yeah, that red hourglass design on your body."

I heard defensiveness in her voice. "Well, what of it? It is certainly distinctive and I think rather attractive —"

I laughed. "Hold it, I didn't say it wasn't attractive or bad or anything like that. I'm just stating a fact —"

"Why should it be bothersome —"

"The hourglass is the classic symbol of the passage of time," I thought. "And of death."

She sipped her coffee reflectively. She lowered it as if considering to say something — then sipped again. Quietly and with great injured pride she said, "But I'm a widow — a black widow to be sure and sometimes my appetite does get carried away I suppose — but time? Time? It's just coincidental that I have a red hourglass."

"Symbolic," I said, "maybe people fear spiders because they associate the hourglass with being overwhelmed by time." I paused. "Or the lack of it. Or the passage of it."

Mrs. Webb chuckled. "Overwhelmed by the Black Widow of Time. My, how sinister and ugly we sound — all we are are life forms just like you — we don't even kill for sport or blow up anyone and yet we're regarded as so horrible." She sighed, finished her coffee and simply held the mug. "More and more," she finally said, "it sounds like the attributes given to spiders — especially Black Widows — are qualities that people hate and cannot accept in themselves."

"Maybe," I replied. "A lot of it sounds like that to be sure. The term, I believe, is 'projection'." I drained my cup. "Well," I said, "as usual, it's been interesting talking with you."

"Thank you," Mrs. Webb replied. "Hope our chat didn't scare you."

"Hardly," I replied. "What is most frightening and always frightening is when things aren't said — then the fantasies, and usually the worst ones — set in."

"Indeed," she sighed, "indeed. Well, I have to get positioned in my web here to see if dinner drops in."

"Let me take your cup," I said and so doing, and dodging thick silky strands, I went to the sink, washed the cups and put them on the drainboard. Then, "Take care," I said as I walked out the door.

"Good-bye," Mrs. Webb said, "do come back; it's always so interesting talking with you."

I went downstairs thinking of many things. When I reached my apartment, I stopped by the mirror—yup, I sighed, a few more gray hairs. I shook my head and, on the way to the kitchen to fix dinner, I glanced to the table at the red hourglass and watched, drop by drop, this mortal blood pass.

The Ring

It is as though Brundool, trade representative from Opayknon, knows by osmosis; while others grapple with symbols and abstraction, Brundool already knows only to consciously become aware of everything later. Thus, when an official of the city of Pantyan approached Brundool at the open air restaurant, Brundool smiled and simply said, "I had a feeling I might be visited by you today." His green eyes sparkled; he sipped his wine, sipped it so carefully.

The official, an overweight, trying-to-hide-concern sort of fellow, dressed in the yellow robes of city official/purple belt for enforcement of laws, sat at the table and stared at Brundool.

Brundool smiled. "I've known you for a long tine, Krelta; I sense you're anxious about something."

"I'm not anxious." Krelta made an effort to still his hands on the table.

"I see," said Brundool, "and the anxiety I experience is self-generated; I'm not resonating with you at all. Is that correct?"

He stopped. "The anxiety I experience has just increased. Are you feeling threatened by me?"

"No," said Krelta, a bit too emphatically.

Brundool shrugged, passed a hand over his baldness, then sat back in his chair and placed his hands on his stomach, over the simple maroon robes of Trader. He smiled. "I fantasize you want me to do something for you that may not be legal." He winced. "My, the anxiety! How *do* you contain it within yourself, Krelta?"

"I'm *not* anxious!" said Krelta, his face growing red, his hands fidgeting.

"I see," said Brundool, "and your hands certainly tell of a vast and wondrous inner peace?"

Krelta scowled.

"Krelta," Brundool said at length, "come now. I *know* you — what is going on?"

Krelta sighed, looked away for a moment, then looked back. "Do you — are you familiar with the name Dasdan? Dasdan Yorko?"

Brundool thought for a minute. "Oh, oh, yes. You directed the detective work which led to his capture. I heard about it not long after I first came here." Brundool looked at Krelta for a long minute. "Ah. I suspect something has happened to him and your political career is in danger?"

Krelta looked chagrined and lowered his head as though feeling somewhat shamed. He swallowed. "That is true. He escaped from detention which is under *my* jurisdiction—he killed several enforcers in his escape—it is not my fault—but *I* must answer for it. Everyone will know the news in several hours. I must go back and answer questions and what I must say is that he *will* be captured soon—" Krelta looked around, then whispered, "Very, *very* soon."

Brundool sighed. "I'm not sure what you mean by soon—but if you can find me some of his victims here in Pantyan or on Prandor—"

"Anything!" said Krelta. "We can find his victims—I know of two—three—right in the city."

"I guarantee I can find him—whether or not I can *help* him—"

"Don't worry about that," said Krelta, "just *find* him—the man is crazy—"

"Crazy?" asked Brundool.

"He loves to torture, to inflict pain—he has dismembered people, animals—"

Brundool looked both sympathetic and repulsed. He nodded. "It's easy to speculate how *he* grew up. And it's fairly easy to see how he can be helped."

Krelta looked puzzled. "How?"

Brundool shook his head. "No, let us wait. I want to be sure. Can you take me to his victims?"

Krelta nodded. "It will have to be tomorrow—I have to contact people. This afternoon, I am going to have to answer many uncomfortable questions."

"Tomorrow, then," said Brundool. "Meet me here at this time?"

Krelta nodded, "if you can help me—"

"Ah-ha!" Brundool smiled. "Bribing an Opayknon Trade Official?"

Krelta flushed, blustered and bristled. "What I mean is—that is—I'm grateful—it's not bribing—"

But Brundool laughed gently and raised his hand. "Tomorrow."

Krelta, smiling tightly, nodded and left.

The next day Krelta appeared on time. He sat warily at Brundool's table and placed his hands, palms down, on the yellow and blue tiled surface. "It's been most difficult," he finally said, not looking at Brundool. His round face somehow seemed much thinner as though what had transpired drew out more from him than just energy. "I did not sleep well. Anxious."

Brundool leaned forward. "From guilt?"

"That and feeling like I'm incompetent and I'm having trouble handling what has happened." He looked up. "Sorry that I wasn't honest with you yesterday about what I was going through—" He sighed. "Felt so overwhelmed, so vulnerable and bewildered. How things change so quickly; I'm very tired."

For a few minutes, Brundool said nothing. Finally, he reached over and placed his hand on Krelta's arm. "I know it is difficult. Let us go and see what we can do."

Krelta nodded; they rose and, some minutes later, were at the dwelling of Saya Kokras—a young female from Suthersland, practically on the other side of the planet.

Krelta said, as he knocked on the door, "She was raped and beaten some time ago by Dasdan. She had to be placed in—" he paused, "—detention— kept trying to kill herself."

Brundool nodded but said nothing. He looked straight ahead to the door. He noticed Krelta seemed ill at ease and looked as though he was trying to distract himself by focusing on the broad walkway, the rounded cubes of dwellings, the luxurious, jungle-like courtyards, the red, brown, yellow and blue cascades of Spadevine growing from balconies on all levels of dwellings—the door slid slowly back a ways and halted. A face appeared. Krelta cleared his throat. "Krelta Tarsda."

The door opened the rest of the way; the figure stepped back from the door.

Inside it was dark; Brundool immediately felt both sad and wary. The female was not emotionally well. On a low, dusty couch the three sat. There was a sour smell in the dwelling like something rotting or profoundly unclean.

"How are you, Saya?" said Krelta, gently.

She nodded. And after a long time, finally said, almost inaudibly, "I do well."

Brundool watched her; something was gone from her; a sparkle, a vividness of life that one so young should have—but did not. Her amber eyes were dilated, dark and sad. She was dressed in a simple dark blue robe— frayed at the bottom. Her dark hair was long and not combed well.

"Saya," said Krelta, "this is Brundool. He is here to ask some questions about—" he hesitated—"about what happened. Are you still comfortable with that?"

She nodded and gave Brundool an utterly neutral look.

No, thought Brundool, *something has not been taken from her nor lost so much as it has been yanked and ripped away. Yes. Yes.* Brundool brought out a ring from his gown; he placed it on his forefinger. Its stone was a small, cloudy sphere. "Saya," he said with infinite tenderness, "I understand what has happened. You needn't speak of it; I just want you to think of it—to feel a bit of it—so that I can understand what you went through—I just need a little bit of it—and that will provide me with all I need to know."

She closed her eyes; Brundool put his thoughts aside; reduced his heart rate, his breathing, became very, very still, opened his mind, his heart, open, open receptive—yes, there—walking home, alone. Evening. Out with Toog Raka—pleasant feelings. Movement. Hand over her mouth. Panic! Bewilderment! Flood of adrenalin! Pounding heart! Wanting to scream! To vomit. To urinate! Bite! Struggle! And laughter... yes, Dasdan's laughter. Arms pinned in front of her, dragged off the street, into an empty dwelling. Too frightened to scream. Fist in mouth. Teeth breaking, warm thick blood in mouth. Clothes ripped away. Darkness. Slowly, slowly, Saya shook her head; tears welled up in her eyes.

"Enough," said Brundool, "enough, I have enough. I can complete the rest."

And Brundool *became* Saya and then, in his mind, he stood back and watched the transformation continue—the pain, the pain, the pain—and complete itself—to wake up, cold, miserable and so broken, broken, broken. Clothes torn. Dried blood. To stagger out of the building, to stagger, stumble, collapse, to wake up in a medical unit...

Brundool looked at Saya. Gently he touched her shoulder, "I'm sorry that happened to you. Are you going to be all right?"

Sobbing silently, she nodded.

"I'd better get someone to be with her," said Krelta. He left and returned a few minutes later with a young helper, about the same age as Saya; she could stay with Saya, observe her and if necessary get further help if Saya showed increasing instability.

Brundool sighed when they left Saya. "Truly ugly," he said. "I found myself fighting to maintain control as I experienced everything she experienced." He nodded. "And now it's all been transferred and faithfully transcribed in here." He lifted his hand; the ring glowed.

"What exactly *is* that?" Krelta asked.

"One function of this is to record. I concentrate, this ring picks up all that I experience. Whoever gets it will experience *exactly* what I have experienced—an impression so vivid that the person who has this ring might as well *be* me—or whose experience it has recorded—like Saya's."

Krelta looked both impressed and taken aback. "Isn't that a bit—dangerous?"

Brundool nodded. "That is why only Opayknons can record with it—" he smiled, "or even make it work."

Krelta looked relieved. "That's good to know."

"And fortunately, or unfortunately, what works well for Opayknons doesn't always work for others. That is why I never sell these." He paused, and looked at the ring. "It also functions as a transmitter/locator. As soon as Dasdan has it, its signal will alter."

"It will be signaling constantly?"

"Yes. So that you can monitor me—then Dasdan."

Krelta looked at Brundool with a mixture of hope and skepticism. Then he shrugged. "Very good. Now, we must catch a transport to south of the city."

They were fortunate; the first transport that stopped for them was going to Kroddasa, a large city of 500,000, that used to be a half day's journey south of Pantyan. They climbed on the long and shining transport and easily found seats; the vehicle was relatively uncrowded so early in the morning. There was the muffled clicks of magnets releasing and quickly they accelerated, soon passing the inner city, the tall, slender, multi-hued structures that graced the air. Soon, they were outside the city; Brundool watched Pantyan receding, noticed how insignificant it was compared to the ragged and snow-covered Pyrntes Pasa mountain range that abruptly rose high and massive just a short distance outside the city.

After a short time, Krelta pressed a blue, glowing button in the wall beside him; the transport slowed and settled in silence. Krelta and Brundool got out and stepped onto a sheltered platform. An old male came up to Krelta; his hair was white and thick. He was short and robust, red of cheeks and wide-grinned. More than a few of his teeth were gone. He was obviously glad to see Krelta. Brundool noticed that old man's robe was of a coarse, brown cloth and none too clean.

Krelta motioned Brundool closer. "This is Garthal Bodroada. His mate was beaten senseless—no apparent motive in the attack. She had gone to Pantyan to purchase gifts for a family gathering."

"Hello," Brundool said.

"He-he-he-he," said Garthal, "he-he-hello. He-he."

"As I told you," said Krelta, "Brundool wishes to talk to your mate about what happened when the man—"

"Oh. Oh," said Garthal. "Yes. Yes."

The three of them walked a path away from the station and the small cluster of buildings. The land here was flat, agricultural. Brundool marveled at the flowers: yellow, red, blue and orange.

"Keethara—" said Garthal at one point, "She—she better—walk now. Yes. Yes. Long, long time has taken. But she better. Yes. Yes." They walked toward four rounded cubicles. The land beyond was furrowed; not far away a crop of antra, still green, grew. One of the immense and glaciated twin summits of Morkova Volcano, a safe distance away, was erupting violently. Smoke and ash boiled into the air. The snow around the crater was blackened.

They went to the nearest cubicle; the door slid open and they walked in. A woman, Keethara, Brundool assumed, had been resting on a low cot. She started when the three males entered; she sat up, involuntarily pulling back, then relaxing. Brundool judged her to be much younger than Garthal. Her hair was darker and pulled back. She was, however, just as short as Garthal, though much more slender. Her fingers were surprisingly long and moved in her lap as though they had a life independent of her.

She smiled shyly; Brundool realized that she once was—and still was—a beautiful female. Her skin was dark, wrinkled about her eyes, her mouth and neck. There were scars on her cheeks and forehead, now healed, but you could see the ragged lines.

She was dressed also in a coarse cloth, but it was pale green and clean. Brundool was struck by how calm she appeared, how warm, yet shy and the fingers, the restless, moving fingers... Krelta leaned to Brundool. "The fingers. Permanent neurological damage."

Garthal went to Keethara. "You—you remember Krelta—he-he brings his friend—Broo—Broondul to talk. Yes. Yes. To talk."

She nodded. With her eyes, she indicated Brundool to sit on the cot. He did.

Brundool spoke slowly. "I've come to hear about what happened—" He stopped, chose his words carefully, "You needn't remember everything—I just need enough of your experience to understand how it felt to you—"

"Of course," she said quietly.

Brundool was somewhat startled. He had not expected such a clear, warm response.

"I'll try to cooperate as much as I can," she said. "What should I do?"

"Just think back to what happened, how it began; you needn't say anything, just think of it—feel it."

Keethara closed her eyes.

It was silent except for the distant *thud-thud-thud* of the volcano. Tremors caused Brundool to start. Garthal shook his head; Brundool relaxed. Apparently the tremors were common; nothing to be concerned about.

Brundool closed his eyes. He opened himself to Keethara—"They shouldn't let old things like you run about—" Dasdan.

"That was very unkind of you." Anger. Keethara.

Images formed in Brundool's mind. Late afternoon. The park near the southern limits of the city Pantyan. Keethara resting, her gifts near her on a bench, waiting for the transport out. Brundool tried to focus on an image of Dasdan but can only see a dark-robed blur; blurred from fear? No, he realized, from hate. She *indeed* knows what he looks like and so loathes his appearance she cannot and will not bring it to mind.

"Unkind of me—" said Dasdan. "Oh, you don't *know* how unkind I can be—"

Intense fear, rage. "Please—I've done nothing to you—"

"Yes, you have," said Dasdan, "you've shown me how disgusting senility and old age is."

"That hurts."

"It's supposed to. Why don't you die?"

"Please leave me alone—I've done nothing to you—"

"I should help you die. That's what I should do."

Fear. Pounding heart. Adrenalin. Need to escape. Wonderment that there is no one nearby. Hope that there will be someone. Hope he will go away. What to do? Get up. Leave. Maybe the gifts will distract him. Why is there no one else near?

Dasdan goes up to the gifts. "Anything here for me?"

"No," she says.

"Oh, come on," he says, grabbing a gift and tearing it open: a new robe. "Oh," he says, "how pretty." He looks at it mockingly. "But I'm sure it won't fit." He tears it in half, then into shreds.

Rage.

"Here," says Keethara, picking up a vase, a beautiful, clear glass vase. "Come look at this," she says, "I'll give it to you if you leave me alone. See the beautiful etched designs?"

He draws close. "Oh, my," he says. "My, but that is *so* pretty," he leans, mocking her and she slams it right in his face; the delicate glass, it shatters; he falls back; she tries to run. He recovers, screams and pain! Pain! Pain! Something breaking! Vivid light, circles of color in her eyes. Then nothing. She wakes up in a medical unit, blind. It turns out to be temporary but her hands have taken on a life of their own.

Brundool shakes his head out of sadness and out of a sense of mystification: there is something familiar about Dasdan. Something haunting, disturbing and perplexing to Brundool. He opens his eyes; the ring on his finger glows. It is all there. It is all taken in.

Keethara fights to remain in control, "if I see him again," she says, "I shall kill him. A person like that who so enjoys his hostility is not a creature that deserves to live. Even mindless insects that crawl and fly through darkness treat each other better. They survive; they are not deliberately cruel and do not seek enjoyment of the other's destruction." She then looked at Krelta. "He's escaped, hasn't he?"

Slowly and with much discomfort, Krelta nodded. "I don't know how it happened."

Keethara nodded. "His character is totally foreign to Prandor. He is not of this world. His enjoyment of his hostility and cruelty is beyond comprehension. If I see him," said Keethara, "I will do all that I can to kill him. There are some who do not deserve to live if their sole purpose in life is to inflict pain."

Krelta smiled hastily. "I understand your feelings very well, but—"

She looked intently at Krelta. "I will kill him. And if I die for killing someone who deserves death, then I will die knowing that I spent my life well performing an act of profound kindness to someone so sick and kindness to others who will be rid of a living death."

Grathal looked frightened but said nothing.

Thud-thud-roar roared the volcano. A shock came that almost knocked all of them to the ground. Keethara looked straight ahead. "This whole planet is outraged at him," she said, whispering, "if only the land could rise, form a fist and smash him into a stain."

On their way back to Pantyan, Brundool and Krelta said nothing. Brundool looked out the window. Keethara's right, he thought, Dasdan is *not* of Prandor. Then where? Of Earth? No. Not even Earth people are as vicious and cunning as Dasdan. And yet why is he so familiar? He sighed and looked to his ring then at Krelta. Krelta simply stared straight ahead as though he was in a stupor. When they reached Pantyan, Krelta took a deep breath. "We have one more stop."

"Another victim?"

"Another victim."

They climbed off the transport in the heart of Pantyan and walked to the immense sprawl of the medical center. When they reached the proper floor, they went to a desk, behind which health care professionals monitored instruments and performed other tasks.

"Hello," said a male, "are you well today?"

"How is he?" asked Krelta.

The health professional looked sympathetic. "No news—I'm sorry. His condition is essentially stable as it has been for quite some time."

Brundool looked very puzzled. He knew Krelta was sad—but unsure as to why. Neither of them talked as they walked down the corridor. They then went into a room; in a bed was a child.

"He was beaten by Dasdan as well?" said Brundool.

Krelta nodded. "Gefta—" he closed his eyes. "My child... beaten on his way home from school... has not regained consciousness..." Krelta then went to his knees, arms folded on the bed, head buried in his arms. "My own child—" He sobbed silently.

Brundool opened himself, opened himself... and there it was: no, not the reactions of Gefta, but of Krelta, of being in the city chambers on a bright day in winter—getting the message—*the medical center has requested your presence*—concern, bewilderment! What has happened? His mate, Ponarla? His child, Gefta? he leaves, hurries. Finds Gefta being readied for urgent treatment. Confusion... enforcers have physical description; Gefta was assaulted. Panic! Anger!

Why Gefta? Gefta! Gefta! My little Gefta! Why this? No one deserves this! Revenge! Will find him! Revenge! Capture! Pound fist in his face! Strangle him!

Brundool then envisions the child: Broken arm, fractured skull, blackened eyes; bruised and beaten. Attacker captured by passersby.

Krelta's mate, Ponarla, rushes in, sees Gefta; her face twists in horror; leans to touch Gefta, places a hand, a gentle, trembling hand against the child's cheek; Ponarla's mouth is open, contorted, no sound emerges. She straightens, places her hand to her face, staggers. Krelta rushes to her, supports her; she turns, they hold each other, weeping. Gefta wheeled away for surgery and urgent care.

At the bedside, Brundool places his hand on Krelta's shoulder; Krelta weeps in wrenching sobs and the child sleeps, arms outstretched on covers, eyes closed, scars almost healed.

Brundool looks from Krelta, from Gefta, across the room, to windows, to the spires of the inner city, to the immense, snowy mountains beyond.

Dasdan, Brundool thinks, *Dasdan, I am coming. I am coming for you. In the name of Gefta, Keethara and Saya, Dasdan, Dasdan, I am coming for you.* He concentrated on the ring; it has taken it all in, all of it and it glows an angry, angry red, like boiling blood, like lava. "Dasdan," he says to himself, "maybe if you truly know how it *really* feels to be hurt by you, you will stop hurting others." He stared at the ring, the glowing, angry ring. *Take me to him.* He felt the ring tug, pulling him, like an animal after prey.

Krelta slowly got to his feet. He looked at his child, gripped his hand and sighing, he turned to Brundool. "Have you had enough?"

He wiped his eyes with the back of his hand. "Have you had enough?"

Brundool nodded. He gave Krelta a small blue sphere. "Let it rest in the palm of your hand," said Brundool. "Now face me."

Abruptly, a high pitched whine sounded and a light appeared in the sphere.

"Turn right," said Brundool. The whine decreased, the light did not change. "Now, turn left, slowly." The whine increased, then faded.

Krelta nodded.

"Both light and sound can be adjusted for distance. The light grows brighter with decreasing distance. When I give Dasdan this ring, the pitch will change to a deeper tone and you will know that I have found him. Come immediately."

Krelta nodded again. "I'll also have three others with me and reinforcements nearby, paralleling us some distance away. We will try our best to keep in visual contact of you as well."

"Let us go," said Brundool.

Later that afternoon, outside the Chambers of Administration, Brundool, Krelta and the others met. Krelta gave orders; the hunt was organized and begun.

Brundool walked at a moderate pace, letting the ring take him, lead him. The second sun set, evening came, the city glowed from indirect lighting, in pale blues, greens, and yellows. Brundool walked through the inner city, then down near the long, curved rectangles of warehouses on the River Manthar. It was quiet; no shipments were being loaded or unloaded from mighty ships. The ring glowed red; the pull became stronger. Past the warehouses, over a bridge, in the direction of the Kroyamatan Inter-Cosmos Launchport.

Ah, yes, thought Brundool, *get money, get aboard, get away. Far, far, far away.* A bulky Earth vessel rose silently skyward.

Brundool walked a pathway in a landscaped area along the river. It was dark, and abruptly Brundool was aware that the tugging stopped. He slowed. The ring had changed back to a beautiful, pale white sphere.

He felt someone draw near. Then a gentle voice: "Shouldn't be walking about with such a strange and lovely ring." The someone came up from behind Brundool. "Someone might try to take it from you."

Brundool did not turn. Instead, he stopped, took the ring off and held it out. "I've done you no harm. If you want this ring, take it and leave me in peace."

There was a long, *long* silence.

"Turn around, slowly," came the voice.

Brundool did. And there was Dasdan Yorko: curling blond hair, dark eyes, yellow teeth, the face strangely clean as though too much effort went into looking neat and clean. The lips pulled into a sneer, the nose wrinkled and his manner became contemptuous. He wore a long, maroon robe.

"Well, well, well," said Dasdan. "A trader you are. My, my, my, how impressive."

Brundool glared. "How *dare* you wear the robes of an Opayknon Trader?"

Dasdan smiled. "Gets me what I want. Besides, don't you understand —"
He stopped. "No, give me the ring first, then maybe we'll talk a little more,
yes?"

Saying nothing, Brundool did.

"Thank you," said Dasdan, "now, I'm sure we have much —" He stopped.
A profound look of surprise came over his face and Brundool could feel all
the pain of Saya Kokras, of Keethara, of Krelta; Dasdan became them, became the victim of himself. He fell to his knees and looked up at Brundool
and Brundool stared. Abruptly Brundool backed away, staggered, as though
physically shoved. "Oh, gods!" he whispered. "Oh, gods! It is not possible!"
He turned, stumbled away, only dimly aware of Krelta and the others running, then carrying a non-resistant Dasdan Yorko to a waiting security vehicle.

Krelta ran to Brundool. "Brundool — what is it — what is the matter? What
is wrong?"

Brundool shivered. "Gods! It can't be possible! I — I was thinking all along
that this person Dasdan Yorko must have been miserable — was inflicting
pain because he was hurt, and truly no greater prison is there than such a
prison, for there is no escape if one is convinced that the world only exists to
hurt — but I did not see something..." Brundool shivered again. "I did not see
that one can be imprisoned — and *not know it!* Dasdan did not at all become
sensitized to someone else's pain..." Brundool shook his head. "He wanted
more. I gave him exactly what he wanted. Exactly! He is insane and has utterly no idea that he *is* insane. No idea at all."

Krelta nodded. "That is the worst insanity of all. But..." Krelta regarded
Brundool carefully, "that's not all, is it...?"

Brundool did not look at Krelta. He watched a massive moon rise over
the Pyntar Pasa Mountains, over their tall and ragged summits. He squeezed
his eyes shut and tears welled up, flowed down his cheeks. He shook his
head. "No, no, that's not all —" he whispered.

Krelta nodded. "When we came over, I heard him talking to you as
though he *knew* you...?"

Brundool sighed. Then he spoke, but not just to Krelta. He spoke to the
sky, the night, the moon, the mountains. "Opayknons are regarded as wise,
powerful, strong and kind. What so many *don't* know is how incredibly bru-
tal and violent we were. We almost exterminated ourselves three times before we learned to understand our violence. No self-aware species likes to
know they are mortal. For some reason, we liked it even less. No greater insult to vanity and pride than death." And Brundool stopped and took a deep
breath. It was silent. The moon had risen fully and Brundool stood in the
light as an actor on a stage. "How much time did it take?" he whispered.

"How much time? How many attempts at immortality? How much rage at the knowledge that there exist only three absolutes: birth, life, death. Somehow we survived to finally accept our mortality. But somehow, at times, there are those born who—at some point—can't—don't—won't accept it."

Krelta nodded. "Like Dasdan Yorko?"

Brundool closed his eyes. "Yes." Tears again. "Somehow to love and be loved is not living. To those like Dasdan, to give pain and receive pain—is. And to see that brings so much shame—so much sadness and bitterness and anger for all the time it took to learn, for all the achievements gained and lost, for all the struggle—to gain then to lose and to lose profoundly—and to see it happen—to see someone who has and acts upon the violence that we tried so hard to leave behind—that we still, even now, wrestle with within ourselves—we don't kill such individuals; we send them away, to a colony, to help them with their overwhelming violence that is so reprehensible to us. Sometimes they are cured, sometimes they are not." Brundool hugged himself. A second, smaller moon was rising over the mountains.

"And sometimes they escape?" asked Krelta.

Brundool said nothing.

"And maybe they end up—perhaps on Prandor?"

Brundool shuddered. The small moon rose full now, as though tailing the large one.

Krelta put his hand on Brundool's shoulder. "It must be very, very difficult to see a little bit of Dasdan in yourself."

"Oh, gods," whispered Brundool, "oh, gods." Then silently, he watched the small moon rise.

Photogenic

In the magazine cover photo, they are climbing a trail. "They" are two women, perhaps twenty-five or so, but the picture is taken back a ways: I can't tell if they have crows' feet around the eyes; they are walking up the trail and the sun is coming from the front and left, the right side of their bodies are cast in shadow. One has a cotton tee-shirt on I think, but it looks like the material is finer than that. Secretly, I curse the photographer for not getting a closer view. Surely he knew that this picture might be bought by the magazine, hence distributed widely to many people, including someone like me who is rapidly falling madly in love with these women, but more the first one; she has bronze skin, like a goddess almost, and blonde hair that hides her forehead. She's looking away, away from the scenery and I want to tell her, "No, look over your shoulder, the other way, that's where the wonderful valley is, that is where that mountain ridge is that is frosted by the last snows of winter. But she does not hear me. She keeps walking up that trail, walking right into the white print that reads "Cardiovascular Health". Please be careful, you'll bump your head right into the "C". I am grateful that the letter isn't an "H" or worse, the lower case "g", "j" or "y" that might put an eye out. And what could I do? As an observer, I could only stare with horror if she got injured. If I tried to dial "911", who would believe me? "What?" they might say, "What? A picture of a woman hiker who got injured on a trail somewhere in British Columbia by walking into a lower case "G" and put her eye out? Don't you think you should talk to someone at Harborview? They got crack psych units—a little Haldol—" No, no, I cannot say that, besides, by the time I got this magazine and really considered the situation, much time has already passed, eight months at least—or if the picture was taken a long time ago, who knows? The woman might have had her eye put out for quite some time, years perhaps. Perhaps she has given up on hiking altogether. I hope not. And her shoulder. What about her shoulder? Walking right into the big red "B" of "Back to School In Health." And there is the C in Calcium Ascorbate which looks like it's going to punch her right in the stomach. Perhaps I should call the Canadian Royal Mounted Police, maybe they can help—but it is January, the area must be covered by snow and if the woman died because of injuries of ill-placed writing on the cover, they would have removed the body long, long ago. I hope they are all right. The woman behind the woman with whom I am bonding strongly—I think her features, her face are airbrushed. It's much darker—almost red, actually; she's right behind the first woman. I think her foot has been cut off by the red horizontal banner at the bottom of the page in which bold white letters that spell out, "Special Convention Issue '93". That's it. I don't have to do anything after all. This happened long ago. The woman I am concerned about is either dead or injured—how sad in either case—but perhaps the lettering is a trick to deceive my eyes: maybe it's actually in *back* of the woman whom I adore. She's not walking into the letters after all; as she walks, they must flow behind her. Maybe she *is* safe. Right now, looking at them, it seems they are enjoying themselves out in the sunlight. I just hope that lettering in the upper left, "Country Health" remains suspended and doesn't deflate, dropping on them. Maybe the letters won't drop—maybe they'll just kind of drift down and cover the women in yellow type-goo. I do hope my fears are unfounded. They look like such nice women, walking on that trail; they must be having so much fun, talking about the things that are meaningful to them...

"... oh, Annie," the one in the blue, the one who has the dark face, probably says, "it's so grand to be outside."

Annie. The one who might walk into the letters and hurt her self—her name is Annie.

"Annie," I whisper, "Annie, do be careful—"

Annie smiles and turns but being careful about keeping her balance on that steep trail. "Yes," she says, "it's fun to be out—if only Richard..."

Richard? Richard? My heart hardens—Richard? I didn't know—

"Ah," says the one in back, "you're better off done with him."

"I suppose." She sighs, stops and looks around.

I smile. Perhaps I am in luck after all.

Annie then frowns. "Sheila, do you believe in spirits?"

Sheila stops, looks at Annie, her look is hard to decipher. Is she thinking Annie is a bit strange? Sheila, I think, Sheila, don't be so quick to judge. Perhaps she has something important to say. Keep an open mind.

"I don't know," says Annie, "it's just that right now, I kind of feel like we're being
watched—"

I back away from the photograph. How could they know? How could they *possibly* know?

"Like right now—I feel like something—someone cares for me, is concerned for me—you know?"

"Like a god—" says Sheila, adjusting her backpack, "a force, a being—?"

"Don't know," says Annie. "It feels nice in a way but kind of smothering—"

I get up out of my chair and back up a few feet. I stare at the magazine cover, to the other words on it, "Shark Cartilage, Bee Pollen, Ginkgo" and the white rectangle with the picture of a thistle in it and the pink lettering inside the rectangle below the flower that says "Milk Thistle" and I wonder, I wonder if all health magazines are this strange and unsettling. Maybe I should dash over and quickly turn the page and find something else, maybe an article that has no pictures, something about Goldenseal with Parthenium extract.

"Don't get me wrong, Sheila," I hear Annie say distantly; I sneak up closer to the cover so I can hear better. "It's nice to be cared for—I don't know—it's just strange."

Sheila smiles. "Maybe you've been eating too many spirulina bars; maybe you need some bee pollen; maybe your Yang did a drive-by shooting on your Yin." Then she snickers. "Or maybe your bra's too tight."

Maybe it is. I can't tell. But both women laugh.

"Well," Annie says, "if it is a spirit. I'm glad it's there—even a somewhat smothering spirit—it's just nice to know that there is more to reality than we can ever imagine—"

But Sheila is a realist, like an American Empiricalist of the worst ilk; if it can't be seen it doesn't exist. "I dunno," she says. "Your electrolytes may be out of whack. When did you last have something to drink?"

And Annie just shakes her head. "Say something," I whisper. "Annie, *say* something. Don't let her get away with that. You're right. Reality is far vaster, more subtle, more wonderful, more insane than we can *possibly* imagine."

But Annie says nothing and they resume hiking, on past the letters (such a relief; the letters go behind them) and then out of the photo, leaving the letters, the valley; they go off the page and the sound of their voices fades, fades, fades away, leaving only the sigh of the wind and the aching sweet smell of pine.

The Hat

Now, it has to be said that there was a hat, a very nice, grey, sporty hat with a little red feather in the band and it was indeed a grand little hat that was worn by Mr. Keen, a banker of the most proper sort in this type of town of S, by the mountains, by the sea. And whenever Mr. Keen wore that hat about the stores, about the bank, oh, such a special person he became. Oh, indeed. This gentleman of age fifty-five almost seemed to become somehow a different person when he put on that hat, yes. His lips would assume a thin line of direct purposefulness, his eyes would narrow down and yes, he would see everything that he needed to see as he went his way through the town of S. by the mountains, by the sea. He once remarked to Elizabeth Daniels in New Accounts that he didn't know what it was about that hat, "But as soon as I saw it in my travels in the country of X, I knew I had to have it. Just *had* to have it!"

Elizabeth, age twenty-three with long brown hair and oh, so big and round eyes, dark as the land on a cloudy day, said, "Oh, my, Mr. Keen, such a fine hat it is, yes it is. It must have cost you a small fortune—"

"Well," said Mr. Keen, "it did. It most certainly did. But it was worth it— oh, when I put this on, nothing seems to ever go wrong. A lucky hat it is. It must be a lucky hat."

"Indeed," Elizabeth smiled knowingly, as if she shared some secret with the wily fates beyond, above our everyday clockwork routine of, say, reading the paper as if that was the only reality that really was, "Well, I heard about your good news," she said, "about landing that Murchanson Account for the bank—"

Mr. Keen laughed and put a hand on his ample stomach and said, "It never fails, it must be the hat. Ever since I've had that hat things have gone so well."

But that afternoon, on this particular day that this story takes place, a wind of all winds was brewing, moving, heavy, vast and strong across the sea, toward the town of S, by the mountains by the sea. The wind, it came, it roared against the mountains, and then slammed into the lands, it curled and pushed into the coves; eddied and swirled around, across the land and like a vast and moving hand, along with all else that it was doing, it flipped off Mr. Keen's hat when he came out for lunch. Just like that, Mr. Keen's hat was lifted by that windy hand that also had lofted shopping bags, papers and such into the air.

Mr. Keen, after making futile grabs and a frantic run, stood and yelled, "Come back!" but the hat was gone. High, high into the air and then the wind—it was as though a lethargy suddenly set in and it abruptly dissipated—the hat dropped—right at the feet of Sid McClure, an ancient person with alcohol for memory and he picked up the hat and said, "Whu." He smiled. "Wha," he said and placed it on his head and for some strange reason that he could not really understand, a memory appeared, somehow, some way, so long ago and he saw himself walking on a beach up in Alaska with a woman whom he adored, saying to her, as they stared out across the bay to the mountains, blue and mighty, icy, high, "You just watch, ol' Sid here, he's gonna make something of himself! Oh, I'll head down to S and get a job in the port unloading ships—they need all the help they can get."

He remembered how Molly smiled at him with a playful softness in her eyes.

"Yes," he said, "get some money ahead, get that nice place right in town, looks over the bay toward a place called Queen Anne—oh, I'll make me a bundle there and then I'll send for you."

And Molly smiled and that playful look became more that of love and she ran her hand down his arm, over the red flannel, down to where it was rolled up revealing the blue tattoo on his forearm, a tattoo of a rose. Then he placed his arm around her and that said it all, in the amber rays of setting sun, on the beach with the whisper of the waves and the *scree* cry of circling hawk, that embrace said it all and—Sid McClure sat down on a bench, hands up to his eyes, mind leached by alcohol and "Why's"—for some reason he could not comprehend, then took the hat off and flung it as far as he could and that wonderful hat then came to rest on the sidewalk. A minute later it was picked up by Sophia Winter, fur-dressed woman extraordinaire, in blue silk dress and high heels. With her blue eyes and cheekbones (delicate as if created of the most delicate china in the world) she appeared to be a refined and lovely lady, yes, and she stopped and looked and why—even she could not say—but she picked the hat up and thought, *Oh, my, such a nice hat indeed. Some wealthy gentleman lost something very, very nice; what a shame.* And she inspected it closely as she walked those breezy streets in the town of S She moved like a cat, sedate and smooth with elegance of step and coolness of look as if everything around her was on display for her to buy with her Mastercharge and at the window of the Bon, she glanced down and gazing at the red feather, looked puzzled and going to the square, sat on a bench in the sunshine of the April afternoon and thought, *Somehow this is familiar but I don't know* – She smiled at a foolish notion, *I wonder how I'd look* – *I know it is fashionable in some circles these days to wear such* –

She smiled and put it on –

Crash! " – you God damn whore!"

" – Daddy – " little Sophia cried, "don't – don't hit Mommy – "

"'Don't hit Mommy –'" her father said, imitating her wailing voice, "Go to your room, this ain't any of your affair – "

And in his distraction, Sophia's mother, tall and thin with features as though delicate as glass, she struck her husband with a skillet black and heavy as his soul and he crashed to the ground and Sophia stared with horror, staring at her fallen father and who knows why but she then focused to the coat tree, to his hat with the little rust-colored feather in the band –

Slowly Sophia took off the hat and bedazzled by she knew not what, looked off to the sun. Blinded by the light, she slowly stood and walking into the blazing light she thought, *I had put that away, I was done with that, I was done with that* – and her eyes burned and something way, way down deep, something finely cut and chiseled and oh, so delicate, shattered once again and her heart ached from that ancient pain and all her furs and jewels and elegance somehow transformed into a demon with a shrieking laugh that beckoned her into that blazing sun.

And on the bench the hat sat, grey, a very nice hat indeed and little Jeremy Smith, age seven and a half, right then, in the square, he was a pirate, yes he was, and the city was his ship, bound toward some southern land. "Avast!" he yelled to his crew, the crowd in the square, but to no one in particular. "Avast!" he yelled again, "Prepare to board that coming ship!" And in his mind, the buildings they were sails, and the city square, it rocked and pitched in foaming sea and then Jeremy saw the hat and in his captain mind, thought, *Yes! For me!* and grabbing it, not concerned of fit or not, continued on, still piloting his mighty ship, in that vast and roiling sea.

Charles and the Protostar

Though Charles Broder sat for endless hours staring out the window, he was not exactly catatonic; he could change his clothes and eat but had to be led about, and talking with him was impossible. It had been that way for the five days he had been on the ward. He was preoccupied; his mind was elsewhere and the staff at Bay Heights Mental Hospital called him schizophrenic. He sat. And he stared. The world went on around him, but he reacted as though he did not see it.

But he did see. And he saw very well. He looked inside himself and watched. And listened.

It was dark inside Charles. So very, very dark. "I am alone," he whispered to himself. "Am I the only one here? Just me? Is there no one else? Please! Please — anyone? Is there anyone to hear me?"

Finally one day, Charles thought he heard something. "Charles? Charles? Can you hear me?"

Charles listened, suddenly intent. Had he heard something that was not there? For it sounded like the wind blowing over grass or water. Charles listened. He peered into the blackness and he listened. He heard nothing. Bitter, he fell back into himself and stared glumly at the darkness.

Charles' parents came up to visit him. Mechanically, Charles looked at them. Mr. Broder slapped his son on the shoulders. "How's my boy doin'?" Charles did not respond. Mr. Broder frowned. He was a husky, thick man with large hands and wearing a ring with a large red stone on one finger of his right hand. On the thick wrist of his left hand he wore a watch; the band was silver and the sunlight coming in the day room window shone on the band, forming a miniature sunburst. Charles looked at the brilliance and slowly blinked. Uneasily, Mr. Broder took off his coat. "Everyone has been askin' about you. The coach is more than willing to let you try out for the team again — but hey..." and he leaned close to Charles, "ya gotta cut down on the book work a little. I know you can do it, Tiger."

Mrs. Broder gave a warning look at her husband. Then, as if preoccupied, she patted the fur piece that draped around her neck and shoulders. Her grey eyes showed concern and worry. She suddenly smiled. "Oh," she said and *she* leaned over as though sharing some gossip, "I talked to your teachers. They understand. You're still in the honors program. Isn't that wonderful?"

Charles turned away and looked out the window again. It was late afternoon and the sun, low in the sky, turned Charles' eyes green and deep, like pools of translucent jade.

Mr. and Mrs. Broder exchanged angry looks; the covert messages flashed back and forth: *Why did you have to mention football? Why did you mention school? It's your fault; he'll never get better. Damn you.*

Mrs. Broder bit her lip. "We'll be back tomorrow. Take care." Mrs. Broder leaned and kissed Charles on the cheek. Mr. Broder ruffled Charles' hair. They left the room. Charles did not turn to see them go. The attendant came in a few minutes later, helped Charles to his feet, and took him to dinner.

That night, Charles lay in bed, eyes open, staring into the darkness, staring into himself. "Charles...?"

Charles stiffened.

"Charles...?"

Charles swallowed. "Yes," he said, "yes—I hear you. Who are you?"

"I am one like you. Look around in yourself. Do you see me?"

Charles looked. At first he saw nothing. The darkness in himself was as indistinguishable as the darkness outside himself. It suddenly occurred to him that he was without boundaries. There was no separateness from the darkness within and the darkness without.

"Do you see me, Charles?"

Charles looked inside himself. Hard. Hard. He blinked his inner eyes. There was something. Something very, very faint—a wisp of a lighter darkness, a strand of darker fog. "Yes," said Charles, "yes, yes. What is it?"

"That's me, Charles."

"But what are you?"

"A protostar."

"Protostar? Protostar? What is a protostar?"

"A stellar fetus, Charles. The mating of atoms, the accumulation of matter, the gathering of darkness into light. What are you, Charles?"

Charles shook his head. "I don't know. Oh, God, *I don't know!*"

The protostar then spoke with a profound gentleness. "Have faith, Charles, have faith. For I can see you. You appear to me as I appear to you, a small, ill-formed island of dark grey. But you have a voice, Charles, you have a voice. All you need is faith in that voice."

The protostar became quiet. Charles blinked his inner eyes again, wondering if, by doing so, the protostar would vanish. It did not.

* * *

The next day, the social worker, Andrea, a short, blonde, and usually bright and sparkling woman, came into the nursing office and, with frustration and exhaustion, collapsed into a chair. The medical student, Mark, a rather lean fellow with glasses and a taste for red ties, glanced up from reading a chart. "What's going on with you?" he asked. "Micro-psychotic break?" He grinned.

Andrea sneered. "Shove it." She closed her eyes. "That does it," she finally said, "That does it." She opened her eyes. "I hate to do it, but Mr. and Mrs. Broder are going to *have* to be restricted from the ward. You have any idea what kind of trips they're laying on Charles? Do you have *any* idea?"

Mark took off his glasses and waited.

"Father wanted Charles to be on the high school football team. Mother doesn't want Charles to play football. She wants him taking all honors courses. So, to please father, Charles tried to make the football team but because he was trying to please mother, he had to study—and to study he had to miss some football practice, which meant he did not get on the team—and because he tried out for football, he couldn't study as much, which meant that he got failing grades in his courses—which means that Charles probably feels he's an utter failure."

Mark sighed. "Would seem to me that Charles is a victim of stereo rejection."

"Oh, yes," said Andrea, sticking the end of a pencil between her teeth. "It's that; it's also confusion between a feeling and one's personality: Charles *feels* like a failure, therefore believes himself to *be* a failure therefore *acts* like one. It makes as much sense as saying, 'I have an upset stomach, therefore my entire personality is an upset stomach.' But with Charles, there's that but also something a little different going on."

Mark cleaned his glasses with his tie and put them back on.

Andrea spoke again. "Mommy and daddy are rejecting each other and doing it through Charles."

Mark just shook his head. "Ouch."

* * *

Night again.
"Charles?"

Charles looked about. There. There it was. The protostar. A little brighter. "Hello," said Charles. "It's easier to see you tonight." He paused. "What's it like being a protostar?"

The protostar was stronger, its sigh was audible across the great distance. "Difficult, Charles, difficult. Forming in darkness. Forming out of darkness. It's so hard, so very, very difficult and it takes so long. And just when I think it seems so impossible, I look around and I see where I am now. And I look to the future and see how far there is to go. But I'm growing, Charles, I'm growing, slowly, slowly." The protostar paused. "I see you more clearly, Charles, you, too, are gathering your form from darkness."

"I am?"

"Yes, yes, I even hear it in your voice. You're stronger."

And Charles thought for a minute and suddenly realized his thinking *was* clearer. "I do feel better," Charles replied. But then there was sadness in his voice, "but what if..."

"Faith," replied the protostar, "faith in the act of creating yourself."

But the sadness was still in Charles' voice. "I can't. I can't! I feel like such a failure. My life is a failure! I can do nothing! Nothing! Nothing!"

Suddenly the voice of the protostar was very far away. "Charles.... Charles... you're fading... fading... darkness..."

"My parents hate me..."

"... darkness, Charles, darkness, darkness."

Suddenly Charles caught himself. "Protostar, protostar — don't go away — please don't go away..."

"I must, Charles, I must. You're turning into a darkness darker than space; you're becoming a massive black star radiating unbelievable coldness and darkness and I'll not let you destroy me. I have faith in the light and the warmth; you have faith in the dark and the cold. No, Charles, no, no, no..."

Inside himself, Charles watched the protostar fade until he could no longer see it. Again he was alone. But not the same. The staff noticed it. Andrea commented to Mark, "Something is going on with him. He no longer stares out the window but he looks down — like he's looking at himself."

"Does that mean he's improved?"

Andrea shook her head. "I wish I knew."

And Charles sat, looking down and in his mind he whispered over and over again, "Protostar? Protostar? Where are you?"

Finally, an answer. "...Charles...?"

"I'm sorry, Protostar..."

"Don't be sorry for what you do to me. Be sorry for what you do to yourself." There was a long, long pause. "You're better."

"How can you tell?"

"You're brighter."

"You're brighter also."

"I know. I'm revolving now, faster, faster, gathering myself about. I grow in strength and as I become assured of that growth, I seem to be able to gather even more atoms, more and more and I keep growing, the temperature within me rises, I become warmer, denser, my gravity increases, I spin faster and attract even more material and the process keeps on until my birth."

Charles thought for a minute. "Your birth? You're already born, aren't you?"

"I know what I am to be. Physically, I'm still a stellar fetus. When I turn into a sun, I will truly be born; the physical and the potential will merge and become real. And Charles, that's what you're going to have to do. You have to be born, too."

"I don't understand," Charles said, "I don't understand at all. I've been born."

"Physically, but not *psychologically.* Do you see the difference? Physically you exist, but who are you? What are you to be? I *know* what I am to be—a sun. I am going to be born! I believe in the process that is occurring within me. I am patient for I know the process takes time. I know the change will occur—my potential will become actual—and when it does, I shall be a star. I'll be born."

"What has that to do with me?"

"Everything! Believe in yourself, Charles. Love yourself. Trust yourself. Believe in your potential! Your worth! That's what I mean by being born! Believe in *you!*"

Charles felt incalculable despair. "How?" He shook his head. "How? How? *How?*"

"The same way I have done it. I have looked at myself and doing so, defined myself. I am a protostar. I shall be a sun. What are you, Charles? What are you?"

* * *

When Andrea and Mark walked out of the day room, they exchanged puzzled glances. They stopped in the hallway, beyond the doorway so that they could not be heard nor seen by Charles.

Andrea leaned against the wall and sighed. "This work can be so hard. I wish he could *talk!*"

Mark frowned. "It's so obvious that something is happening. I can't help but feel that he's perplexed..."

"Yeah," Andrea nodded quickly, "yeah, like he's really puzzled about something..."

Mark shrugged, took off his glasses and cleaned them. "At least he's showing some emotion—as far as I'm concerned, it's the best he's looked since he's been here." He put his glasses back on.

Andrea again nodded. "Oh, yeah, I agree. But what is changing? What the hell is he going through? What's happening? That's what's so frustrating. We don't know."

Mark smiled. "I thought psychiatry had all this stuff figured out."

"How I wish," she laughed, "how I wish." She pushed herself away from the wall and they both walked down the hallway to the office.

* * *

That night, Charles lay in bed.

"You're looking much brighter, Charles."

"Been thinking." For the first time in a long, long time, Charles laughed. "Gathering light from the darkness. How are you doing?"

"My time draws near. Very, very near. A little more time, a little more substance. It is difficult to wait; I am eager to be born. I want to be a sun. And you, Charles. And you. You, too, can be a sun. Believe in yourself, Charles, believe, believe, *believe* in yourself."

Charles did not answer, but felt reassured. And as he lay in bed, he became suddenly aware of the pressure of the covers; slowly he rubbed his hand on them and felt the texture. He placed his hand on the wall and felt the smooth coolness of it.

The next day he was moving about the ward. He looked about himself in the dayroom; to the blue-green carpet, the pictures on the wall, the wall shelf cluttered with books, games, music and puzzles and he constantly touched things: chairs, tables. He stopped and listened. Someone was playing Bob Dylan's *Ballad of a Thin Man*. He smiled. He liked the music. The meaning of the words escaped him but he liked the song.

Often he would stop and simply look about with an expression of surprise. It was as though the world about him was a sudden occurrence; that it had just happened and he was only now aware of it.

Finally he went to the window. With fascination, he looked out over Seattle; he watched the water of Puget Sound sparkle, he stared at the Olympic Mountains and studied their snowy ruggedness. He looked to the partly-clouded sky and was as amazed to see the sky blue as he was fascinated to see the seeming impossibility of such bulky and heavy-looking clouds— floating. In disbelief, he watched the clouds move and saw the intensity and pattern of sunlight change over the city, the water, the mountains. Once he glanced to the sun and, before he sneezed, found himself amazed that it was so white and bright.

Mark and Andrea watched all this—utterly mystified. "Well," Andrea said, "what can you say?" She watched a while longer, then turning to Mark said, "Hey, look. Will you call up Charles' parents? They're going on a two week vacation the day after tomorrow and before they go, we need to get ourselves, Charles and his parents together to decide what Charles is going to do when he leaves the hospital."

Mark made a note in a little memo book which he kept in his breast pocket. "Will do," he said.

* * *

Again, that night Charles listened and watched. The protostar was now very bright and it spoke with eagerness. "My time comes, Charles. I feel it. I feel it."

Charles was excited. "Your birth? You are going to be born?"

"Yes, yes—it's coming—deep within—the conversion is taking place—the nuclear fires are transforming—yes, yes, the heat, it's coming—yes—yes—almost—ah! Now! Now! Ah! Ah! AHHHHEEEEIIIIII—" Then an explosion of light—bright, intense, white, white, burning, burning white. And slowly it faded, faded, and there, there, still surrounded by the whiteness and heat of birth—a new star, a new sun and a voice: "I am! I am a sun! My photons race from me carrying the message of my new being to the entire universe! From the darkness I have come! I have gathered the darkness and turned it into heat and light! Oh, galaxies! The power! The beauty! Oh, galaxies, galaxies, galaxies! My birth! My being!"

Charles watched the white fires of the sun dance and he felt the heat and the joy and his own tears at seeing the stunning beauty and elegance of being. "Oh, galaxies!" he heard the sun sing, "There's never been one just like me before; I am unique in my own awareness! My own fire burns between the night of what was before me and the night that shall come after me! And for now—this moment! This heat! To *truly* be what I have waited and worked and wanted to be! I have arrived!" And then, softly, softly, gently as wind on a kitten's fur, "And now, Charles, now, now *you!*"

Charles could say nothing. But within him he felt resolve and a sudden power. "Yes," he whispered, "yes, yes. Oh, yes!"

* * *

The family conference was at eleven o'clock the next day. Mr. and Mrs. Broder were ushered into the conference room by Mark and Andrea.

Mr. Broder walked over to Charles and presented him with a stack of sports and football magazines. "Here, son; your mother and I had quite a tussle over whether or not I should bring them, but I felt that while you were up here, you might want to read up on plays and positions—it will help you when you try for the team when you get out."

Charles held the magazines. He looked at them as though they were utterly alien. And as he looked at them, something within him moved—the conversion—the melting—the heat!

His mother then gave him his school books, stacking them neatly on top of the sports magazines. "I don't know if you're going to have time to play much football, dear," she said, "I signed you up for all honors classes next quarter and brought your books so that you might begin studying."

Charles looked at the books—what were they? And something within him—something boomed and thudded and shrieked and atoms were stripped and the sudden heat was intense. Charles shook his head. He handed the magazines back to his father. "I..." It came out a squeak. He had not used his vocal cords for several weeks and his voice seemed strange to him. He took a deep breath and began again. "I *hate* football."

The melting! The fusion! The intense, frightening, burning light and the heat! The heat! *The heat!*

"And I *hate* school!" He handed the books back to his mother. Suddenly, within him—a blinding light, brilliant and searing! He closed his eyes and, looking into himself, saw no darkness and it was done. Within himself he heard a voice, "Ah, Charles, Charles! You burn with the light of a billion stars! You are a sun! You are born! We are brothers in being, sisters in light! Ah, Charles, Charles, Charles, such shining, brilliant beauty!"

"Oh, God," Charles replied, "the heat, the heat, the beautiful, beautiful heat. And all around me, all within me, light, light, light!"

Charles stood in the conference room and smiled. Mark and Andrea looked at each other with profound surprise and awe. Charles' parents looked utterly devastated. And they all stared at Charles and no one, no one could understand that strange and beautiful light, burning, burning, in his eyes.

New Patient Interview

Harborheights Hospital Psychiatric Inpatient
Service Bruce Taylor, Interviewer

Form 747: *Identification and Problem List*

Patient: Clark Kent (also known as Superman)

Problem List:
1) Possible delusions
(Patient claims he's Superman. This interviewer laughed when patient said that. Mr. Kent then asked me to remove my watch. Upon doing so, patient then stared at the watch. It melted ($234.00 Omega). If this gentleman wants to claim he's Superman, I'm not going to argue.)
2) Support System
(Mr. Kent refuses all visitors except for a Mr. Perry White and Lois Lane.)
3) Diagnosis
Adjustment Reaction to Old Age/Possible Psychotic Depression or ?
4) Disposition
Unknown at this time

Form DC-10: *Record of Valuables and Clothing*
One Timex watch
One boy scout knife
Grey coat, hat, pants, white shirt, black tie, belt, shoes
Underwear: red cape, blue/red costume with large "S" on front of tunic (costume badly worn and frayed)
Red (badly scuffed) shin-high boots

Form 312: *Observation of Patient*

Elderly white male in frayed and torn, red and blue Superman costume. Patient claims to be Superman. Looks confused, sits forward on chair, obviously tense and anxious.

Sensorium:
Date: "October, 1954"
Place: "Metropolis"
President: "I like Ike"
Assessment: Not very well oriented.

Concerns: "...fighting for truth, justice and the American way."
Assessment: Does not understand personal limits of responsibility. Delusions of Grandeur (I must save world to feel worthwhile).

Form 98155: Harborheights Mental Health Clinical Data

I. *Chief Complaint – Patient's Stated Reason for Seeking Help*
Brought in by Seattle Police for disrobing in phone booth and then trying to leap over a building in a single bound.

II. *Present Life Situations*
A. Describe Relationships with Significant Others
Has good relationships with Lois Lane, Jimmy Olsen, Lana Lang, Perry White (former editor of *Daily Planet* in Metropolis). Had warm, close relationship with foster parents in Smallville. Biological parents allegedly killed when home planet, Krypton, exploded.

B. Housing
Apartment by self on Skid Road

C. Education: Describe Learning Deficits and/or Strengths
12th grade, Smallville ("I was good in sports, journalism, astronomy.") Might have had some college (patient could not remember). Seems to have ability to learn quickly.

D. Past and Present Employment and Economic Status
Was mild mannered newspaper reporter for *Daily Planet* paper in Metropolis. Has been retired for last 18 years. On welfare, presently. Seems to have had no difficulty surviving up to now.

E. Social and Societal Activities

Spends some time with Lois Lane at Golden Age Villa. Plays checkers with former editor Perry White at Happy Time Nursing Home. Says that, until last five months, "flew around the country" and used to "occasionally tour the galaxy."

III. *Past History*

A. Significant Developmental History (Early Family, Childhood and Adolescent Problems)

Allegedly was born on Planet Krypton. Was sent to earth at age one month because Krypton was going to explode. Mr. and Mrs. Kent found baby in wreckage of rocket and discovered baby had "super powers". Gave the child a double identity: Clark Kent and "Super(baby)(boy)(adolescent)(man)". Even though it would seem that the child would grow up in constant role conflict and identity crises, he apparently adjusted to the problem and was able to work for the *Daily Planet* newspaper. Said to have habit of jumping into phone booths and changing clothes (exhibitionistic tendencies). In childhood, was very attached to a dog, Krypto. Nature of attachment seems questionable.

B. Family History — Medical and Psychiatric

Biological parents — little known.

Client claims that biological father "was great scientist, Jor-el, on Krypton. Mother was housewife." Foster parents are dead. Father died of heart attack. Mother of "old age". No psychiatric histories.

C. Past and Current Medical History — List Major Illnesses Operations and Hospitalizations

Perfect health.

D. Allergies

Kryptonite.

IV. *Review of Systems* — Sleep Disturbance, Weight Loss, Sexual Problems, etc.

Sleep: 2 to 3 hours a night for last five months.

Weight Loss: Twenty pound weight loss.

Sexual: "Havin' a bad time gettin' it up. Guess I'm not a super-stud any more."

V. *Mental Status*

A. Appearance and Behavior

Unkempt and disorganized. Overall affect is depressed.

B. Speech and Communication — Coherence, Pace, Organization

Varies between totally disorganized to the obsessional. For example: "Faster than a speeding bullet! More powerful than a locomotive! Able to leap tall buildings in a single bound!" (Patient then stood and pointed) "Look! Up in the sky! It's a bird! It's a plane! No! It's SUPERMAN!" (Patient then leaped through glass window in admitting office. He snagged his cape and tripped. Was more cooperative afterwards.)

C. Emotion/Affect — Anxious, Depressed, Elated, etc.
Labile — very quickly changing.
Impulsive. (See above).

D. Special and/or Unusual Perception, Experiences, and Preoccupations

Hallucinations ("I can see through your pants. You're wearing purple boxer shorts with yellow flowers. You a queer?" He was right about the underwear. Coincidence?)

Suicidal (Said that he tried to commit suicide but "my superskin busts razor blades.")

Obsessions ("I have this thing with phone booths.")

Special Fears ("I'm scared of old age.")

E. Sensorium and Intellectual Status — Secondary Evaluation; Orientation and Level of Consciousness

Question: "What state is this?"

Answer: "I don't know. Alberta?"

Question: "When did the Viet Nam War end?"

Answer: "I didn't know it began! Was it a good war? I'm always glad when we win..."

Question: "Name a recent great American."

Answer: "Joe McCarthy."

Ability to Abstract: Similarities and/or Proverbs.

Question: "What does this mean: 'A rolling stone gathers no moss'."

Answer: "Gotta keep flying or be grounded."

Question: "How are apples and oranges alike?"

Answer: "I can crush both in my fists with equal ease."

Question: "What does 'Water over the dam' mean?"

Answer: "It means a disaster! This is a job that calls for SUPERMAN!"

Superman jumped up, ran out the door, became confused and ran into woman's bathroom where a paranoid schizophrenic clobbered him with a plumber's helper. A dazed Superman was led back to his room.

VI. *History and Summary of Present Problems*

Basic problem seems to revolve around loss of self-esteem due largely to onset of old age and subsequent decrease in super powers which has resulted in depression.

Patient is bright (though confused). Should present few problems in learning new skills. Main problem will be dispositional. No one is exactly certain how strong he is. It seems that he cannot fly anymore (which further increases depression and feeling of failure and loss of "hero image") however, his strength must be taken into account.

In regard to his stay at Harborheights, it seems that supportive therapy is the key.

He needs to be told that he is still a capable person and that, for his numerous good deeds, the world will always be grateful.

It seems also wise to avoid any confrontive therapy. Should be started off on a high dose of medication in order for us to combat not only his confusion but a possible management problem.

Plan: Orientation, Medication, Evaluation, Discharge to safe environment.

Form 1040: Psychiatric Inpatient Service Admitting Orders

A. Should Commitment Officer be called if patient wishes to leave? Yes; may need Seattle Police and U.S. Army as well.

B. Will this patient require restraints? Possibly, but without Kryptonite, doubtful how useful restraints would be.

C. What medications are to be used? Thorazine, 1000 mg. every 4 hours.

D. Strong man. If acts out or becomes violent and there is no Kryptonite available, strongly suggest hospital be evacuated.

Sub. "I can fly! Look at me! Faster than a speeding bullet!"

Obj. Superman, during morning group, was telling about himself. Became agitated when confronted by one of the other patients that he (Superman) was no longer as super as he thought he was. Superman jumped up, broke a chair into splinters with one hand and then made a leap for the windows. He knocked himself unconscious. About 25 square feet of the wall was knocked out. Superman was taken to seclusion and after becoming conscious, was given medication by mouth (injections won't work; needles don't pierce skin). He then wept.

Asses. Self-esteem very touchy subject. Suggest we concentrate on building up his ego and not confronting him.

Plan. Supportive therapy. Avoid agitation. Locate Kryptonite—may be only way to manage him.

Bruce Taylor
Primary Therapist
12/21

S. "You think you can lock me into seclusion? I'm Superman! More powerful than a locomotive. Able to leap tall buildings in a single bound!"

O. Superman was put into seclusion after using his super breath to blow the clothes off Ms. Chestly, Nursing Supervisor, and Dr. Jetlaag, chief of psychiatric Services for Harborheights, San Martin Hospital, Brazil and Queens Hospital, Perth, Australia. After Superman was put into seclusion, and the door locked, he laughed, turned around, dropped his trunks and suddenly passed a great deal of gas which blew the door off its hinges.

A. I think we're going to have problems.

P. Use scan line to call Smithsonian or *National Geographic* – we need to locate some Kryptonite—fast.

Bruce Taylor
Primary Therapist
12-22

S. "I always have liked to help people."

O. Superman was using his unique vision to light patients' cigars and cigarettes.

A. Encourage constructive use of super powers. He seems to like the positive response. Help him see that any type of destructive behavior is not to his benefit.

P. Give positive feedback whenever he uses super powers appropriately.

Brucia Talorez,
RN
12-23

S. "It's tough gettin' old, you know? It really hurts. Can't fly worth shit now. Every day I get weaker. What a God damn drag. And I can't even kill myself because I'm indestructible! Wish I were young again."

O. Sitting in day room. Sad as he discussed his problems. Looked frustrated when he talked about inability to kill self. Body posture was forward, stooped.

A. Looks about the same. Has not been violent in last couple of days. Seems under good control. Certainly his depression has real roots. Encourage talking; it seems to help him a great deal. Discourage suicidal ruminations; since he can't harm himself, there's little point in talking about it, other than pointing out that suicidal talk, as well as suicide itself, is, generally speaking, somewhat self-defeating.

P. Continue to talk with him. Incidentally, Primary Therapist was contacted by *National Geographic*. Kryptonite has been located. Being flown in; Should be here tomorrow.

Dr. B. Tai-Lor
Attending Psychiatrist
12-24

S. "What a great book!"
O. Sitting in room, reading *Conscience of a Conservative*.
A. Status quo.
P. Try to keep more involved with others; has tendency to withdraw and judgement becomes impaired.

Bruce Taylor
Primary Therapist
12-26

S. "I was a great reporter for the *Daily Planet*. Wanna see how fast I can type up a story?"
O. Smiling, sitting at keyboard.
A. Does not recognize his own strength. Typed so hard and fast that the keyboard and table melted ($600.00). Superman was appropriately apologetic.
P. Do not allow Superman to demonstrate typing ability.

Brucia Talorez,

RN
12-27

S. "I'm going to leave, dammit!"

O. Superman began going for the door. Stopped when he saw I was holding crystal of Kryptonite.

A. Kryptonite controls Superman better than medication. Became immediately docile when confronted with the mineral.

P. Use Kryptonite whenever Superman becomes agitated. It's in the medicine cupboard next to the milk of magnesia and ExLax.

Bruce Taylor
Primary Therapist
12-28

S. "No great chance at anything anymore. Nobody wants me. Nobody cares. I used to be a supersuccess—now I'm a superfailure. I'm sorry I'm crying—I realize men aren't supposed to cry but God damn it, I just can't help it."

O. Sitting in day room, crying.

A. Crying becoming more infrequent. Gradual overall improvement. Earlier today was playing ping pong with Dr. F. B. Skinny. Game came to end when Superman hit ball so hard that it bounced off Dr. Skinny's forehead.

The Dr., startled, stumbled backwards into upright ashtray, fell, and was knocked unconscious. (Dr. came to a few minutes later; when asked if he was hurt, he said, "I think I'll stick to pigeons.")

P. Needs to be with people who can appreciate his powers.

Brucia Talorez,
RN
12-28

S. "It used to be so great looking down and seeing people pointing up at me. Oh, the thrill of it! I could always hear them yelling, 'Look, up in the sky.' Of course, when I flew over South America or Africa, I had to fly pretty high to dodge the bricks and bottles and I guess it was just as well that I couldn't hear what they were saying but it sure hurt my feelings. Did you know that there are some people in the world who don't like America? How can there be so much communism?"

O. Showing amazement, surprise, concern. Good affect.

A. Self-esteem still very touchy subject. Wants to be liked and loved by everybody and seems to not understand that others don't think and feel about issues the way he does. Very sensitive to rejection. Extremely insecure.

P. May have to be confronted with fact there are some people in the world who don't want or need his help and that such rejection doesn't necessarily imply that he is not worthy.

Dr. B. Tai-Lor,
12-29

S. "The Circus? You can get me into a circus? Who? What? When? Where? Why?"

O. Eager. Grinning. Sitting forward in chair, pulling on end of cape.

A. Contacted Ringling Bros, and Barnum-Bailey circus. They were most interested in giving Superman a job and title of Star Attraction. Superman seemed somewhat interested.

P. Arrange for discharge.

Bruce Taylor
Primary Therapist
12-29

S. "Superman! I'm a Superman again! Oh, God! I can hear it now —'Look! Up on the highwire! It's a clown! It's an acrobat! No! It's SUPERMAN!' Thank you! Thank you! Thank you!"

O. Smiling, laughing, rubbing hands together, jumping up and down, punching holes in floor with feet.

A. Seems pleased.

P. Discharge as soon as possible to circus.

Brucia Talorez,
RN
12-30

S. "Whoops!"

O. Superman, as he ran out the door at discharge, snagged cape on door lock and yanked door off hinges. At that point, all the patients ran off the unit.

A. Seemed somewhat eager to leave.

P. Total cost of damage done to Harborheights Hospital by Superman: $41,704.63. Send bill to Ringling Bros, and Barnum-Bailey Circus.

Dr. B. Tai-Lor
Attending Psychaitrist.

One Day at Glasnost

Mr. Gorbachev, dressed in a pink ballerina *tutu* dances with the spider to the music of *Swan Lake*. I sit in the bleachers, along with Thomas Jefferson, Alexis de Tocqueville, and just to my right, John F. Kennedy and we watch the ballet of Mr. Gorbachev and the spider, beneath the star-studded tent and oh, how quiet is the audience as it watches the show.

"Profiles in courage," whispers Mr. Kennedy.

"Merde," whispers Alexis, over and over again, "I *knew* this was going to happen. *Merde, merde, merde.*"

The music changes from *Swan Lake* to early sixties rock and Mikhail Gorbachev does the watusi. The spider backs away and some people cheer. Not too far away, I see Dostoyevsky taking notes and then scratching his head. He frowns, looks confused, then hesitantly smiles. Solzhenitsyn fervently underlines some words on a yellow legal pad and ends up ripping the page.

Jefferson, sitting next to Benjamin Franklin studies the spider, then he looks to his notes. "Ben," I can hear him say, "I really don't understand what went wrong. I really don't understand. I thought we created something elegant, that soared and was proud—not—not something that's dark and scrambles. What'd we do wrong? I don't understand!"

"Nor do I," sighs Ben, "nor do I."

At this point, three clowns in scorpion suits rush out and try to assail Mr. Gorbachev; but he laughs, grabs each one, rips off their costumes; Brezhnev is revealed, naked, and he runs to the shadows. Gorbachev rips off another costume and Stalin is revealed wearing a red and white fur-trimmed g-string. He is laughed at and, covering his groin with bloody hands, he alternately backs away, turns about confused, and makes it to the shadows. Mr. Gorbachev grins and does a beautiful turn on one foot as though he had been a ballerina since birth. The last clown comes at Mr. Gorbachev, a fearsome scorpion indeed and Mr. Gorbachev simply grabs him as the others; off with the costume, and Beria, with a necklace of guns, is flipped by Gorbachev, and goes head over heels, lands with a *wham;* he stands up, dazed, rubs his behind and begins to cry and wail like a child, "Staaaaaaleeeeeeen!" And runs into the shadows.

Then Khrushchev bounces out in an ill-fitting tutu and wearing a necklace of missiles. He means to engage Gorbachev in *pas de deux*, but trips, stumbles and before he can stop himself, he gets too close to the spider—it attacks, bites; Khrushchev screams once...

Kennedy looks down. "I don't know..." he whispers. "I don't know." He sighs. "Even now, I don't rest easy; my flesh does not decay, held together by doubt, by remorse... those advisers in Viet Nam. Am I less guilty than Khrushchev? If he is devoured by the spider, shouldn't I be as well?" He begins to stand, then sits, and shakes his head. "I don't know. I don't know. Maybe I *was* devoured by the spider and didn't know it."

"Your problem," I whisper, "may be that you experience emotions and guilt in a mercantile society that has no use for emotions other than profit."

"Dear God," whispers Kennedy, "what went wrong? What went wrong?"

The music has changed; it's now the *Blue Tango* and Gorbachev changes his dance. He goes up to the spider, grabs two front legs, and tries to get it to dance; instead, the spider tries to attack. He gives a shout of delight, yells, "*Glasnost*" and flips the spider over on to its back; the spider lands with a *whump* and the whole place shakes. Enraged, the spider rises and tries to attack Gorbachev again, but he deftly grabs the spider by its front legs again and spins it about, then he lets it go and it slides across the floor and slams into the wall. *Crash!* And the body of the spider obscures a bright Coca Cola sign. Then the body abruptly bloats and explodes in dishwashers, toasters, jogging shoes, tires, VCRs, televisions and finally three smaller spiders, with the heads of Reagan, Nixon and Bush, come scampering out from the body. The one with the face of Nixon screams, "I am not a crook!" The crowd roars in laughter as he goes up to the body of the spider and begins to push it. The spider with the face of Reagan says, "Well, I don't know, I just can't remember. You know how it is," and the crowd applauds and yells, "Hooray!" The spider with the face of Bush says, "No second-rate Slavic is gonna make a fool of us! We gotta get a proper spin on this." And the crowd laughs again at the humor and Nixon scampers over, manages to awkwardly throw junk bonds toward Gorbachev and screams, "We will bury you!" and the three spiders drag the big, dazed spider away into the shadows.

"Come on baby, let's do the twist..." The music roars and Gorbachev dances. He does the twist better than Chubby Checker.

I hear fervid whispering in the back and turning about, I see Arnold Toynbee talking to Lenin, "... it's all the same, be it the new Soviet Man or the Rugged Individualist. It's impossible for two mirrors to have a dialogue and yet—"

Lenin answers, "...and yet we must dance, mustn't we? Until all workers of the world unite, we still must dance, mustn't we?" He stands, grabs Arnold by the hands and says "My dear comrade, shall we?"

"Nyet!"

Gorbachev is standing there, looking at them, waving his hands and repeating, "Nyet! Nyet! Nyet!"

He then points.

To the left, where the scorpion clowns emerged — movement.

The music to the final act of *Swan Lake* is playing and Gorbachev does the ballet beautifully and Kennedy whispers, "...and the torch is passed to a new generation?" But I notice that he says it in the form of a question.

Thomas Jefferson and Benjamin Franklin look at their notes and continue to mumble, "What the hell happened? What happened? I thought we had it all figured out..."

Alexis De Tocqueville continues to rock back and forth, covering his eyes, muttering, "*Merde, merde, merde.*"

The music soars and swells, and Gorbachev continues to dance and the darkness moves. It moves, it flows, it congeals.

"Ahh," I hear Lenin. "Ah. The partner that Mikhail must dance with or not dance at all. This is truly the dance of the hour, of the ages, of history."

Which history? I wonder. Whose history? Is he dancing with that which creates the spider or some Russian monster? Or that which creates both? I glance to De Tocqueville, to Toynbee and I shudder.

The darkness oozes out to Gorbachev. And stops. Gorbachev turns to face it. The darkness moves and takes on form, a hunched, broad shouldered, brutish dark form that keeps changing. And it is impossible to say exactly what it is. Its eyes are dusky and distinct and they watch Gorbachev. And Gorbachev, in his pink tutu, with *Swan Lake* elegant and majestic, tries to get the beast to dance. But the beast just watches. And watches. And waits.

Movies

Alex, his parents and sister, sit in the back of the dark theatre in lounge chairs. They are fighting again. Alex glances to the screen and the screen hasn't changed. It is dark blue and familiar constellations are on the screen: Cassiopeia, the Big Dipper, the Southern Cross. Alex wonders if this is going to be a foreign film. He glances to his father—a tall man, big boned, big jowled and his gray hair is crew cut. His nose is off side a bit, broken from a scuffle while waiting in line for an earlier movie. He's gesturing to Alex's mother, a stout lady whose jaw line is firm as granite. Her black hair is curly and cut close and she doesn't say anything.

"I toldya, ya shoulda bought the tickets first," he says, "we almost didn't make it to this show because of that dumb mistake."

"We got in, didn't we?" says Alex's mother finally. "So what's your problem?"

"Yeah," Alex says. He's sitting between his mother and father. "Yeah, what's the big deal here?"

"Lissen," his father says, leaning real close to Alex, "you keep outta this."

Missa, Alex's sister, sits on the right of Alex's mother. She looks like her mother, that firm face, those eyes staring ahead, watching the movie screen and the tranquility of it and the never-changing constellations.

Down in the front, a family has started to sing and they abruptly go off key and laugh. In another part of the theatre, someone is crying then sobbing hysterically. But Alex pays little attention to that. "You're always picking on Mom," he says, "why don't you leave her alone?"

"Listen, Buster, you keep outta this. This is between me and my wife, your mother, you got that, twerp?"

Just then, Alex's grandfather turns around. "You don't call Alex a twerp. You've been petty all your life. Why don't you just shut up and watch the screen."

And Alex's father explodes. "What is this? Pick on Daddy day? She made a mistake and how can I watch the screen while I'm upset? You want I should sit on my anger like on a turd all evening?"

Missa laughs and Alex's mother turns, seething. "I'll not have you use that language in public at this theatre."

"Oh, Jee-zuz Christ you dumb bitch—"

Someone in the back row throws popcorn on Alex's father. "Sexist pig!" someone whispers.

"Hey, looky there," says someone down front, "boy, ain't that a scene?"

Alex looks around but can't tell what the person is referring to. The screen remains blank except for the constellations.

"God damn it, who threw popcorn?" Alex's father turns around in the seat and glares into the darkness.

Someone else whispers in the back, "Turn around, bozo, and quit being such an asshole."

Alex's father stands, turns around again, and yanking up a frail old woman with round glasses and black veil by the arm, he then stares. "Oh," he says, "sorry, Sister."

"Jesus be good to you," she says. "Young man," she continues, "you must learn to control that temper."

"Fuck you, Sister."

Alex shoves his father down in the seat. "Jesus Christ, Dad, are you nuts?"

Down front, there is hysterical laughter which changes to a sob.

"Don't you Goddamn shove me, you little asshole." And Alex's father shoves back.

"Oh," says the mother, "can't we just watch the show? It's always like this. All this fighting. Can't we stop the fighting?"

"Hey," says Alex's father, "I grew up in the front row. I fought all my life. I fought for the seats, the place in the ticket line. You gotta fight to survive, gotta be tough. This movie house here don't do nobody favors, got it? No favors, no way." He folds his arms across his chest in the darkness, obviously self-righteous. Finally he says, "Oh, hell, who wants popcorn?"

But everyone is angry at him and nobody says anything. "Oh, hell," he says, "the silent treatment. I'm supposed to feel shitty now, huh?"

He gets up and goes for popcorn. In the rest of the theatre, another argument breaks out, this time between kids. It turns into a fight and The Management comes flapping down the aisles whispering urgently, "Shush, we can't have this fighting, you can argue all you want but you can't fight like this. Not in this theatre and since this is the only theatre there is, we can't have fights."

"Bullshit!" someone yells, "people fight all the time here. Always have. Always will. You know it. Take your flashlight and stick it up your ass."

Alex's dad returns with a big bowl of popcorn. For himself. "Greedy son of a bitch," says Alex. "God, you're greedy."

"Bullshit, you long-haired frog. I asked you if you wanted popcorn. You didn't say anything. What's your problem?"

The mother shakes her head. "You two are always fighting. Can't you stop fighting?"

"Sure," says Alex, "when Dad grows up and stops being such a god damn buttfucker."

The father laughs, "Boy. That's a joke, I mean, who's the one who has to grow up around here? Hey, punk," and then the father leans over. "Want popcorn? Here." The father takes a handful and dumps it on Alex's head.

"God damn it!" screams Alex and he yanks the popcorn away from his father and sends it flying and spilling over the audience.

"God damn it!" someone yells.

"Whoopee!" yells someone else.

And somewhere else, someone has taken up the guitar and plays a lovely Spanish ballad. The father turns to Alex and grabs him by the collar. "Listen sonny boy, you're getting too big for your britches. I don't care if you are just fourteen, and I don't give a fuck what the laws are here but you've just pushed a little too far and—"

There is applause. The main show has begun. Both Alex and his father turn to watch—turn to see a ghostly blue hand come drifting out from the screen, over the audience, over to Alex—the hand engulfs Alex, then crushes him; his eyeballs pop out of his skull and arc high out over the audience. The hand turns a deep red and pulls back into the screen and Alex's father screams, "Oh, no, oh, no, one less person to fight with! Oh, no!" And the rest of the audience cheers wildly and enthusiastically. A couple dances in the aisle.

"Great show," someone yells.

"Four star!" yells someone else. And the applause is deafening.

Friend

Caterwauling, puking, stalking,
It climbs upon the garden wall,
Howling, baying, peeing, shaking,
Making the night so very long,

Making the day so far way, you wonder if it
Will *ever* come. Beast is out there,
Scaly, furry, eyes a-flashing in thin
Crescent light of moon.

God, you wonder, what did I do
To deserve this loathsome cartoon with
Voice and song all so wrong like the
Devil is serenading you with

Tortured songs like sounds of
Shearing gears or metal that is
Convoluting, bending, breaking, a full
Assault on the ears and still the

Creature sits there howling, howling,
Retching, screaming, with energy and
Morbid delight, and hearing it you know,
It's gonna be a long, *long* night.

Dawnscape III

Dawnlight coming, pale goblin
Of the light to be,
Sends shadows slowly to existence
Then devoured in degrees.

Dawnlight coming, things of
Night scamper to the dark,
Hiding beneath bark or leafen
Cover, scuttling in chitinous flee.

Dawnlight coming, coolness calm
Is a lie for the rampant bestial
Darkthings scrambling into the still,
Nightdark soil

Way down deep and below
Along with slippery, sliming things,
The bugs with legs blurry
Moving, going deeper, deeper

And for a moment, all is as still
And taut as spider's web but not
Asleep, oh, no, no—all is but
Waiting for the glowing globe

To go, to go, to go away, to get
Beyond another day, to wait until
The twilight comes a-creeping
Like a princess with dusky key

To slip into the lock of earth,

Whispering in an insectile voice,
"Come out my brothers, my crawly
Friends, it's dark again, be free.

Be free—" And then with odd,
Attentive ears, the strange forms hear;
Earth vomits chitin; crawly,
Hissy and bitey things, into the

Night; the night is here, is present again
With mad, flighty, crawly presence
Until the dawn light in the east
Creates, then shrinks shadows

By degrees, by degrees
And makes that multi-eyed night flee,
Take flight
Into the leaf-mold, soil night.

By Ring Bound and Unbounded

Now this is how it was on that great Saturday in early May; oh, you know those days when you bounce out of bed and the day looks vast and glorious like some sort of sentient jewel playing in light and wanting to play and maybe there is something perhaps a bit strange but not dangerously strange, oh, no, not that at all, but just a *little* strange, like the universe is sitting there beside you and whispering, "Hey, come on out and play and I might just show you a little something divine, something so fine that you wonder why you never saw it before but once you've seen it you are changed forevermore in a way that you didn't even think that you could change." And in some way Edward knew, hence this hunch that the universe was whispering something to him, something eerily grand but he did not know yet what it was and his speculation was interrupted when he heard the phone and it was a call from his friend Roy and it went like so:

"Hey, whatcha doin'?" Roy said.

"Not much yet, but maybe we can change all that!"

"Yeah. Well. Hey you can help me with something."

"You got your lawn to mow."

"Nah. Something better."

"Yeah? Well, it better be."

"Just come on over."

"Yeah, well, O.K. See you in a bit."

"Yeah."

And so Edward, he gulped down his oatmeal and chomped down those eggs and his mother said, "Well, what is your hurry?" as she picked up the dishes and took them to the kitchen and she was still dressed in her forest green gown with a pink towel wrapped around her head.

And Edward said, "Roy just called and I'm gonna go over to his house."

"Well," his mother said, "before you go, you energetic thirteen year old, clear the rest of the dishes and take out the garbage."

"Aw—" but he did and it took considerably less time than he thought it would and then it was on foot up to Roy's house, oh, yes, he could have taken his bike and it might have been considerably faster, but something about this day whispered in a sly way, "Part of the secret is doing this by foot."

And so, Edward walked, walked past the market with big Larry there, with his front tooth missing but he smiled anyway as he helped Mrs. Appleton, who always was dressed in a faded gray coat, (her eyes were aquamarine blue) and her hair, ah, so white and she got into her washed-out beige, fifty-three Ford and Larry helped her with her groceries and he said, "There you go," and she replied, "Thank you."

And he said closing her door, "You have a safe trip now." (She lived all of three blocks away.) And she said, "Thank you." And Larry said, "Y'all come back again."

And she started up the engine on that faded Ford, looked out the rolled up window and quite silently said, "Thank you."

And Larry said, "See you real soon now." And Mrs. Appleton said Thankyou and thankyou and thankyou and she backed away and Larry looked at Edward and then looked away and snapping his fingers, went into the store and Edward considered the sense of the sly shifting of air and wondered, *Was that it? Was there a little secret there?*

But he went on. And in just a few minutes, he was at Roy's place and Roy came to the door, yanked Edward inside and said, pointing to a bill in his tight fist, "Ten bucks! My aunt gave me ten bucks."

"Wow," said Edward, "not because you were good."

"Nah," said Roy, "I'd owe *her* a bunch! Got this for my birthday."

"Well," said Edward, thinking ah? this is the something I've been looking for? "Whatcha gonna do?"

"My aunt, she wants me to get something nice. Real nice."

"Wow," said Edward, "nicer as in a box of Mounds Bars and Milky Ways?"

"Nah," said Roy, "nice like in — uh — um — "

"That would getcha in four or five movies."

"Yeah," said Roy, "that's nice all right but — " and he rubbed his hand over his crew cut hair and his gray eyes looked about for a minute and then he said, "My aunt wants me to get jewelry. A tie clasp, ring or something or other."

"A ring?" said Edward. "That's kinda neat. Let's go over to the McKessons' and see what they got."

So they walked over to the store but they didn't really hurry all that much. And they talked as they walked and when they passed Mr. Gwin's house, Edward said, "Hey, have you seen him recently?"

"Yeah," said Roy, "he's as fat as Miss Cheldon, the geography teacher."

"Naw," said Edward, "she's not fat. Naw, he's the kinda fat where if he painted his stomach green it'd be a watermelon. Now *that's* fat!"

"Yeah, that is," said Roy. "Yeah, a watermelon for a gut, painted green. Or like a pumpkin at Halloween! Yeah, *that's* fat."

And they walked on, under that splendid turquoise sky, so serene with a few white clouds floating like pale islands on a wondrous sea and Roy said, "Look, don't that cloud look like a battleship?"

"Naw," said Edward, "looks more like you!"

"Hey," said Roy, "ha!"

"Ooo," Edward felt the sharp elbow in his side.

"You ain't gonna die."

"I know that. You couldn't hurt me if you tried. No, siree! Hey, you smell that?"

And Roy stopped and sniffed. "Oooooo," he grinned, "cinnamon rolls — Andy's Bakery, a new batch! Watcha say? How much money you got?"

Edward stopped and looked, "Enough for one. Gotta remember, we can't spend that money that you got."

"I know," said Roy, "Dad'd skin me alive."

"We can split," said Edward, and he thought, maybe this is it. Perhaps there is something that will happen here...

So they went into the bakery, and there was Mr. Grsten, a sulfurous old coal of a man in a dirty brown coat and black framed glasses with little specks of paint on the frames and his gray hair mowed short and the little lines on his nose like red streets on a map, arguing as usual with old Sally Mahoney, behind the counter.

"These biscuits aren't fresh!" whined Mr. Grsten, "Taste them and you'll see."

And Sally leaned on the counter, her gray eyes weary like this was really too much or maybe it was oh, cripes, here we go again, "Mister, I baked them myself yesterday. They was fresh when ya got 'em."

"No," And Mr. Grsten, he stood there. "They're stale as can be."

Sally shook her head. "No, hon, they're not. Really they're not."

"Well," said Mr. Grsten, "I want my money back."

"Well," said Sally, "you ain't gettin' it back. Not at all. We went through this last week. I did it before, but I won't do it again. So take your biscuits and get out the door."

And Mr. Grsten just stood there, his mouth making small twitches, and he then grabbed the bag and said, "Dang robbers."

But Edward and Roy noticed that he didn't throw them away as he rushed past the waste basket near the door and he left and *wham* went the door and *clintinkletinkle* went the ornamental little bells dangling from the top of the door.

And Sally sighed, "Oh, my Lord," and suddenly she looked like she was real old, like a roughed-over ruby but she saw Edward and Roy and said, "Well, look who's here."

"Hiya," said Edward.

"Like a cinnamon roll?" said Mrs. Mahoney.

"Yeah," said Roy.

"Sure thing," she said and brought out a big one. "Biggest one that I got and that'll be—" and she looked out the window to Mr. Grsten stomping down the street, "Here," she then said, "after someone like him, this is my treat."

"Wow, hey, neat," said Roy.

"Thank you," said Edward, grabbing the roll.

"It's okay," said Sally Mahoney, "after someone like him, serving you is a pleasure, a pleasure indeed. Say hi to your moms and do come back."

"Yeah," they both said, and then it was out the door and Edward thought, was there something there that I didn't see? He puzzled about that just a bit but smiled to himself and thought, just wait and see. And in a few minutes more, they were at the McKesson's and once inside, after wiping their hands on their pants from the butter and cinnamon of the roll, they went to the glass-enclosed jewelry display with seventeen year old Molly Peterson standing right there, seemingly perfecting a look of professional disdain. "Yeah?" she said like she was saying, Oh, god, whataya want? Edward pointed to the display tray of rings. "We wanna take a look at all of those."

Molly looked at Edward and Roy for a very long time. "They're outta your price range."

Roy stiffened a bit and said, "I wanna look." Molly, trying to perfect her act, waited a few seconds more and then opened the case and brought out the rings and, ah, Edward sighed: agates, tiger's eye, jade and diamonds too, and Roy said, "What are the prices?"

"Twenty-five, thirty, forty-two-ninety-seven."

"You got anything for ten?" Edward asked.

"Yeah," sniggered Molly, "out in the gumball machines."

Neither Edward nor Roy said anything to that, but they looked a bit longer at the display until Molly let out a sigh that was sure filled with exasperation, "Through gawking and wanting whatcha can't have?" And she smiled a smile that was as counterfeit as could be.

Both Edward and Roy just looked at Molly and finally they just walked away and outside they sat down on the curb and Edward said, "Rings are really kinda expensive."

"Yeah," said Roy, "darn it all to hell." He smiled a bit as he said the last word.

"So what to do?" Edward then said.

"Dunno," said Roy. "Sure want a ring. Be nifty to have."

"Geez," said Edward, "can you imagine forty bucks for a ring? How much are the tie clasps? Fifty or so? Surely there's something beautiful your money can buy! I mean, there just has to be jewelry that looks great that really doesn't cost all that much."

Roy sighed. "Well, I sure don't know where it is."

So they got up and began the walk on toward home, both feeling a bit on the dejected side, and Edward wondered about that sly message of morning. What was that special sparkle of sun? Did the sudden shift of the breeze bringing on it the scent of roses and trees in luxurious bloom—was there nothing to that? And they dropped in to Margaret's Ice Cream Confectionery, and with Edward's grand fortune of all fifty cents, they got a big double decker ice cream cone, with a scoop of chocolate on top which was for Edward and scoop of strawberry which was Roy's favorite flavor and they went to the magazine rack again (again after wiping their hands on their pants, after all, who wants to read a chocolate/strawberry version of the latest *Batman*?) they read comics until they both fidgeted and sensed that Margaret Trillip was getting ready to say something to them about reading and not buying again and they timed it just right, turning right before she could speak; they caught her off guard and said, "Thanks for the ice cream, it was great! See you again—"

To which Margaret said, suddenly a bit awkward and she fumbled with her necklace of gold, "—uh, okay boys, thank you and do come again—"

And Roy and Edward looked at each other and grinned and Edward whispered, "Uh-huh—"

"Sure," Roy responded, and they wandered out, and Roy began to look dejected again. "Geez," he sighed, and they stopped at McAllison's pond, "I sure wish I could have bought that ring—that green one—gee, that was grand."

"Yeah," said Edward. "What a great ring, but God, thirty-one sixty—but that was such a great shade of green."

"Or that one of the agate, with all the browns and the tan?" They sat on a log and looked out over the blue of the pond to the rich jade of trees on the opposite shore.

"What was that blue one?" Edward asked.

"I think it was sapphire. God," he said, "like wearing a chunk of the sky on my finger."

"And there was that diamond; God! It was a bright as the sun."

"Or that Alaska black diamond," said Edward. And he pointed to a reflecting flash of the water, "Just the color of that."

And they both sighed right then, thinking of the jewelry that was in that store. And after a while they began the walk home, past Mr. Crysi's place and on that May afternoon, he, incredibly thin, and pale as mushroom, was washing his new 1956 Studebaker Hawk and in the background, Elivs belted out *Heartbreak Hotel* and Mr. Crysi washed his car to the rhythm and he waved and yelled, "Hiya, kids, how's it goin'?"

And Edward and Roy, they smiled and waved but it was gesture, just gesture, and Roy was still sad about the ring and they went past the house of the Millers just in time to see four year old Jerry bonk his sister, little five year old Peggy on the head with a plastic play bucket and she went screaming and crying into the house and Jerry looked like he utterly could not understand just what the heck the commotion was all about and in that strange gem of a moment, Edward wondered again, *Was this it? Was this it? What was that sly twist of the events of the day? What was the smile behind all of this?* And Edward sighed, utterly unable to sort it all out, feeling like the universe had something to say but somehow missing the message some way and in the topaz light of the late afternoon, talc colored clouds dusted the sky and Edward pointed, "Ring around the sun, rain coming soon."

But Roy didn't say much; he simply replied, "Geez, it would have been great to have one of those rings. There must be neat jewelry that ten bucks can buy."

And Edward said nothing but smiled without quite knowing why, while behind them, the elegant pearl of the moon rose in the sky.

Kafka's Uncle Publication History of Excerpts

Busride, published in Dreamcon 7 program book, October 1992.

The Crossing, published in *Westwind,* Magazine of the Northwest Science Fiction Society #179, August 1993.

Somewhere Around the Square Root of X, as above, # 189, June 1994.

Bushwacking, as above, #192, September 1994.

Job, as above, #194, November 1994.

Pet, as above, #196, March 1995.

Kafka's Uncle (Chapter 1), as above, #201, June 1995.

Elvis Martian, as above, #237, February-March 1999.

...Other Strange Tales Publication Credits

All the Stars in the Sky, to have been published in *The Land of Nod,* 1991. (Magazine ceased publication before story appeared.)

Nightscape II, published in *The Olympic View Anthology, October 1991.*

The Eyes of Little Juan, with Marie Landis, self-published. 1989.

No Matter Where, Perhaps the Same, published in *Heliocentric Net #9, 1994.*

Jack of the Lantern, published in *Blood Review,* Issue #4, October 1990. Nominated for the Nebula Award.

Blue Dinosaur, published in *Heliocentric Net,* Summer 1992.

Fishin' Off the Starry Stream, to have been published in *Aberrations,* 1996. (Magazine ceased publication before story appeared.)

Stardance, accepted for publication in *Wiggansnatch.* (Magazine ceased publication before story appeared.)

Dreamscape I, to be published in *The Raven.* (Magazine ceased publication before story appeared.)

Horrorscape IV, published in *Midnight Zoo,* Vol. #2, Issue #1.

The Christmas of Eddie McGrew, accepted for publication in *The Year In Darkness* Wall Calendar, 1992 (project cancelled before publication). Published in *Heliocentric Net* #13, Winter 1995.

Darkscape V, published in *MIDNIGHT ZOO,* Vol. #2, Issue #2.

The Master Goes Whacko, first published in *Seattle Arts Image,* Newsletter of the Seattle Arts Commission-Special, August 1986. Reprinted in the *World Fantasy* program book — *The Roots of Fantasy, the book of the World Fantasy Convention,* Seattle, WA, 1989.

Fidene Knows, published in *tomorrow SPECULATIVE FICTION,* Vol. 3, #1, February 1995.

A Little Spider Shop Talk, published in *The Olympic View Anthology; October 1991.*

The Ring, published in *TALEBONES,* #11, Spring 1998.

Photogenic, published in *Seattle Writers Association Anthology,* 1999.

One Day at Glasnost, to have been published in Pulphouse. (Magazine ceased publication before story appeared.)

Movies, published in *TALEBONES,* #2, Winter 1996.

Dawnscape III, published in *The Olympic View Anthology; October 1991.*

About the Author

Bruce Taylor, known as Mr. Magic Realism, was born in 1947 in Seattle, Washington, where he currently lives. He was a student at the Clarion West Science Fiction/Fantasy writing program at the University of Washington, where he studied under such writers as Avram Davidson, Robert Silverberg, Ursula LeGuin, and Frank Herbert. Bruce has been involved in the advancement of the genre of magic realism, founding the Magic Realism Writers International Network, and collaborating with Tamara Sellman on MARGIN (http://www.magical-realism.comwww.magical-realism.com). Recently, he co-edited, with Elton Elliott, former editor of Science Fiction Review, an anthology titled, *Like Water for Quarks*, which examines the blending of magic realism with science fiction, with work by Ray Bradbury, Ursula K. LeGuin, Brian Herbert, Connie Willis, Greg Bear, William F. Nolan, among others. Elton Elliott has said that "(Bruce) is the transformational figure for science fiction.;

His works have been published in such places as The Twilight Zone, Talebones, On Spec, and New Dimensions, and his first collection, *The Final Trick of Funnyman and Other Stories* (available from Fairwood Press) recently received high praise from William F. Nolan, who said that some of his stores were "as rich and poetic as Bradbury at his best.;

In 2007, borrowing and giving credit to author Karel Capek (*War with the Newts*), Bruce published *EDWARD: Dancing on the Edge of Infinity*, a tale told largely through footnotes about a young man discovering his purpose in life through his dreams.

With Brian Herbert, son of Frank Herbert of *Dune* fame, he wrote *Storm-world*, a short novel about global warming.

Two other books (*Mountains of the Night, Magic of Wild places*) have been published and are part of a "spiritual trilogy.; (The third book, *Majesty of the World*, is presently being written.)

A sequel to *Kafka's Uncle* (*Kafka's Uncle: the Unfortunate Sequel and Other Insults to the Morally Perfect*) should be published soon, as well as the prequel (*Kafka's Uncle: the Ghastly Prequel and Other Tales of Love and Pathos from the World's Most Powerful, Third-World Banana Republic*). *Industrial Carpet Drag,* a weird and funny look at global warming and environmental decay, was released in 2104.

Other published titles are, *Mr. Magic Realism* and *Metamorphosis Blues*.

Of course, he has already taken on several other projects which he hopes will see publication: *My False Memories With Myshkin Dostoevski-Kat,* and *The Tales of Alleymanderous* as well as going through some 800 unpublished stories to assemble more collections; over 40 years, Bruce has written about 1000 short stories, 200 of which have been published.

Bruce was writer in residenc at Shakespeare & Company, Paris. If not writing, Bruce is either hiking or can be found in the loft of his vast condo, awestruck at the smashing view of Mt. Rainier with his partner, artist Roberta Gregory and their "mews,; Roo-Prrt.

More books from Bruce Taylor are available at: http://ReAnimus.com/store/?author=Bruce Taylor

ReAnimus Press

Breathing Life into Great Books

If you enjoyed this book we hope you'll tell others or write a review! We also invite you to subscribe to our newsletter to learn about our new releases and join our affiliate program (where you earn 12% of sales you recommend) at www.ReAnimus.com.

Here are more ebooks you'll enjoy from ReAnimus Press, available from ReAnimus Press's web site, Amazon.com, bn.com, etc.:

Kafka s Uncle and Other Strange Tales, by Bruce Taylor

Coming soon: KAFKA'S UNCLE: The Unfortunate Sequel

Edward: Dancing on the Edge of Infinity, by Bruce Taylor

Magic of Wild Places, by Bruce Taylor

Mountains of the Night, by Bruce Taylor

Side Effects, by Harvey Jacobs

American Goliath, by Harvey Jacobs

The Bleeding Man and Other Science Fiction Stories,
by Craig Strete

Wyoming Sun, by Edward Bryant

Cinnabar, by Edward Bryant

Fetish, by Edward Bryant

Neon Twilight, by Edward Bryant

Predators and Other Stories, by Edward Bryant

Trilobyte, by Edward Bryant

Darker Passions, by Edward Bryant

Among the Dead and Other Events Leading to the Apocalypse, by Edward Bryant

Particle Theory, by Edward Bryant

The Baku: Tales of the Nuclear Age, by Edward Bryant

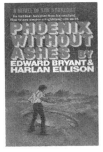

Phoenix Without Ashes, by Harlan Ellison and Edward Bryant

In Hollow Lands, by Sophie Masson

Journals of the Plauge Years, by Norman Spinrad

Fragments of America, by Norman Spinrad

Pictures at 11, by Norman Spinrad

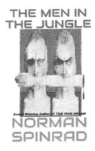

The Men from the Jungle, by Norman Spinrad

Greenhouse Summer, by Norman Spinrad

Passing Through the Flame, by Norman Spinrad

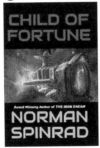

Child of Fortune, by Norman Spinrad

Mexica, by Norman Spinrad

Songs from the Stars, by Norman Spinrad

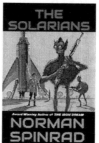

The Solarians, by Norman Spinrad

The Void Captain's Tale, by Norman Spinrad

Staying Alive - A Writer's Guide, by Norman Spinrad

The Mind Game, by Norman Spinrad

The Children of Hamelin, by Norman Spinrad

The Iron Dream, by Norman Spinrad

Bug Jack Barron, by Norman Spinrad

Experiment Perilous: The 'Bug Jack Barron' Papers,
by Norman Spinrad

The Last Hurrah of the Golden Horde, by Norman
Spinrad

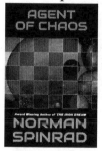

Agent of Chaos, by Norman Spinrad

Russian Spring, by Norman Spinrad

Little Heroes, by Norman Spinrad

A World Between, by Norman Spinrad

Anthopology 101: Reflections, Inspections and Dissections of SF Anthologies, by Bud Webster

Past Masters, by Bud Webster

Of Worlds Beyond, by Lloyd Arthur Eshbach, ed.

The Issue at Hand, by James Blish (as William Atheling, Jr.)

More Issues at Hand, by James Blish (as William Atheling, Jr.)

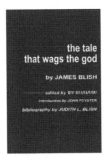

The Tale that Wags the God, by James Blish

The Exiles Trilogy, by Ben Bova

The Star Conquerors (Collectors' Edition), by Ben
Bova

Colony, by Ben Bova

The Kinsman Saga, by Ben Bova

Star Watchmen, by Ben Bova

As on a Darkling Plain, by Ben Bova

The Winds of Altair, by Ben Bova

Test of Fire, by Ben Bova

The Weathermakers, by Ben Bova

The Dueling Machine, by Ben Bova

The Multiple Man, by Ben Bova

Escape!, by Ben Bova

Forward in Time, by Ben Bova

Maxwell's Demons, by Ben Bova

Twice Seven, by Ben Bova

The Astral Mirror, by Ben Bova

The Story of Light, by Ben Bova

Immortality, by Ben Bova

Space Travel - A Science Fiction Writer's Guide, by
Ben Bova

The Craft of Writing Science Fiction that Sells, by Ben Bova

How To Improve Your Speculative Fiction Openings, by Robert Qualkinbush

Ghosts of Engines Past, by Sean McMullen

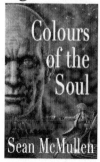

Colours of the Soul, by Sean McMullen

The Cure for Everything, by Severna Park

The Sweet Taste of Regret, by Karen Haber

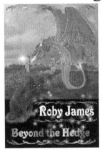

Beyond the Hedge, by Roby James

Commencement, by Roby James

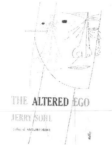

The Altered Ego, by Jerry Sohl

The Odious Ones, by Jerry Sohl

Prelude to Peril, by Jerry Sohl

The Spun Sugar Hole, by Jerry Sohl

The Lemon Eaters, by Jerry Sohl

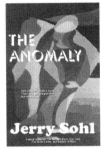

The Anomaly, by Jerry Sohl

I, Aleppo, by Jerry Sohl

Death Sleep, by Jerry Sohl

In Search of the Double Helix, by John Gribbin

Fire on Earth, by John and Mary Gribbin

Q is for Quantum, by John Gribbin

In Search of the Big Bang, by John Gribbin

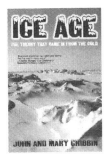

Ice Age, by John and Mary Gribbin

FitzRoy, by John and Mary Gribbin

Cosmic Coincidences, by John Gribbin and Martin Rees

The Sad Happy Story of Aberystwyth the Bat, by Ben Gribbin

A Guide to Barsoom, by John Flint Roy

The Gilded Basilisk, by Chet Gottfried

William J. Hypperbone, or The Will of an Eccentric,
by Jules Verne

The Futurians, by Damon Knight

Shadrach in the Furnace, by Robert Silverberg

Xenostorm: Rising, by Brian Clegg

Bloom, by Wil McCarthy

Aggressor Six, by Wil McCarthy

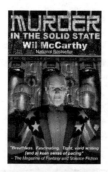

Murder in the Solid State, by Wil McCarthy

Flies from the Amber, by Wil McCarthy

Dear America: Letters Home from Vietnam, by edited by Bernard Edelman for The New York Vietnam Veterans Memorial Commission

I've Never Been To Me, by Charlene Oliver

Steep Deep & Dyslexic, by Jeffrey Bergeron

Innocents Abroad (Fully Illustrated & Enhanced Collectors' Edition), by Mark Twain

Local Knowledge (A Kieran Lenahan Mystery), by Conor Daly

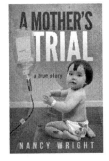

A Mother's Trial, by Nancy Wright

Bad Karma: A True Story of Obsession and Murder,
by Deborah Blum

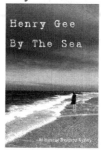

By The Sea, by Henry Gee

The Sigil Trilogy (Omnibus vol.1-3), by Henry Gee

Made in the USA
Charleston, SC
17 June 2016